Sex,
Drugs
and
Blueberries

Also by Crash Barry

Tough Island: True Stories from Matinicus, Maine
a memoir

Second Edition
Copyright 2011 by Crash Barry
All rights reserved.
Published by Maine Misadventures.
mainemisadventures.com

ISBN 978-0-615-38529-7
Library of Congress Control Number: 2010911681

Cover by Patrick Corrigan

Thanks to Shana, Sharyn and Tom Sexton, Harold and Kim Crabill, John McDonald, The Bollard, Green Acres, Buzz, Jenny and Fuvvie, Kipper, the Farm, Patty and Pete, C. Delles, Mark Baldwin and Petunia.

This is a story about how quickly things can go wrong. The characters and events are inventions of the author.

August 2006
Washington County, Maine

Everything seemed normal. The thin line of white powder felt granular going up my nose. I shook my head, sniffled loudly, rubbed my nostrils then fell back into the depths of the comfy couch. Cough. Cough. Swallowed and closed my eyes. Tasted a quick tickle of bitterness in my throat. Sprawled on the giant sectional in the candle-lit, ancient Grange Hall, hanging out with two hot chicks and a couple cool dudes in the town of Irwin in rural Down East Maine, I was feeling fine. We had already smoked two huge blunts and drank many beers. After the snort, I waited for the cocaine to reach my brain and deliver that frenetic energy I occasionally enjoyed.

I kept my eyes closed. Not because I was tired. (Though I was exhausted by the first three days of the blueberry harvest. Three long days of bending, stooping and reaching under the hot sun.) Closed my eyes because my eyelids suddenly weighed a ton. Closed my eyes to focus on the sweet laugh of the girls and the boom of Ganeesh's deep chuckle. Closed my eyes, waiting for the buzz to arrive, trying to forget betraying my wife 20 minutes earlier.

The super speedy rush didn't come. Instead, I started to float. Warm and fuzzy. The Pink Floyd on the stereo softly throbbed in one part of my brain, while another lobe enjoyed the pale red light show being projected on the insides of my eyelids. I realized, for the first time since the harvest had started, I was not in pain from the stoop and bend of raking blueberries. My lower back, spine and legs didn't hurt. The rake wound on my finger didn't throb. My wrists weren't sore. I couldn't move off the couch.

I opened my eyes to a flashing world. Lights. Sound. Smell. Touch. Everything flickered. Candles strobed, then dimmed. Took a couple seconds to dawn on me. This snort wasn't cocaine. I should have known. Prescription drug abuse is huge in Washington County. The powder was most likely Oxycontin, ground and razor-bladed into a long thin line. Snorting a crushed opiate, "cracking it," as the kids say, cancelled the pain pill's time release coating. I laughed at my mistake.

"What's so funny, dear?" the lovely Missy asked. Standing, she towered above me, with a wide grin on her freckled face. Like many people in this part of coastal Maine, as far east as you can go in the States, on the border with New Brunswick, Canada, Missy frequently used the endearment "dear," though she pronounced it "dee-uh."

I'd spent a dozen hours with her over the previous three days and every minute was fun, flirtatious and enthralling. She liked me too, and was affectionate and playful. Even though she was just 19-turning-20 and I was 37, it felt like

I'd known her forever. On this night, she glowed. Her blue eyes shone round and big. Wearing a pair of cut-off coveralls and her red hair in pigtails, backlit by a couple dozen candles scattered around the room, the glitter and pixie dust on her dimpled cheeks glimmered. So did the tiny jewel stud in her slightly crooked nose. Through my eyes, she looked like a soft and warm farm girl.

"Why are you laughing?"

"Oh," I said, slowly shaking my head. "Guess I thought I was doing a line of cocaine. But that wasn't..." My voice trailed off and my eyes closed.

Everyone laughed. Gentle laughter. Not mocking or unfriendly. Since the snort, everything felt nice. I heard my name. Ganeesh was speaking to me. I opened my eyes.

"You're right," he said. "Not blow. Just enough Oxy for a good time."

"Yeah." I closed my eyes again, forgetting the ache from raking blueberries. I was pain free now. An out-of-body experience. An excruciating suit of armor had been removed from my soul. And floating felt great. Much, much better than bending over among berries. "Right on."

"I love it," Missy said. She took a seat on the couch. Right next to me. Not touching, but close enough to feel her heat and smell her sweetness. "I love how my body feels after a snort. Tingly." She giggled. "I love how other people's bodies feel, too." She touched my arm with the electrical charge I'd felt each time she made contact with me. This time, though, her power didn't startle. Something to do with the snorted opiate? Or was it more spiritual, now that we were closer? Intimate. Her electric shock was a series of delicate warm pulses, merging, all the way to the tips of my ears and toes.

I enjoyed sitting close to her. I'd also enjoyed the mind-blowing powerful orgasm she'd given me twenty minutes earlier.

Her fingers traced an electric line down my forearm until she reached my hand, which she grabbed and held with both of hers. High as a kite, I closed my eyes. Together, we levitated, then soared, then began to fly. Over a rolling blue field of the ripest, juiciest, heaviest blueberries in the world.

Sounds great, right? Problem is, I was married and madly in love with my sexy and sweet poetess of a wife. Yet Missy owned my heart for that moment. Possibly forever.

In the very back of my brain, I knew this joy was derived mostly from the magic of the opiate and Missy. I also knew the joy would be fleeting. One way or another, I'd pay. No doubt. My Catholic upbringing guaranteed all illicit pleasure would eventually mean pain. And, inevitably, guilt.

But, at that moment, under the influence of sex, drugs and blueberries, I didn't care.

Sweat and Bloodberries

The very first time I bent over with a blueberry rake in my hand was easy. At a little past seven on the morning of August 7, I was standing in the middle of shin-high blueberry bushes still wet with dew. The metal rake given to me by Larry Staples was the size of a bread box and weighed a couple pounds. I bent at the waist, the way Larry showed me, and dragged the short-handled rig through leaves and vines. The rake had 53 six-inch long, dagger-sharp tines. I pulled it like a comb, through the bushes.

Silverish blueberries, ripe and fat, tumbled into the rake. That's the theory, anyway. It took several minutes of reaching, stabbing and dragging through the surprisingly resistant leaves for me to fill the rake. I straightened my spine and dumped the contents into the five gallon bucket the way Larry did, letting the slight southwesterly breeze winnow away the worthless leaves and vetch. The pitter-patter of berries falling into the bucket was a sweet sound. The rat-tat-tat of money. I smiled and looked down. My bounty barely covered the bottom of the bucket. I sighed, grin gone, since Larry had explained a whole heaping bucket was worth a mere $3.50. Fourteen cents a pound. That's what the raker in the field gets. It would take me forever to fill that bucket.

The second time I bent over with a blueberry rake in my hand hurt like a son-of-a-bitch, like someone jabbed me in the lower left side of the back with a stick. I looked around, but I was all alone. The 20 or so other rakers on this part of Larry's rolling 100 acres were scattered across part of a corner of field. Framed on one end by an ancient stone wall and a spruce, poplar and white birch forest at the other, the section we were raking was about the size of four football fields divided into six foot wide lanes, clearly marked with endless pieces of white kite string. The rakers closest on my left and right were a hundred feet ahead of me. I bent over again to reach with my rake. The stabbing returned instantly.

It's tough to accurately retell pain. Intensity. Duration. Location. You really need to experience pain yourself to comprehend the anguish. The measure is so personal and subjective, specific to individual tolerances and history. Some are immune, or at least resistant, thanks to misfiring brain synapses or wounded nerves. Others cry and sob from a paper cut. For me, the pain of raking hurt.

The pain of raking was a deep, dull throb, mixed with a soreness and constant stabbing in my lower back on my left and right side. A pain horizontal and vertical. Circular and square. The awful ache felt by a billion workers since the birth of agricultural hard labor. The sting of the bent spine. The stoop and twist and the reach and pull. A million times worse than any sorrow from office or factory. The spread of the pain from raking surprised me. Fiercely radiating up and down my spine and across my nervous system. Shoulders. Arms. Wrists. Feet. Knees. Ankles. Brain. Concentrated, extreme and severe. How would I last three weeks?

By the end of the first hour, I decided to give up and go home. Unfortunately, I overestimated my preparedness for the stoop and constant motion, the bending and reaching necessary to rake berries. That and the low pay, bugs, heat and humidity also sucked. Obviously this wasn't a job for a man of my height and inflexibility. My six foot two frame was better suited for reaching high, not stooping low. I decided to tell Larry thanks, but no thanks. He could have my semi-full bucket. If I left the fields immediately, I'd make it home in time for a nice long soak in the bathtub before lunch. Then Monica and I would have to brainstorm – big time -- on a new way to make ends meet.

We needed cash. Immediately. We'd nearly emptied our savings account to pay August rent; leaving us with a little food money, enough to pay the power bill and buy gas for Floyd, our fuel-guzzling blue Ford pick-up. We were very close to totally broke. Monica's part-time job at Goose Island High didn't start for almost another month. Then it'd be two more weeks until her first payday. So I had to rake berries. No question. But due to the pain, I felt like I couldn't continue.

For that first hour, my take was an almost full bucket of berries. A lousy three bucks for my hard labor. After a long drink of water, I dropped my bottle to the ground. People have been raking blueberries in Maine for a century. No doubt other tall people have done the job over the years. What was their secret? Why was I such a terrible raker?

I leaned over, once again willing to capture the elusive berry, and pulled the rake through the plants. My back instantly spasmed. A jolt of pain. A donkey kick. A sucker punch.

Almost crying, I dropped to my knees to reach my water bottle and took another long drink, then noticed a fella who just started raking a new row a couple strips to my left. Super-fast and graceful, at 50 yards away he appeared to be dancing, effortlessly bent, almost sweeping the berries from the vines and dumping the fruit into his bucket in one fell swoop. As he grew closer, I heard his rhythm. The swish and drag of his rake through the bushes was a song with a beat. Then I noticed his headphones. I wondered what sort of music allowed him to dance among the blueberries. What tunes inspired him through the pain? When he was about ten feet away, he dropped his rake to the ground, straightened his back and stretched his hands towards the sky.

"Yes sir," he yelped, wiggling his fingers. "Wouldn't you just love to have sex with Britney Spears? Mmmm. Yeah." He removed the headphones and looked at me, nodding. "Wouldn't cha?"

Standing straight, he was maybe 5'8". For the first time in my life, I wished I was shorter. This guy was the perfect height for raking. Short enough to reach the ground easily. Arms long enough that his rake reached lots of berries each time he bent over. He was about 30, tanned with a mop of curly black hair sticking out from under his blue bandana. He wore a pair of tight black leather gloves, the type a race car driver would wear. He peeled them off, delicately, like a surgeon.

"Uhhh, uhhh," I stammered as I rose from my knees. "Sure. I guess I'd..."

"I'd do Britney in a heartbeat," he interrupted, unzipping the fanny pack around his waist to take out a pack of Marlboro Reds and a lighter. "First day, right?" He pointed at me with his smoke. "Aren't you kind of friggin' old to be raking?"

He laughed and I noticed he was missing his right front tooth. He lit his smoke.

"Kinda tall, too. You gotta bend quite a-ways to reach them berries."

"I'm feeling pretty old right now," I said, stretching my arms over my head. "Does it get any easier?"

"Not really." He pulled a piece of sandpaper out of his pouch and rubbed it, back and forth, across several of the rake's tines. "Gotta keep your rake sharp and clean. Goes better through the leaves and vetch. But raking don't never get easy."

I groaned.

"Well, maybe a little bit easier." He laughed. "But I gotta tell ya, your muscles never really get used to bending over a million times a day. Want some advice?" He took a second drag off his smoke and didn't wait for an answer. "Keep your rake clean and keep moving and keep stretching. Drink lots of water. And if you gotta take a break, never sit on a bucket. Only idiots sit on buckets. Drives me friggin' crazy." He shook his head. "Worst thing you could do. Sit on a bucket. If you've been working muscles hard with your stooping and bending, then suddenly stop and sit on a friggin' bucket, you'll get all friggin' tight. When you start back up, you're gonna be sore and hurt like a son-of-a-gun." He grinned. "No reason to make raking more painful than it already is. 'Cuz it's bad enough, that's for sure. When you take a break, keep stretching and moving around." He inhaled again and reached for the sky. "Another bit of free advice. Hold on to your rake. You lose it, Larry charges you fifty bucks. And if any of those young punks lose their rake," he pointed to a couple of teenage boys 100 yards down the field, sitting on their buckets, smoking, "they're gonna try to steal yours. Easy to lose a rake around here." He grinned. "My name's Richard, by the way." His cigarette dangled from his lips and he pointed at me with both index fingers. "Who the frig are you?"

"Ben Franklin." I offered my hand. "Nice to meet you."

"Ben Franklin? I thought you died way back in the olden days. And where's your wig? You planning on flying a kite?"

"Nope," I said, deadpan. "Must have me confused with someone else."

We shook hands.

"Seriously," Richard said, "what the frig are you doing on Larry Staples' blueberry farm? I know you're not from Washington County."

"I just moved to Goose Island..."

"Goose Island," he waved a hand in my face. "Goose Island! You must be friggin' crazy. The government's declared Goose Island a 'slum and blight zone.' You know any of my posse? Maxine Marie? Paul Pants? Bob Carter? Gutta? Wilbur Rosshole? Or Madman Don Hanson? Justin Craiger? Big Frank? Or that fat perv, Hughie French-Fry?"

"Nope," I shook my head. "Don't really know many..."

"Crazy island. Lots of people there are pretty screwy. Something to do with all the lead in the ground from the sardine canneries. They used lead solder on the cans." He nodded. "I've spent lottsa time on Goose Island because I lived there with my grandparents so I could go to Goose Island High. Graduated way back in '94. Though I don't remember much. *Hah*!" He took a final puff off his smoke and flicked the butt towards the center of the field. "Tended urchin divers back in the late 90s. Three different times I worked for Bonner Brothers flinging bait on salmon cage sites over by Lardford Head. Got laid off for good a couple years ago. Replaced by a robot. Couple winters, I worked on a scallop dragger outta Goose Island. Been known to occasionally clam those flats – during the midnight low tide -- on the back side of the island, near my secret place to find wrinkles." He pointed at me. "The city manager, that fat idiot thief, Fuddy Binch, is my dad's second cousin. Why the frig did you move Down East? I know there ain't any jobs or opportunities on Goose Island, that's for sure."

"My wife and I were done with Portland. Normal people can't afford rent, let alone buy a place." That was always the start of the answer as to why

Monica and I moved from the largest city in Maine to Goose Island two months before the blueberry harvest. I had decided not to reveal my former career as the lead singer in an emo rock band that almost (should have, could have) made it big. Instead, I told people about my second set of skills, which earn me good money in exchange for short bursts of hard labor.

"I'm a wood floor refinisher." I paused. "I thought with all the old houses on Goose Island, I'd have tons of work. Never imagined I'd be raking blueberries. Bit slow right now. But once it gets going, we're gonna save cash so we can buy 10 acres, build a little house, have a big garden."

"Right on," Richard said. "That's exactly what I'm doing. I've got a market garden. Grow all my veggies with enough extra to trade and sell. I live right on the line with Perry and Irwin." He pointed through the woods. "On the tippity top of the Steep Ridge Road." He smiled. "Want to see it? 'Cuz me and my family need a ride home after raking." He paused and shook his head. "'Cuz I totaled my friggin' Chevy a couple of weeks ago." He laughed wistfully. "So now I gotta use my friggin' blueberry money to buy wheels."

"That sucks." In rural Maine, a vehicle is essential. "Sure, I'll give you a ride."

"Right on. Thanks." He nodded and smiled. "Smashing the friggin' Chevy was a blessing in disguise. I hated that truck. Piece of junk. Gas guzzler. Gonna get me a little friggin' Jap truck that gets a friggin' million miles a gallon."

"I wish I had a smaller truck," I said. "I betcha I'll burn 15 bucks for the round trip from Goose Island. What's that? A hundred pounds of berries? Five hours, at the rate I'm going…"

"I've had it up to here," Richard tugged at his bandana, "with George Bush and Dick Cheney. They're just out to make their buddies fatter and richer than they already are." He spat. "I don't get it. Fuel prices in Washington County, poorest part of the state, are the friggin' highest in Maine. And our gasoline comes from New Brunswick. Just an hour away." He shook his head. "Electric prices are just as friggin' bad. I really want to get off the friggin' grid. Screw paying for what Mother Nature gives away for free."

"Yeah." I nodded in agreement. That's what Monica and I intended to do.

"Was gonna use my friggin' blueberry money to buy a nice little solar panel kit," Richard said. "But now I gotta use the money for wheels." He reached into his fanny pack with one hand and pointed at me with the other. "You're not a cop are you?"

"What? Me? A cop?" I was surprised, but could see his point. Slightly suspicious for a nearing-middle-age white fella, who happens to be tall and unfit for stoop labor, suddenly showing up to rake blueberries. "I'm not a cop. I'm a floor refinisher."

"Cool," Richard said, pulling out a nice fat joint from his pouch. "I didn't think you were a pig. No cop is gonna rake blueberries just to make a bust. A friggin' gazillion other ways to do it." He paused and looked at me. "You smoke herb?"

"Yes sir."

Richard sparked, took a long, deep puff and handed it to me. I looked around, surprised to be toking in the middle of the field. But the gentle southwesterly wind blew the smoke away from the other rakers. I puffed. Puffed again. And again. For one long moment, everything was all right. This was seriously good weed. Just a couple hits gave me a body buzz that calmed down my pain and my brain. Suddenly, the harvest didn't seem so overwhelming. If I could rake and smoke herb the whole time, it might turn out okay. Of course, that probably meant spending more money on weed than I was actually making raking. I took another drag and handed the reefer back to Richard.

"You have no idea how much I needed that," I gave him a little bow when I finally exhaled. "You're a lifesaver."

"No problem." He puffed again and gave the joint back. "You're gonna give us a ride home, right?"

"Yes sir." I inhaled again, then tried to pass it back to him.

"No thanks." He held up his hands. "I'm all set. That's your gas money. Finish it. I gotta rake some money." He pulled on his gloves while I inhaled again. "Can't believe how few berries there are," he said. "Larry thinks it could be the worst year, ever."

"Great." I exhaled a cloud, then took another puff. "That sucks..."

Richard's pot was some of the best ever and I've smoked a ton of good reefer. The marijuana made my skeleton feel light. My feet, too. I wished for my guitar. And a chair. Then I'd be better. Playing music, right there in the middle of the field. I'd be happy. Of course, if I had my guitar, I couldn't rake berries. Suddenly I realized I was really high and that Richard was still talking to me.

"What were you saying?" I said. "That's some good herb."

"I said not a friggin' good year," Richard grinned, "to start in the blueberry business. Not many friggin' berries..."

"Oh yeah." I took another hit. "I gotta rake. We totally need the cash." I laughed. "I haven't had any work since we moved." I shrugged, with a huge smile on my face. "We're almost broke."

"Hey hey, Ben, don't let me harsh your friggin' chi." He put up his hands. "It's only the first day. Harvest might turn out great." He pointed at me. "But at the same time, you gotta be realistic. Last winter was super-cold and windy. And there wasn't a lick of snow on the ground. Then spring was way too rainy. Then there's the bees. Bees are mysteriously dying off. Getting more expensive to rent hives. And Larry thinks the bees he rented were lazy and didn't pollinate that good. Plus Larry thinks the idiot who sprayed the herbicide watered it down, 'cuz we're seeing lots and lots of weeds." He pointed across the fields. "Way too much vetch considering all the poison sprayed." He frowned. "Yes, sir, you might have chosen the worst friggin' year possible to start in the blueberry biz."

"Great." I exhaled a cloud, then took another puff.

"Remember, drink lots of water. Don't get dehydrated. You don't wanna get the runs out here. That nasty sani-can," he pointed to the other side of the field, near where Floyd stood, baking in the sun, "is always either occupied or a mile away." He laughed and picked up his rake. "All right, break's over. You just watch how an experienced professional rakes blueberries."

We both laughed. I inhaled again. Richard bent over. His work became art. Dance. He held the rake at a slight angle and pulled it through the berries, in a continuous motion, right-to-left across the strip of bushes. Then he took a step forward and raked from left-to-right. After swaying back and forth with a half-dozen swipes, his rake was full. He tilted it and the fruits of his labor dropped into his bucket. The gentle breeze coaxed the tangles of grass and weeds away.

His technique seemed so effortless. Graceful. Would I eventually rake with such skill? The joint went out. Still a half-inch long, I tucked it in my pocket for later and took a long sip of water.

"Okay." He pointed his rake at me. "Let me see your stuff."

Actually, I wasn't ready to start. Didn't want to waste the buzz from the reefer on hard labor, but feedback from Richard on technique would be valuable. Took another swig of water, then dropped the bottle next to my bucket and slowly stretched my hands over my head, reaching for the sky. A final stretch. A deep breath. I exhaled, picked up my rake and leaned forward, holding it the way Richard did and began to sweep.

Immediately, the shooting pains started in my lower back on the left, followed by pulsing pain on the right side. Ignored it. A second later, my rake got hung up, hard, on tangles of stems, leaves and weeds. Both hands tingled. And not a pleasant tingle. Felt like I'd smacked the rake against a brick wall.

"*God-damn son-of-a-bitch*," I yelped. All the marijuana-inspired joy vanished in an instant. "*That fucking...*"

"*Dude, dude,*" Richard said, rushing toward me. "Chill out. Watch your language. There's kids out here. Seriously, I don't need my five-year-old nephew learnin' how to swear. Chill out. You just gotta slow down. Let me see you do it again. But do it in slow motion this time."

"What?"

"In a perfect world, I'd videotape your technique and slow it down to analyze your swing. Like a golf pro. But we don't have a friggin' camera. I gotta see how you hold the rake when..."

"Okay, okay." I shook my head. "This fucking sucks."

I bent over and tried again. The pain returned instantly. At that moment, I was so tempted to jump in Floyd, drive back to Goose Island. There had to be an easier way to make the cash we needed. Maybe hold up a drug store?

"*Fuck!*"

"Dude, it's totally obvious," Richard said. "You're going too deep. You can't go too deep, because you'll get stuck on the vetch and vines. Anyways, you don't need to go deep to get the fruit." He walked toward me. "This ain't like sex." He thrust his pelvis back and forth. Side to side. "Plenty of fruit on top. Near the top. Yeah. Yeah. On the top. No need to go so deep." He pointed at me with his rake. "Give it another try."

"Gimme a sec." I pulled the tangles of stem and leaf from my rake, then bent at the waist and held the rake slightly forward and started to sweep. This time, my rake traveled a couple feet across my strip before getting hung up in a bigger mess. "Motherfucker."

"Ben, dude. Language." Richard held his rake in front of his chest and shook his head. "I think the sweep might be a little advanced for a beginner like you. You should try combing. Much easier than sweeping. That's the way kids and ladies do it." He lifted the rake over his head with his right hand and flexed his muscles, his bicep hard and strong against his tight tee-shirt. "Sweeping is for professionals. Maybe someday you'll get it."

I grunted.

"Combing just takes longer." Richard smiled. "But at least you won't get hung up so often. Watch." He stepped into my strip and bent over, parallel to the white string, and with a long series of short stabbing and pulling motions he combed a patch the size of a twin mattress and had a half-rakeful. "See, it's easy, just takes a little longer. If I'd been sweeping, I'd have a full rake." He poured the berries into my bucket. "You owe me a dime. Hah. All right. I gotta get back to work. Just take your time and perfect your combing technique, then you'll be able to speed it up a bit. And then you'll rake real money. I'll talk to you later."

Richard put on his headphones and turned back to his strip. He stretched to the sky, then bent over and started sweeping. Again, he was a smooth machine, back and forth, in sync with his soundtrack. I watched for a couple minutes while taking long sips of water. Richard seemed to be in a trance while raking.

How I wished to rake like him.

So I bent over and started to comb with short forward stabs. Sure enough, I didn't get hung up (or hung up as much) and soon my rake was full of fruit, with only a few tangles of weeds and vines this time. I was still slower than everyone else on the field, but at least I was getting some berries. Forty-five minutes later, my first bucket was heaping, my second bucket was three-quarters full and I felt a better mood approaching. Seven bucks an hour was better than the three I made in my first hour. Things were looking up.

All good things come to an end. First, I twisted my left ankle after stumbling into a hole half-hidden by a blueberry bush, which disturbed an underground wasp nest. The inhabitants were pissed and swarmed. I turned and ran. Got about 20 feet away, half-hobbling, before I tripped on another bush and fell to the ground. I rolled over and dozens of wasps were on me. I writhed and tried to swat them away. Unfortunately, I was still holding the rake in my right hand. So in the midst of my flailing, I stabbed the middle finger of my left hand.

Stabbed is putting it mildly. Impaled would more accurate. I was surprised by how easily the rake tine tore through my skin. A single tine was able to puncture, then rip an inch long jagged gash all the way to the tip of my finger. Before I could even consider the wound, though, several new pains struck.

Right cheek. Left forearm. Left side of neck. Right side of neck. Left leg. Then I felt the rest of the swarm discovering me, like Lilliputians on Gulliver. I knew I had to get the hell out of there, otherwise the attack would be debilitating. I struggled to my feet, left the rake behind and sprinted toward my truck, hobble-running away from the hive and swarm.

A minute later I was sitting in Floyd with my first aid kit on my lap. Hot as hell. My puncture bled. Gushed. Throbbed. I was surprised by the amount of blood. The wasp stings made me temporarily forgot my aching lower back. Taking account of my injuries, I realized I was lucky. The puncture wound wasn't fun, but it wasn't life-threatening either. As for the wasps, it's not like I was allergic and swelling. So after applying pressure to my finger for a couple minutes, I made mud, mixing dirt with drinking water and applied it to the stings. Ate one sandwich, drank water, then smoked the rest of Richard's joint while watching the other rakers.

Easy to tell the workers versus slackers who spent half the time sitting on an overturned bucket, smoking cigarettes. Workers, like Richard, seemed relentless. And Richard was slow compared to this one kid with a huge black beard, who raked robotically. Looked like one of those retro-hippie teenagers into Phish or Bonnie Prince Billy. Wore flannel on a hot summer day. A trucker's cap and thick black rimmed eyeglasses. This kid didn't stop for a second the whole time I was watching, sweeping and filling bucket after bucket.

Sitting there in my truck, I became inspired. To make the harvest worthwhile, I would transform myself into a raking machine like that kid. Otherwise, why bother showing up? Another long sip of water. Then back to my strip, energized, intent on raking some money.

It took fifteen minutes to find my rake after the wasp attack. Also took awhile to fine tune my combing technique because of the finger injury, which slowed me down a bit. Mix in the sweat, bugs and sun, and the afternoon was extremely unpleasant.

By four p.m. I was nearly dead. With another hour left in the workday, my right arm was about to fall off. My punctured finger still throbbed. Dehydrated (despite drinking a couple gallons of water) sun-burned and bug-bitten, my back was killing me. Felt like I'd been kicked a couple hundred times. For a second, I closed my eyes, rake in hand, and teetered, about to faint.

"Well, Mr. Franklin," Richard came up from behind, startling me back into consciousness. "How many berries did you get?"

"Ahhhh," I stammered. "About nine or ten buckets, I think..."

"*About?*" He shouted, shaking his head. "*About?* Dude, you gotta keep track of your berries. Anna writes the numbers down in the book, but you gotta keep your own total. Ask her for the weight when you take 'em off the scales." He shook his head. "I'm not saying she's a cheat or a thief, but you can't be too careful. Gotta make sure they don't make a mistake." He patted me on the back. "Ready to get the frig outta here?"

"I thought we raked until five?"

"Hah!" He shook his head, grinning. "That's what Larry wants you to think. Remember, he ain't our boss. We're independent contractors. We can come and go as we please. And he can't say nothing about it, 'cuz he needs us in order to get all the berries raked. Yeah, sure, he'd like us to work from six until six. Maybe Mexicans will do that, but no one from Washington County is gonna spend more than eight or nine hours raking. More than that," he nodded, "you'll wear yourself out. What's the friggin' point? You gotta finish the harvest in order to get to the best strips and the good money. The last fields are always the best. You still gonna give us a ride?"

"Oh yeah," I said, remembering my promise to bring Richard home. "Let me get these buckets to the scales."

"I'll meet you at your truck." He pointed toward Floyd. "I gotta talk to someone for a sec."

I was ready for a good night's sleep. My feet ached. I was exhausted, hungry and thirsty. My hair and fingernails were filthy. My hands were stained blue. I desperately needed a bath and dinner. But first Richard needed a lift, then a 45-minute trek back to Goose Island.

Richard appeared, followed by a little boy, a woman and a teenaged male who was dressed all in black.

"How many pounds you get?" Richard asked.

"Not many," I sighed. "Ten buckets. Two-hundred and forty-five pounds."

"Wow. That sucks. That's what? About..." He wrote the numbers in the air using his forefinger. "Thirty-four bucks?" He shook his head. "And it cost you $15 bucks on gas to get here and home. How many hours did you spend raking?"

"Well, if you don't count the wasps and looking for the rake and lunch and breaks..." I paused to do the math. "About eight hours."

"Plus a half hour commute each way."

"Actually, about 45 minutes."

"Man, you're driving too slow. Should barely take a half hour to get to Goose Island." He shook his head. "Anyways, not to make you feel bad, but you made about two bucks an hour. That really sucks."

"Yeah, that sucks," said the little boy, grabbing Richard by the hand. The kid was cute. Huge green eyes. Goofy grin. Big cowlick. "That really sucks, don't it Unk?"

"This fella here," Richard said, "is my main man, my top dog, my one and only nephew, known throughout Washington County as Captain." With his free hand, he tousled the kid's tangled mess of black hair. "Captain, this is Mr. Franklin."

"Hello, Mr. Franklin. Pleased to meet you." He offered his hand for me to shake, which I did.

"Nice to meet you, Capt..."

"Hello Mr. Franklin," the woman interrupted, "Nice to meet you."

"Ben, this is my sister." Richard stepped in between us. "I've been ignoring her for years, but she refuses to go away."

"Fuck you, Richard!" She shook her head angrily. "You can call me Buffy," She reached around him and extended her hand. "Pleased to meet you, Mr. Franklin."

"Call me Ben."

Her hand was sweaty. Buffy was hot, in a slutty, bad-girl way. In her early-20s, wearing cutoff shorts and a blue tank top, her long brown hair sticking out beneath a Boston Red Sox baseball cap. Sweet body under those clothes.

Maybe five foot tall with curves in all the right places. Firm breasts. Small ass. Not bad for a blueberry farm in the middle of Down East Maine.

Her face, though, was a little off. Her eyes were slightly crossed, seemingly in a permanent glare. Her lips were frozen somewhere between a half pout and sneer. When she opened her mouth, you could see the empty space where her left canine had once been. And her tattoos were bad. Jailhouse bad. The one on her right forearm looked like a blue carrot and the mottled two-inch crucifix on her left forearm, with "Big Paul" below it in messy handwriting, was green and fading fast.

"And this freakazoid," Richard pointed to the forlorn-looking teenage Goth boy, wearing sunglasses and big black boots draped in heavy chains. "This is my brother Jazz. Can you believe the get-up he's wearing? Probably sweating his balls off in there..."

"Lay off me, Richard, will yah?" the kid muttered. "Hey," he said to me, head downcast, with a half wave.

"Hey Jazz, nice to meet you." Up close he looked like a cross between Richard and a skinny vampire with spiky blue hair. Definitely not your average Washington County teenager. "How you doing?"

"Buffy and Jazz will ride in back," Richard said. "Me and Captain will be up front with you."

"I don't wanna ride in the back," Buffy whined.

For a split second, I hoped Richard would change his mind.

"Buffy and Jazz in the back, for frig's sake," Richard repeated, giving his sister a hard look. "Captain and I ride in front with Mr. Franklin."

"On the right," Richard said, 15 minutes later, while Floyd groaned climbing Steep Ridge Road. He shook his head and grinned. "Not to bust your chops, Ben, but you drive like a friggin' old lady. Takes me less than 10 minutes to get home."

"Look," Captain pointed. "Unk's truck."

"Oh," I spotted a crunched red Chevy on the side of the road, just below the crest of the hill. "Here?"

"Yeah," Richard said. "Did I mention we live in a old church?"

"Nope." This place wasn't a classic New England church, though. On the front of the single-story, prefab steel building, I could just barely make out the faded silhouettes of capital letters spelling the former church's name on the yellow sheet metal: Kingdom Hall. I counted six windows. "Interesting."

"My old man bought this place for nothing 10 years ago." Richard gestured toward the building. "Friggin' Jehovah Witnesses abandoned it. Poor bastards couldn't keep up on the mortgage." He pointed to the birch and spruce tree line on the other side of the parking lot. "Plus 15 acres back there. Half woodlot and half vegetables. That's where I stay, most of the year."

Buffy and Jazz climbed out of the back of Floyd as soon we stopped. Captain climbed over his uncle's lap, scrambled out of the truck and ran to the yellow building, entering through a side door. Jazz was right behind him.

"They're checking on the puppy," Richard said. "Rottie and Shepherd mix. Named Pigeon. Gonna be a huge dog."

"We gonna smoke a joint?" Buffy asked, appearing at the door. "'Cuz this morning you promised we was gonna smoke one if I lasted all day. But I gotta take a shower 'cuz I got plans."

"I'm afraid to ask where you're going." Richard turned to me. "How about it, Ben? Smoke a joint?"

I hesitated for a moment. Exhausted. Hungry. Thirsty. Sore. My finger throbbed. I didn't want to drive home. I wished instead to be instantly transported to a hot bath in my tub on Goose Island. But that wasn't going to happen. Besides, a chance to smoke Richard's killer weed while checking out his homestead was very appealing.

Monica and I moved to Washington County because it was the last part of Maine, near the ocean, with affordable chunks of land. Plus, Washington County, the size of Rhode Island and Delaware combined, had a population of only 35,000. A good place to homestead, far enough away from the masses who would be on the prowl when our petro-fueled economy collapsed.

Monica and I were eager to do what humans have done for centuries. Tend to pastures, raise livestock and grow veggies, plus have a 5 acre wood lot. Apple trees. Maybe a cow, a mini-Jersey we'd call Petunia. Chickens for eggs and roasting. Pigs. And two goat herds. One meat and one dairy. Or, perhaps, a single breed of goat with a good reputation for both. Goats were a constant topic of discussion between Monica and I, augmented by many hours of reading and research.

But buying land was still another year off, at least. Monica's job at the high school was gonna pay $11 an hour. Awesome by local standards, though only part time. Barely covered rent and half our food budget. But the principal had promised a full-time gig in the spring. And floor refinishing jobs would start coming my way. Hopefully.

Once we were in the cash and had saved enough for a down payment, we'd find some owner-financed land, ten or more acres. Monica would continue working at the school. I'd do the chores, tend the animals and build a little studio. Just a shack, really. Big enough to set up keyboards, drums and my guitars. Plus mics and recording gear. Tiny, but big enough to give me a place to think and work on my music.

"C'mon. I've got a 12 pack in the cooler," Richard grinned. "Nothing like a cold brew after raking blueberries all day. Plus you can check out my garden."

"Yes." A drink and garden tour cinched it. "A beer would be great."

"OK, Buffy," Richard pointed at her. "Go feed Captain. Your kid is friggin' starving. Meet us at the camp in about a half hour. I'm gonna show Ben the garden. And if you're good, maybe I'll get you high."

Richard walked me through his rows and rows of vegetables. A micro-farm, not a garden. Several types of corn. Six tomato strains of determinate. Six indeterminate. Red and white beets. Cauliflower. Broccoli. Broccoflower. Shallots. Onions: red, white and yellow. Carrots, two kinds. Many rows of potatoes. And rows and rows of rich orange and yellow marigolds which, he said, kept away many bugs.

"Eventually, I'll have a greenhouse for the tomatoes and salad greens," he said. "Can't wait to have lettuce and spinach, year round."

He showed me his old red tractor, then we walked along a small pond at the bottom of the sloping field. Richard pointed toward a mishmash of hoses and water pipes connected to a rough pump house he used to send water uphill during the dry times.

"Over there, that's where the garlic was. Planted 10 pounds of seed, harvested about 50 pounds of some nice Russian and Red Bohemian in mid-July. It's still drying." He pointed to the other corner we hadn't visited. "That's my pumpkin patch." He grinned and, with his missing tooth, was a jack-o'-lantern. "Gonna be one of my cash crops." He nodded. "Yup."

We ended up at Richard's campsite, on top of the hill, at the edge of a forest of spruce, birch and maple lining the path back to the parking lot. We relaxed at his picnic table and drank a beer.

"I call this a market garden. Too small to be considered a truck farm," Richard said while trimming several beautiful marijuana buds. "A buddy of mine over in Charlotte has a farm stand where he sells just about everything I give him. Except pumpkins," he sighed. "I need a market for my pumpkins."

"I could totally live here." I said, looking around. Pots and pans hung from nails on a trio of small spruce trees on the other side of Richard's two-room canvas tent with a small canopy that extended toward the fire pit in the middle of the camp. Two big metal coolers were chained to the legs of the picnic table. "Food" was scrawled on one in black magic marker. On the other, "Beer." Both coolers had padlocks which Richard unlocked with a key from his pouch. A slight wind cooled the campsite. "This is awesome," I sighed jealously. "Real great."

"Thanks. Over there," he pointed to the tree line on the other side of the field, "if I cut down a whole bunch trees, we'd have an ocean view. Twenty-five miles away. On a clear day, you'd see the cliffs of Grand Manan."

"Wow."

"Breeze keeps most of the mosquitoes away." Richard put a joint in his mouth. "Only bad thing is the black flies. May and June is wicked thick with the bastards. I set up a screen house then. Only way you can be outside. Friggin' black flies are awful."

"Where do you live in the winter?"

"Ugggh. Hell." He shook his head. "In the basement of the church. A friggin' cave. Every summer I think about building a teepee and trying to stay out all winter, but I usually head inside when it gets real cold. Mid-November. After I'm done tipping in the woods for Christmas wreaths." He shrugged. "Maybe December, at the latest. Could be worse." He shook his head again and pointed toward the path. "In the basement, I got a little wood stove. Cook soups and stews on it. A dorm fridge. Microwave. Hot plate. Couple friggin' lava lamps. It's dark and warm and I can lock the door. Basement has its own private entrance. For the ladies." He grinned and slapped his knee. "Yes sir! But most of the winter, I just chill out. Hibernate. Listen to music. Plan my garden. Read the seed catalogues. Smoke dope." He paused for a second. "I gotta get my own land, though. Gotta get me a yurt. Or build a little shack. Don't need anything too friggin' fancy. Last seven years I've focused on this garden. Which benefits my old man." He sighed. "And I'm not a fan of his." He shrugged. "Took a couple years just getting the soil right. Lots of experimenting and friggin' around." He sparked the joint. "Covered some of the rows in seaweed for two years before I even planted. That's why living near the ocean is great. Tons of free fertilizer. Go to the shore and get seaweed. There's a bunch of places where you can drive your truck right onto the beach. Get the seaweed that washes above the tideline. Bring it home and set it out in the dooryard for a couple storms to let the rain rinse the salt away. I use it as mulch and in my compost." He pointed. "And I'm making my own liquid fertilizer out of it. Put the seaweed into a trash can, fill with water and cover. Stir occasionally. A month and a half later you got liquid gold."

"Wow." Even though he was a bit of freak, I knew I could learn a lot about gardening from him.

"I've dried seaweed and ground it into powder and mixed it into the soil. And we've added a lot of compost to these fields. Our chicken poop and seaweed combination has turned out to be the perfect mix, turns into great compost. Super soil." He took a quick puff and handed me the joint. "You could eat my dirt, so moist and rich. Lotta work, let me tell you."

"Sounds like it's worth it." I inhaled. "I can't wait until me and Monica move to the land."

"Since this is my old man's land, I don't really wanna make too many more improvements. Rather spend my time and energy on my own spread. But that takes cash. And it's tough for me to save much money, considering we're in Washington County. But I got my eye on a nice piece."

"Really? Around here?"

"Down the road a little ways and over the other ridge."

He took the joint back.

"Well," he said after a long puff. "Everyone has a tough time making it in Washington County, but after a while, I'm hoping for a payoff from the veggies. Right now, this," he gestured toward the rows, "feeds the family and some friends, then I make four or five grand after that. Trade with my buddy Buzz down the road for milk, cheese and butter. Plus I have a couple rich folks out on the lake that stop by here for fresh veggies. I rip them off for prices higher than the IGA and they don't care. Everything else goes to the farm stand. Especially my taters and tomatoes. 'Cuz I get a good price for 'em."

"Do you have blueberries?"

"Are you friggin' kidding me?" He shook his head. "Tough to make a profit with berries, unless you're a processor. The only reason Larry is still doing 'em is because it's his family thing and he didn't have to pay for the land. Though on the property I wanna buy, there's a couple acres of berries. Probably rake enough to pay the taxes and sell the rest to my rich customers." He sighed. "I've got a couple other schemes, but this year, I'm hoping my friggin' pumpkins turn into a real cash crop."

"Really?"

"Yep. My second year of pumpkins. Me and Lora are doing 'em together."

"Lora?"

"She's my girlfriend. Wait a minute, you're from Portland, right?"

"Yep."

"If I brought a couple thousand pumpkins down to Portland, could I sell them?" He took a puff and handed me the joint.

"Good question," I said, inhaling and wondering what a couple thousand pumpkins looked like. "I don't know. Why?"

" 'Cuz me and Lora were thinking. Around here, we're lucky to sell a couple hundred pumpkins for a buck a piece. But Lora read online that people in Portland don't think nuthin' of spending 10 bucks on a pumpkin. So we're thinking of maybe trying to sell ours there. Or maybe go down to Boston. Or New York City. Even if we just unload 'em at five bucks wholesale that's ten grand. That's a down payment on the land."

"Sounds like a good idea..."

"Oh Lora is full of good ideas. She's wicked smart. And hot too! Hold on. Let me get her picture."

Richard got up from the picnic table, ducked into his tent and reappeared with a piece of paper.

"This is her." He unfolded the paper. "My Lora."

"She's cute," I said, though he only showed me the top of the photo. Her face and shoulders. Lora looked pretty enough, with a nice smile, slightly chunky cheeks, librarian glasses and long blonde hair.

Richard grinned and unfolded the rest of the photograph. Lora was naked and sitting, spread-eagle, in a chair. Her arms were sleeved with snake tattoos. Both nipples were pierced. She had a finger inside herself.

"She's so friggin' hot," Richard said, pointing. "And she shaves for me."

"I bet," I said, not knowing what to say. I kept looking at the picture and took another puff. "Great."

"We'd love to get her pussy pierced," he said, taking the joint back. "Can't find anyone to do it around here. They say the insurance is too expensive. You know anywhere in Portland that would do it?"

"Oh, I'm sure there's plenty of places."

"Right on. When we sell the pumpkins down there, she can get it done."

"Where is she now?" I asked, swapping him the photo for the joint.

"Down in Machias. For a couple more weeks."

"Oh, what's she doing down there?" I took a drag, but the joint was out.

"A month."

"Huh?"

"It's a bunch of bull." Richard put the photo on the picnic table. "Bunch of trumped up charges. I can't visit her because I don't have wheels. And 'cuz I've got a record. I'm out on bail, myself." He shook his head. "All a bunch of malarkey. She was just chilling with friends and they all got busted for possession and..."

"Hello boys," Buffy interrupted, surprising me and snatching the joint from my fingers. "Hey, you assholes started without me."

She must have snuck along the fringe of the forest into the campsite. She had a comb in her left hand, a pack of Marlboro Lights 100s and a lighter in her right. Her hair was wet. She looked great. Sexy. Her firm breasts pressed her nipples hard against her tight pink Red Sox shirt. Her denim mini-skirt barely covered her ass. Her lacy pink tights made it easy to ignore her cross-eyed stare.

Head to toe, she was quite hot. A raunchy, sleazy hot.

"Oh shut the frig up, Buffy," Richard snapped. "Quit your whining. I'm gonna smoke another one."

"Good." She lit the roach, took a couple puffs and then handed it back to me, all while running the comb through her hair. "Any beer?"

"Sure," Richard nodded, taking the joint from me. "I hear Mary's Market has a whole fridge of 'em."

"C'mon Richard," she whined, "just one. I'm going out."

"Where's Captain?"

"Just finished supper. I told him to put that damn dog in the crate and then he could come out here." She stopped combing and picked up the paper portrait sitting on the table. "Oh, the lovely Lora. Looking good." She stared at it for a second. "When did she shave her bush?"

"None of your friggin' business," Richard said, grabbing the picture. He folded it and shoved it into his back pocket. "What did you feed your son for dinner?"

"I nuked 'dogs and beans."

"Really? You are such a great mom." Richard shook his head. "How about vegetables? Plenty of carrots. Beans. Cukes. You ever think of that?"

"I nuked tater puffs, too." She stuck out her tongue. It was pierced with a silver barbell. "And he had lots of ketchup. That's some tomatoes." She nodded. "Can I have a beer, Richard? Please, just one?"

"Oh, all right." He was annoyed. But I felt that he was being polite and generous because I was there. "One beer." He lit the second joint. "Where you going anyway?"

She popped open a Bud and took a long sip. "See someone about..." she paused, "some work."

"Who?" Richard stood up. "Who would hire you?"

"People. Friends of Buzz. You don't know 'em."

"Where you meeting them?" Richard asked.

"Down," she said, taking another long sip, "at the Black Bear."

"A job interview in a bar?" He shook his head. "How you planning to get to Roosevelt?"

"I thought maybe," she looked at me, "Mr. Franklin could give me a lift on his way back to Goose Island."

"Oh," I said, "well, I..."

"Listen Buffy," Richard cut me off. "Roosevelt ain't on the way to Goose Island." He handed me the reefer. "Ignore her, Ben. Hopefully she'll disappear."

"I know it ain't on the way," she said, "but if he brought me, probably add maybe 20 minutes to his trip. Would you mind?" She fluttered her eyelashes at me.

"Ignore her," Richard said. "So what kinda job?"

"You know," Buffy said. "House cleaning for rich people who need..."

"*Hey Unk*!" Captain shouted, suddenly appearing on the edge of the campsite, like he dropped out of a tree. "Can I get a helicopter ride?"

"Hey buddy! Sure thing." Richard stood. "Get over here." He walked to the open area by the side of his tent. "First helicopter ride is free. Second costs you."

"*Hah*!" the boy laughed and ran toward his uncle, reaching for the outstretched hands. Richard began to spin. "*Hah hah*!" went the little boy as he went round and round.

"Listen Ben." Buffy came close and took the joint from me, then took a deep puff. She leaned closer, her breasts stressing the Red Sox logo, pressing against my arm. "Could you give me a lift? I'll make it worth your while."

"*Hah, hah*," squealed Captain. "*Hah, hah*!"

"I'm sorry, Buffy, but I..."

"I'm serious." She took another puff, then leaned closer. "I'll suck you off."

I took a long sip of beer, stalling, despite the erection that appeared instantly.

"You'll really like it."

"I'm sure," I said. My erection, hung up in my sweaty boxers, was at an uncomfortable angle. My mind began to linger on her mouth. "I'm..."

"I'll make you cum so fast you won't even believe it!"

"Ahhhh," I stammered, further aroused by the seediness of the possibility. We'd park on a dirt road. We wouldn't kiss or touch or caress. She'd lean across the front seat and unzip me. Her head would bob up and down, back and forth, side to side, barely missing the steering wheel until I finished in her mouth. She'd gulp loudly and the act would be followed by a silent ride into Roosevelt, where I would drop her off at the bar. A quick exchange for transportation. Like the joint Richard gave me for the ride home from the fields. Gas money. Gas blowjob. Barter. Trade. Not really sex. Not cheating. Not much more than masturbation.

Of course I couldn't give Buffy a ride. My beautiful wife was waiting for me at home. I took another sip of my beer. She looked back anxiously at her brother.

"Really," she said, "how 'bout it, Ben?" Buffy again batted the lashes of her crossed eyes at me. She opened her mouth and flickered her tongue at me like a serpent. "Wouldn't that be good? Nice and clean. Very hot. I'll swallow and everything."

"Wheeeeee!"

I turned in time to see Richard let go. Captain flew through the air and landed on his feet almost 10 feet from his uncle, then stumbled and tumbled onto the ground. The little boy started laughing and giggling and couldn't stop.

"Hey Ben," Richard called out, "I don't care what she says, don't give her ride."

"Fuck you, Richard," she snapped. "Stay out of this, you asshole."

"Language!" Richard snapped back. "How many times are you gonna swear in front of your kid? You want him to sound like a friggin' piece of white trash?" He pointed at his sister. "You're such a terrible mom."

They stood there and glared at each other. My opportunity to leave.

"Thanks, Richard," I took a couple steps away from Buffy. She flashed me the hopeful crossed eyes again. "Gotta split. Thanks for the beers and for the smoke and for the tour. Pretty awesome place. I'm wicked impressed. Can't wait 'til I get my own spread of land." I turned back to Buffy and gave her a half wave. "Sorry I can't give you a lift," I said, wondering if my erection was visible. Wondering if my walk would look odd because of my hardness. "Maybe next time. I'm already late. My wife's probably freaking. I gotta get home."

"Oh." She stared at me and shook her head sadly. "Guess I'm gonna have to hitchhike."

"Yeah," Richard said, "you'll catch a ride dressed like that." He nodded. "If I'm lucky, it'll be a crazed serial killer."

She flashed him a sour look.

"All right," I said, "I'll see you guys tomorrow."

I walked, almost jogged, down the path and jumped into Floyd and took off quick, just in case Buffy decided to give chase and divert my drive back to Goose Island.

Getting behind the wheel made my finger throb, my back ache and feet hurt. Despite all that, I had a pretty good buzz from the beer and killer weed. A mile from Richard's house, I impulsively pulled over and parked at the boat launch on the east side of Sutherland's Lake. I jumped out of the truck, stripped off my tee-shirt and jeans, shoes and socks. Wearing just my boxers, I ran and dove into the lake, scaring and scattering the huge flock of ducks floating and bobbing in the warm water.

From the bottom, I scooped up a handful of sand and gravel and rubbed my grubby palms together. The tiny rocks scraped the blueberry and dirt stains from my skin. The lake was purifying, cleansing me of the fields and thoughts of Buffy. I pulled the band-aid from my finger. The puncture still hurt, but was clean. I started to swim. Kicked, crawled and pushed through the slight resistance of the lake. A hundred feet later, I finally felt better, my muscles enjoying a strain and pull different from raking.

I flipped onto my back and started to float aimlessly, staring at the occasional cloud slowly crossing the late afternoon summer cerulean sky.

As Richard pointed out, I made $34 from my ten buckets. Minus gas, I made $20 for a hard day of labor and pain. But it was my first day, so a learning curve was to be expected. Hopefully, the wasp attacks and self-inflicted stabbings would come to a stop. And my technique was bound to get better.

What about Richard? I couldn't figure him out. Obviously, a decent human since he was basically raising his sister's kid. And his lack of vulgarity struck me as oddly quaint. And I knew he was a hard worker. A garden like his didn't come easy. Plus his weed was top notch. Still, I wasn't sure I liked him.

Buffy freaked me out. I had time for a swim call, so I could have driven her to Roosevelt and still been home around the same time. The guilt would have lasted longer than any fleeting orgasmatic pleasure. Floating on my back, staring into the clouds, I saw Buffy's long tongue appear and wiggle at me.

Instantly, I was aroused again. Her mouth. Her lips. Her studded tongue. That short skirt. Those pink tights. In my brain, I heard her promise to swallow me. None of these thoughts, though, were conducive to swimming.

I needed to get rid of the erection and I needed to go home. I flipped over and breast-stoked my way towards shore. When I was 25 feet from land, I noticed a couple kids fishing near where I parked the truck. Which was problematic, because even while swimming, Buffy lingered in my brain and loins. I was stuck in the water because of a hard-on.

I dove deep, held my nose, kept my eyes open and looked up. From below, the lake's surface was a warped window into another world. The sky was blueberry, dotted with two blurry, fluffy clouds.

I surfaced for more air, then dove again. This time, I went straight to the bottom, eyes wide open, and spotted an extraordinary number of snails. The lake floor was covered with shell. Almost no plant life. Distracted by the snails, my erection disappeared. Finally, I could wade ashore without worry.

The swim was rejuvenating. Free of dirt and sweat, the rest of the drive home looked easy. I could listen to the CBC news and savor dinner with my sweet wife. I vowed to take a dip every day after raking.

"Hey fellas," I waved to the two boys fishing. They were maybe 12 or 13 years old, casting their lines into a patch of lily pads. "Catch anything?"

"Nope," the taller one said.

"But you might," the other added, pointing at me with a short laugh. "Maybe you did."

"Whaddya mean?" I asked.

"Not supposed to go swimming in the lake because of swimmer's itch," said the taller boy. " 'Cuz of all the duck shit."

"Plus there's lots of leeches around here," said the other boy, shaking his head. "Man, I hope the leeches didn't get you. Better check your privates."

I spun around, away from the boys, and pulled my boxers down to examine my crotch. Nothing, luckily.

"I'm fine," I said to the kids. "No leeches."

As I climbed into Floyd, they were laughing at me.

Ganeesh and the Girls

Usually I don't remember my dreams, but I couldn't forget two from the night after the start of the harvest. The first was ultra-realistic. I was raking alone in a field of the most succulent, heavy blueberries imaginable. The blue went on forever, uninterrupted by weeds or wildflowers, and looked more like the ocean than solid earth. Berries bigger than grapes rolled off the stems with amazing ease, cleanly filling the rake. After a while, I looked into my bucket, expecting it to be full. But the berries barely covered the bottom. I was confused. I bent over again and combed, faster and faster. Suddenly, I was in severe pain. I fell to the ground. On my knees, it felt like an unseen assailant was trying to snap my arm off. I was in agony. A heart attack? About to die? Then my vision went blue, the exact shade of berry.

Woke up soaked in sweat. Laying on the edge of the bed, my right arm, my raking arm, was twisted beneath my body. Hurt like a son-of-a-bitch. I untangled and looked at the clock. Two a.m. Three more hours until the beginning of another day of blueberry torture and I was wasting precious slumber by sleep-raking. For several minutes, I stared at the ceiling, listening to the steady breaths of Monica and our two dogs. My back hurt. My arms hurt. But my feet didn't. And for that I was glad. Then the bad thoughts started entering my head. Would raking get any easier? Would the pain go away? Would I make enough to pay the bills? In the last moments before drifting off to sleep, the image of Buffy flickering her tongue invaded my brain. What if she offered another blowjob?

Then I dreamed about her. She and I were alone in a field where the berries were scarce and the only ones we found were tiny blue raisins. In the bucket, they rattled like dried beans. After hours of endless raking, I collapsed onto the hard ground. A million different crawling bugs covered me in an instant. Mosquitoes and wasps followed and screamed and buzzed in my ears. Buffy stood above me, wearing a gingham house coat. She pulled the coat up, slightly, and curtsied. She was naked underneath. And shaved. Just as she climbed atop me, I noticed a huge wasp – the size of a small bird -- hovering, circling over her head. And I heard the swarm following, growing louder and louder until I woke to the alarm clock buzzing.

A wet dream about raking blueberries would have been a first. Certainly for me. I slapped the alarm silent and tried to roll out of bed. But the pain stopped me. My body had a sore ache both dull and sharp. Took a deep breath and tried again, gritting my teeth through the anguish and up and out of bed, onto to my feet. Went into the bathroom to take a leak, which was cumbersome due to an incessant erection. Pissing didn't make the arousal disappear. I was still hard a minute later when I put the tea kettle on the stove. Despite my sore wrists and swollen fingers, I was able to masturbate while looking out the kitchen window into the dark backyard, visualizing Buffy's head bobbing in my lap in the front seat of my truck.

I finished long before the kettle whistled, so I turned on the radio. The BBC's *World Update* was talking about more death in Iraq. I clumsily rolled a joint of shitty weed. The lousy pot I brought Down East, courtesy of Sammy's Stems and Seeds in Portland, was a letdown after Richard's sweet marijuana. No comparison. Like instant potato flakes versus garlic-mashed new red potatoes. Kraft Mac and Cheese versus Monica's homemade cheddar and shells.

I smoked the joint and drank two cups of tea in quick succession. I made and ate a couple egg sandwiches, then filled a gallon jug with water and grabbed the bagged lunch Monica packed the night before. By quarter of six, I was in the truck, headed off Goose Island via the seven miles of causeway and small islands. The fading rosy-fingered dawn was in my rearview mirror as I drove through the Passamaquoddy reservation and started my back road odyssey.

Driving magnified the pain in my back. Gripping the steering wheel, the puncture wound resumed its throbbing. My other fingers were swollen sausages. My whole body was sore. Arms. Knees. Shoulders. When my feet touched the gas and brake, I discovered my soles were quite tender.

Forty-five minutes later, I made the turn onto the last leg of the commute, a quarter mile-long series of potholes and washouts with thick walls of spruce lining each side. To call this a road is a lie, but halfway down, I had to stop because a giant bull moose (bigger than Floyd!) blocked my route. I shut the engine off. For a minute, we stared at each other. Then the majestic animal looked over his shoulder and effortlessly pushed through the spruce, disappearing into the forest.

The road eventually became a wide path, then briefly, a narrow creek. Floyd splattered mud, like we were four-wheeling. A hundred yards later, the road opened up and made its way across the lower blueberry fields. I parked near the port-a-potty. Rake in hand, I jumped out. I didn't see Richard or Buffy. Actually, I didn't see many rakers. The day before there were 20. This morning, I counted eight.

Larry was surprised to see me.

"Didn't think you'd make it, " he called out, smiling, as I walked toward the bucket pile. "Thought yesterday had been enough. Lottsa people would have quit. Hah! But you're a tough sonofabitch, aren't yah? I can tell." He patted me on the back. "Don't worry, today will be better. We'll make sure you get some berries. Gets easier as you go along." He nodded and lit a smoke. "So tell me, what do you think is harder? Floor refinishing or raking?"

"Blueberry raking. Without question, blueberries."

"Sore this morning?"

"Well, I've got a constant stabbing in my lower back on both sides. My neck's killing me. Can barely turn it left or right. My knees ache and my feet are swollen and throbbing." I didn't mention the wasps or finger wound. "Besides the sunburn and bug bites from yesterday, that's about it. But I don't want to complain."

"Too late." Larry laughed. "Raking is supposed to hurt, but not that much. Maybe you should try stretching before starting. And drink lots of water. Hotter than a sonofabitch. And if you really start to hurt, take a break. Don't want you dying out there." He pointed at me with his smoke. "I'm serious."

"Not many people here, huh?"

"Nope." Larry shook his head. "Pillheads don't work the hot days. Only the truly dedicated or truly desperate are here today. Which one are you?"

"Ahhhhh." I paused for a second. Did I want to admit to being desperate? "Dedicated."

"Good, so I won't bullshit you." Larry pointed at me again. "This ain't gonna be a banner year. Hell, it could turn out to be the worst year, evah. That being said," he smiled, "I'll let you in on a little secret. There's still real good patches out there. We do the worst places first. To weed out the riffraff." He took another puff of his smoke. "The good patches are for those who last. And then the raking is real good. Blue, blue, blue. A real dream."

Day two was a lot like day one, except for a few things: no wasp attacks, no stabbing myself with the rake and by nine a.m., I was averaging almost seven dollars per hour. Jazz, without Richard and Buffy, showed up at some point. He was raking a couple strips away from me, side by side with an older woman, a golden blonde wearing a tank top and a pair of cut-off jeans one size too small. She could have been pushing 40 after hard living or she could have been a youthful 70-year-old hippie. At one point in her life, she was a great beauty and still had a sexy aura, despite her crackled face and slouch.

Larry stopped to talk to them. From where I raked, I heard every word.

"I'm sorry, Peggy, You know the rule." Larry shook his head. "No advances. But I can have my sister pay you for what you rake today. Only 'cuz you're one of the best rakers, evah. And I know you're gonna do the whole harvest, right?"

She nodded.

He handed her a smoke and lit it for her. "A day's pay should get you some food, cigs and gas in your tank."

Larry patted her shoulder and started across the field again. He barely made it 20 feet before another raker stopped him for a smoke. A ridiculous-looking teenager, maybe 16 years old. A Down East homeboy. Pale, white and skinny, he wore an oversized Patriots' jersey, a Red Sox hat cocked to the left and several earrings in each lobe. Baggy jeans hung down past his ass. Serious bling around his neck. Fake or real, didn't matter. He seemed out-of-place on the field carrying a bucket and rake. Probably would have been happier rapping with his homeboys in a suburban mall food court or kicking back on his mom's couch watching TV or playing video games.

At high noon, after raking 192 pounds (2/3 of day one's total), I sat on Floyd's tailgate. Hidden by a couple other trucks, in the shade, with a clear view of the water cooler, the fields and the port-a-potty, I ate my ham sandwiches and eavesdropped on the homeslice who bummed the cig from Larry. The kid apparently went by the name "Hip-Hop." He and a couple other teens took a smoke break standing around the water cooler. From what I gathered, the trio attended the same middle school, but hadn't seen much of each other since.

"9-11 really sucked," Hip-Hop said. "Fucked me right up."

Did he lose someone in the attacks? Was a parent or sibling off fighting the war on terror? Was he more sensitive and aware of world events than my preconceived notion of him allowed? Nope.

"They never used to search me at the border in Roosevelt. Used to walk right across the bridge and they barely even looked at me. Now on the way back in, the guards are real pricks. The American border guards can't seem to touch you enough. Friggin' perv faggots. Shit, I wouldn't be surprised if this whole terrorist thing is a scam. A stupid excuse to look for drugs and to grab the cock and balls of good-looking kids like me." He took an exaggerated puff on his smoke and nodded vigorously. "And to steal our liberties. Before 9-11, me and my bro were smuggling, big time. We'd make a couple hundred bucks for each pound of weed we brought across. And I was just 12 years old." He pointed north. "Shit, one time I made a cool grand carrying a big bag of pills in my underwear. Looked like I had a huge cock." He grabbed his groin and his buddies laughed. "Bigger than my already huge cock. But since 9-11," he shook his head, "if the border guards are suspicious, they can make you bend over and they can look deep into your asshole. Twice, already, they looked in my asshole. For what? Bombs? They really think me and my bro are terrorists carrying assbombs?" His audience laughed again. "I said to the guard, what makes you think I'm a fucking sand-nigger Muslim? Crazy. I just can't make the cash I made when I was a kid. That's why I'm stuck raking friggin' blueberries and selling dime bags to you guys." He shook his head. "Busting my balls under a hot sun for 14 cents a friggin' pound. Fourteen cents! Shit! Shit! *Shit*! *Shit*!" he said.

I laughed and took a long drink of water. I couldn't tell if this kid was a liar or braggart. No matter, he sounded like an asshole white boy poseur.

"Hey look," Hip-Hop said. "Here comes Buffy Buffster. She's a mom I'd like to fuck. For an older bitch, she's hot. Yes sir."

Richard was carrying Captain on his shoulders. Buffy was five feet behind, with a deep scowl on her face. If they'd walked all the way from the church, it would have taken hours. Buffy was probably super-pissed.

While Hip-Hop and the other boys laughed, I saw the door to the port-a-potty swing open and Peggy appeared through a cloud of blue smoke. She looked around, checking if the coast was clear. Then Jazz stepped out. A second later, Peggy lit a smoke, took a long drag and handed it to Jazz. Wished I had a camera. Teenaged Goth and tired beauty, standing close, leaning on the port-a-potty on a blueberry field, sharing a smoke. Intimate. Raw. Real and surreal simultaneously.

I watched Richard and Buffy walk toward the bucket pile. Hopefully Richard had a joint he wanted to smoke because I wasn't even remotely interested in getting back to work. If I was high, might be a different story. Weed might motivate me. I'd been perched, on my ass, on the tailgate for almost 20 minutes. My muscles were frozen stiff. Worse than a bucket break. Rolled my shoulders and rotated my head and neck to loosen up. Tried to walk, but I was clumsily rigid and unbending for each robotic step toward the bucket pile.

"Hey Ben." Richard knelt so Captain could climb down from his shoulders. "How's it friggin' hanging?"

"Great," I said. "Nice of you to show up. You raking today? Christ, almost time to go home."

"A little bit of a late start. Had some business to attend to, but I'll still rake more than you." He laughed. "Pretty tough to get around in Washington County when you don't have wheels."

"You guys walked here? Man, that must have taken..."

"No friggin' way. It's about five miles or so, even with shortcuts through the woods. Too far for Captain." He patted his nephew on the head. "Can't ask Captain to walk to work. Then he'd be too tired to rake berries. I need his help raking, so I can buy me a new truck. Ain't that right, Captain?"

"Yeah, Unk." The kid yawned, walked over to his mother and grabbed her hand. Buffy didn't acknowledge me. She pushed Captain's hand away and walked over to Hip-Hop and his posse. With a tilt of his head, Richard told me to follow him. We went behind the farm truck. My spirits rose. Time for a joint.

"Our neighbor Sally dropped us off. And we hiked the last half-mile." He shrugged. "Not fun. My sister friggin' whined the whole walk. Listen, I need a favor. In exchange for this," he pulled a fat joint out of the pouch around his waist, "could you help me out this afternoon? I'm really in a jam."

"How?" I asked, staring at the marijuana. The favor was sure to involve a ride. Even though I was dying to get home after raking, I also needed to get high, otherwise the afternoon would be hell. The joint was an irresistible carrot. Giving Richard a lift would be a quick detour before a hot bath with a glass of cheap red wine, then dinner, relaxing and hopefully sex with my wife. As long as I didn't have to be alone with Buffy, everything would be okay. "Whaddya need?"

"Well, a ride home would be great, since we've got Captain. By the end of the day, he'll be wicked tired. Then I need a ride to my buddy's house. Ten minutes from my place."

He handed me the joint.

"Yeah, no problem." I was both weak and cheap. "Sure thing. Should we spark this?"

"No time for me." Richard held up his hand. "I'm wicked behind." He looked down at his nephew. "All set, Captain?"

"I'm ready, Unk!" The little guy smiled up at Richard. "I don't even have to go to the bathroom."

"Good boy." Richard smiled and gave me a salute. "See you around 4."

I smoked half the joint and got super-high. Unfortunately, I had to get back to raking. Stoop labor. Combing. Lugging full buckets across the field to the weigh station.

Kept hearing the chorus in my head. Rent coming. Bills due. Plus, I knew the larder was getting close to bare and we only had a hundred and fifty bucks left in the bank. Monica's first paycheck was still far in the future. Raking sucked.

In Portland, I never worried about making ends meet, because, when things got tight, I'd take on more work or book an extra musical gig. Living in Washington County, however, on the edge of the United States of America, surrounded by 30 percent poverty and the highest unemployment in Maine, making cash wasn't gonna be so easy.

It was either the reefer or reality, but suddenly I feared ending up completely broke with no prospects. And that made me nervous. Very, very nervous.

I walked to the bucket pile. Larry stood there, smoking, looking across his fields.

"Go west, young man," he told me and pointed up the long gradual slope of blue. "You're gonna have a great time over there. Blue, real blue. Start in the strip next to Lil' Luke."

"Luke?"

"Kid with the half-cocked baseball cap and all sorts of earrings."

"Oh. I thought his name was Hip-Hop."

"No. His name is Luke." He pointed west. "Little Luke, actually. His dad, Big Luke, used to work for me. For a long, long time. Mean sonofabitch but a helluva raker."

"Used to?"

"Locked up down in Windham for kicking the shit out of some rich architect from Brewer in front of the Black Bear. Fella's still a vegetable. Two witnesses swore Big Luke kicked the man in the head dozens of times. Wouldn't stop. Real brutal. But Big Luke pleaded not guilty. Claimed it was mistaken identity."

"You think he did it?"

"Sure. 'Course he did. Big Luke's a wicked asshole and a liar. But he's got a wife and a couple boys. I feel sorry for them 'cuz times are always tight 'round here. But they're a lot better off with him locked up. Funny, huh?" He paused for a second, then nodded. "Oh well. You'll be next to Little Luke. You'll be pleased with the patches. A whole bunch of blue. Bring extra buckets."

"Yes, sir." I saluted him. "I'm just gonna have some more water."

"*Hey Larry!*" Someone shouted for him. "*Take a look at this...*"

"See you later." He turned around and walked into the fields. Could he tell I was stoned? Did it matter? I was probably more sober than half the other rakers on the fields. Almost impossible, I realized, to do this job without some sort of pain reliever.

The afternoon wasn't bad. The reefer helped me find my rhythm. Also helped that every single part of my strip was thick with juicy blueberries. I got so many berries, the muggy weather and the throngs of flesh-devouring insects barely bothered me. By half past three, I was wiped out and lugged my final two buckets over to the scales for a grand total of 545 pounds. About $75, twice what I made on day one.

Perhaps raking wouldn't be so bad after all. If I kept improving and averaged a hundred bucks a day for the next three weeks, Monica and I could pay the bills and relax, enjoy the rest of the summer, until I got some floor refinishing work and school started.

At four, Richard and Captain arrived with Jazz in tow, who was still wearing his chains and boots and trench coat.

"My god, Jazz," I said. "You must be sweating your balls off. Gotta be a hundred degrees under the sun."

"Not so bad," Jazz answered with a mumble. "Doesn't bother me."

"Friggin' crazy, dressing in all black," Richard said, shaking his head. "Boy, you are a freak! What would Momma think?"

"Layoff, Richard," his brother said. "Ain't none of your concern how I dress."

"Once my sister shows up," Richard said, "we'll drop these jokers off at the church. Then head over to Ganeesh's."

"Sounds good. I'm wiped out. Can't wait to get home."

"You boys waiting for me?" Buffy rounded the corner with Hip-Hop in tow. "We can drop off my friend," she said sweetly. "Can't we, Mr. Franklin?"

"No way," Richard said, shaking his head. "Little Lukey Frigface, we ain't gonna bring you home."

"First of all, Richard, I've asked you a million times to call me Hip-Hop. My name is Hip-Hop."

"Okay Frigface," Richard said. "Regardless."

"C'mon Richard. Let me come over to your house. Closer for my mom to get me."

"Of course you can, Little, I mean," Buffy giggled. "Hip-Hop. You can ride in back with me and Jazz."

"Whatever," Richard shook his head. "Get in the friggin' truck. We don't have all day. Already been keeping Ben waiting."

Buffy stuck her pierced tongue out and wiggled her barbell at me before jumping into the back of Floyd. Jazz and Hip-Hop followed. Captain climbed into the front.

"Don't trust that little jerk," Richard nodded, pointing to the back of the truck. "No good thief and scammer. His dad's a bad, bad man. Evil. That kid is already trouble. That's one of the problems with Washington County. Population is so small, you know everything about everyone." He shook his head. "I can't wait until I buy my land. Then I'm gonna build a friggin' fence to keep everyone out. A ten foot tall fence, that nobody can see over."

"That lake could have swimmer's itch," Richard said 20 minutes later, after dumping our passengers. He nodded and took a long puff from a huge joint. We were driving past the Sutherland's Lake boat ramp where I'd swum the day before. "Or maybe those boys were just friggin' with you."

"Really?"

"Yeah, sometimes there's swimmer's itch. From the duck poop. I haven't heard of an outbreak, but if it starts to itch, don't scratch. Makes it worse. I usually go swimming at Pocomoonshine." He nodded. "Much better lake. Much cleaner."

"Okay," I sighed. "I hope I don't get it."

"Take a right here," he directed. "End of the road, take a left."

"So who is Ganeesh?"

"Oh man, we've been buddies forever. Went to first grade together. He's more like a brother than that freakazoid Jazz. Me and Ganeesh," Richard laughed, "we've had some wild times. He's a lucky man. He's always been lucky. Except the day he got hurt working out on the cage site."

"What happened?"

"Three years ago he practically got crushed to death between a couple salmon pens. This guy Artie, a huge friggin' idiot, messed up big time and Ganeesh got caught in the middle. Hurt real bad. In the hospital for almost six months. Amazing he's alive." He shook his head. "But because he's Ganeesh and he's lucky, got a huge settlement from the insurance company. Used some of the money to buy the old Grange Hall and fixed it up real nice. That's where we're going. Almost there. Take a left."

We turned onto a road bordered with giant red maples dwarfing the intermittent stands of spruce, birch and poplar. Richard pointed to a huge clapboard building – church-like, but without a steeple – surrounded by an acre of red and yellow wild flowers. The building glowed, magically almost, luminescent even though only flecks of the building's white paint remained. All the windows were covered in plywood, except for an enormous octagonal stained glass window above the front entrance.

"We're here," Richard said, taking a final drag on his smoke and flicking it out the window. "Park anywhere."

I parked to the left of the front stairs, next to a weather-beaten sign with faded words that read "Grange."

"This is his house?"

"Yup." Richard turned to me. "Oh yeah, I meant to tell you. He's been acting pretty paranoid lately. Don't be surprised if he pats you down looking for a weapon."

"What?"

"You carrying a piece? Leave it in the truck."

"No, no," I stammered, "I'm not!"

"Then you don't have anything to worry about. Couple weeks ago, someone tried to rip him off. If the dude's gun hadn't jammed, Ganeesh woulda been dead."

"Wow." Certainly didn't expect gunplay when I signed on for the blueberry harvest. "That's good."

"The Grange ain't a place for little kids. Captain don't hang out here, that's for sure."

"Oh," I said. "Probably a good idea."

I have to admit I was curious about Washington County's world of thugs and gangsters, but had no interest in hanging out after a long day of raking. I was tired and wanted to go home to Monica. Take a bath. Chill. Eat a tasty dinner. Smoke the sizable roach Richard had placed in Floyd's ashtray. Enjoy a good night's sleep.

"I can't stay long," I said, "Monica expects me for supper."

"There's a special treat." Richard leered and grabbed my arm. "You'll meet his girlfriends. They're friggin' hot."

"Girlfriends?" I asked. "Plural?"

One of my many weaknesses was pretty girls. I've loved attractive females of all types. Every type. Which worked out great back in my rock 'n roll days. Not so great now that I was married. And tired.

"Yeah." Richard smiled. "Like I said, Ganeesh is lucky, lucky, lucky."

"Right on," I said, nodding, suddenly energized. "Lucky."

The front door was actually two doors. Huge. Oak. Richard tapped the door buzzer with a rhythmic staccato of Morse code. He waved upwards toward the video camera hanging from the roof over the entry. The door responded with a long buzz and click, then popped open, slightly. Richard pulled the door the rest of the way open.

"Look, but don't touch," he said with a wide smile. "Unless, of course, it's offered." And he disappeared inside.

I followed him into the pitch black. Blinded instantly by the sudden darkness, I looked over my shoulder to catch a final glimpse of daylight as the door automatically swung shut behind me. I stood, motionless, waiting for my eyes to adjust. No use stumbling around in the dark. My other senses took over. The place smelled of incense mixed with the aroma of pungent marijuana. The Grateful Dead played softly on a stereo. Across the room, in the direction of the music, candles flickered like a faint, faraway galaxy. The octagonal stained-glass window above me glowed, a filtered hint of sun.

"Hey Richard," I called out. "Richard, where are you?"

"Over here, dude," he said.

I started walking, tentatively, toward his voice and the music and candles, worried I'd trip over something and look like a knucklehead. My eyes started adjusting and I could make out silhouettes seated on a huge sofa in the corner, backlit by the candles. According to the tell-tale trail of orange glow, they were smoking a joint. Richard stood beside the couch.

"Want you to meet some friends of mine." Richard pointed to the pair of shadows rising from the couch. "Missy and Savannah, this is my pal, Ben."

"Hi Ben," they said in unison.

They were two curvaceous shapes perched on the couch, sitting close, softly lit by flickering candles.

"Ladies," I said, relieved to be in the dark. Under a bright light my ogling would have been too obvious. And I said what I say to every beautiful woman I've ever meet. "I'm honored."

"Hello Ben," one of them replied, standing and giving me a wave. Tall. Beautiful. Blonde. Killer body. Total knockout. Personification of the American male version of an angel. "I'm Savannah. Welcome to the Grange."

"And I'm Missy," said the other. Super-cute and tiny. Red hair with bangs and pig tails. Huge eyes and smile. Dimples. Jeweled stud in her nose. "Nice to meet you, dear." She shook my hand.

"Where's G?" Richard said.

"Right here!" A deep voice boomed from the darkness behind the couch. One of the girls flipped a switch and a red light overhead bathed us as he stepped from the shadows.

"Ben," Richard said, "I want you to meet a legend among men, a giant above giants, my very good friend, the King of the Grange, Ganeesh."

Ganeesh pointed at me with his left hand which, I soon discovered, held a gun. He was a giant, but moved quickly around the couch to tower over me. His barrel chest and massive arms made me feel tiny. (And I never feel tiny.) He seemed ten feet tall. His long, black hair was pulled back in a ponytail as thick as a beer can. He leaned down to peer into my eyes. For several seconds, he stared deep, almost reaching my brain. I stared back. He was a member of the local Passamaquoddy Indian tribe, I could tell. The broad forehead. The dark eyes. The chiseled chin. His people were the first to interact with the French explorers back in the year 1604. They've been fucked over by the white man, and many of their own leaders, ever since.

"I'm sure Richard explained," he said, reaching toward me. "Hands over your head."

My arms and fingers reached for the ceiling while the gun, a 9 mm, was pointed right in my face. Might have been all the excellent pot I'd been smoking, but it took several seconds to comprehend the situation. By the time I realized I was scared, he'd already handed the gun over to Missy. She pointed the weapon at me, at my head, as Ganeesh started the pat down.

"Reach higher," he barked. "Higher."

And I did. I stood on the tip of my toes, trying to touch the ceiling 15 feet above. His frisking was quite thorough.

"He's clean," he said, taking the gun back from Missy. "Clean."

"That's good," Missy said. "I didn't want to have to shoot him."

"How ya doing?" Ganeesh asked more calmly. "Ben, right? How ya doing?"

"Fine," I squeaked. "Yes, fine."

"That's good," he said, "that's good. I'm glad you're fine. Richard says you're all right. And normally that's good enough for me."

"Good," I said.

"Normally, I said. Normally that's good enough. But these aren't normal times. These days, your fucking government is murdering thousands of people in Iraq. And don't even blame 9-11. Nine–eleven has got nothing to do with Iraq... 9-11 was an inside job. Listen to Alex Jones. Have you seen the movie *Loose Change?*"

"Uhhh, nope."

"You should. Learn the truth about your government." He pointed his gun at me. "The way I'm normally seeing things, since you're a white guy, you probably can't be trusted. My tribe is selling my homeland to a bunch of white assholes from Oklahoma so they can build a fucking giant Liquefied Natural Gas terminal on sacred land. All you white guys look alike." He pointed at me. "And everywhere I look, I'm seeing white guys in Down East Maine driving black SUVs. Bastards see dollar signs. Seeing money in my homeland." He suddenly stuck the gun in my face again and was almost screaming. "*What about you white man?*" His spittle flew into my mouth. His saliva tasted metallic. "*Are you a white thief? Are you? Are you?*"

He fired the gun three times in rapid succession. After the first shot, I dropped to the floor and curled into a ball. My hands covered my ears. The shoot-out was over in five seconds, but it took a half minute for me to withdraw from the fetal position. Richard, on the couch, was laughing. Even though my ears were ringing, I could hear his laughter. And at that moment, I decided I hated the bastard. He was an annoying asshole who got me into this mess. Served me right for trying to be a nice guy, giving a fella a lift in exchange for high quality reefer.

"Dude, you okay?" It was Ganeesh, bending over me. "Dude, I was totally fucking with you. Just playing. You okay?"

Ganeesh grabbed me by the shoulders and almost lifted me off the floor.

"Yeah, yeah I'm fine," I said, standing and brushing off my forearms like I was dirty, so relieved I hadn't pissed or shit myself in terror. "Just surprised the fuck out of me."

"Dude, I shot way over your head," Ganeesh said, pointing. "Only trying to scare you."

"It...it worked," I stammered. "Worked."

"Good," he nodded and looked at Missy. "Did you find it believable?"

"Yes," she said. "I just wish, dear, you'd remember to give us the warning line just before you shoot. My ears are still ringing."

"I'd like to wear ear plugs," Savannah said. "But then I wouldn't hear the dialogue. That's why you're supposed to give us the warning line."

"Ladies," he said, outstretching his arms, a huge wingspan, and they both came over to him. "I'm sorry. I just get so excited. I flubbed the line. I started saying something about the white man and it just motivated me..."

"Well, the line is 'Do you understand what I'm saying, *white boy*?' " Missy smiled. "If you'd said 'Do you understand what I'm saying *white man*!' I would've plugged my ears."

"Me too," Savannah said. "*Understand* is the key word..."

"Sorry," Ganeesh shrugged, "I'm new at this. What about that pattern? Pretty tight for an amateur."

He pointed at what appeared to be several holes in the plywood covering a missing window. Tiny beams of light streamed into the dark room. Hard to believe the sun was still out. Felt like the middle of the night. What the fuck was I doing here? Time to go.

Ganeesh stood in front of the couch, backlit in red. His left arm was wrapped around Savannah's waist. The gun, still in his right hand, was draped over Missy's shoulder. Richard was sprawled on the couch, still occasionally giggling. The room smelled of gunpowder.

"Well, dear, all in all, you did excellent," Missy said to Ganeesh. "Look, this poor fella totally flipped." She walked over to me and grabbed me by the arm. Her touch was both soft and electric. "And that's no reflection on you, Ben. I mean, out of nowhere, this crazy Indian shoots at you. If you didn't freak, there's something wrong. Rolling into a ball on the floor in the fetal position is totally instinctual."

"I'm not sure that's instinctual," Savannah added. "That's learned behavior. Probably media-derived. Very 'victim on tv-ish'." She nodded. "Instinctual would have been to run for the door or fight. And who wants to fight a crazy giant Indian? So running for the door would be instinctual, but it's really dark in here and he probably doesn't know where the door is." She shrugged. "But it's totally impossible to gauge without a control group. Control group is essential. And how do we do that?"

"Hmm." Missy put her hands on her hips and pursed her lips. "You're probably right, dear. There's no real way to establish a control group."

"But was I believable?" Ganeesh turned and put the gun on the coffee table and plopped onto the couch. "That's why we're doing this."

"Yes dear," Missy said.

"I believed what I was seeing," Savannah said. "And I like it when you talk tough."

Ganeesh laughed.

"Sure was believable," Richard said. "You were totally a friggin' crazy man with a gun. Like I was watching a movie."

"Right on. That's the point." Ganeesh said. "Sorry we had to scare you, Ben, but it's absolutely necessary. A dress rehearsal."

"Listen dear," Missy said, grabbing my arm. Electricity again. "I've got an idea for a movie starring the sweet Ganeesh." She pointed at him with her free hand. "We need him to have a tough guy persona."

"People gotta be scared by our gentle giant." Savannah nodded. "It's real acting, because he's totally kind and tender."

"Well Ben, what did you think?" Missy asked. "Was he believable?"

"Ahhhhh," I paused for a second. My ears were still ringing. "Pretty fucking crazy. And believable."

"Good!" Missy laughed. "We love fucking crazy."

"And crazy fucking," Ganeesh said.

Everyone laughed.

"Hey, any cold beer here?" Richard asked. "I'm dying of thirst."

"Cold beer, yes," Ganeesh said. "Ben, would you like a beer?"

"Ahh," I said. "Sure."

I forgot about the dreaded 45-minute commute and giving Richard a lift back to his place. Forgot about Monica waiting with a supper of spaghetti and meatballs and garlic bread. Missy and Savannah were enchanting. Ganeesh, intriguing. And a cold beer sounded great. I couldn't leave.

"So Ben," Missy said as Ganeesh opened the fridge, light spilling into the dark room. "Were you freaking out when he had the gun in your face?"

"Uhh, yeah. Yeah."

"We're really sorry to put you through this," Savannah said. "See, he's too sweet. People around here aren't scared of him."

"Do they need to be?"

"Yes. He's a dangerous motherfucker." Missy paused. "In this movie."

"Yeah," Ganeesh laughed as he handed out beers. Then he opened a can of Moxie, the semi-official soft drink of real Mainers. To me, undrinkable. Tastes like bad cough syrup. "I'm a dangerous motherfucker."

"You're wicked tough," Richard said. "Where's that joint?"

"Not sure," Savannah said.

"No problemo," Richard said, opening his cigarette pack and pulling out a new one. "More where that came from..."

"There better be more," Ganeesh said. "Ben, why did you move to Washington County?"

"My wife and I want to get back to the land. Grow our own veggies. Raise chickens. Have a woodlot and a gun tower." I looked at Ganeesh. I liked him. He seemed cool, despite the gunplay. "So I can shoot the crazy locals who try to fuck with me."

"Ha-ha." Ganeesh smiled. "But why Washington County?"

"Because land here is still cheap and the rest of society is on the verge of collapse."

"I'll smoke to that," Ganeesh said, taking the joint from Richard. "Better buy your land pretty quick, before nothing is left." He took a puff, then exhaled with a sigh. A sad sigh. "Things are changing in Washington County. And not for the better." He took another puff. "Oh well."

For a moment there was silence. Then he exhaled again.

"All that shit don't matter." Ganeesh shook his head. A smile formed on his face. "We're here for a good time, not a long time, just like the song says."

"That's right, dear," Missy said, grabbing the joint. "A good time."

"I'm just hoping," Ganeesh continued, "it's awhile before all the shit goes down. I know this sounds selfish, but I'm hoping it's at least another 50 years before the air and water become too dirty to support human life. I mean, I don't want it to happen at all. But it would be nice if we're able to enjoy ourselves. Isn't that right, ladies?"

"That's right," Missy said. "Here for a good time."

"And I didn't pollute this planet. We didn't," he gestured around the room. "But we're paying the piper."

"You are one hundred percent right," Savannah said. "Life is so unfair, isn't it?"

Everyone, but me, laughed. A private joke?

"I'm just trying to get through," Ganeesh said and reached and grabbed the gun off the table. "Just trying to have as much fun as possible while hurting as few people as possible." His voice grew louder with each word. "Do you understand what I'm saying, *white boy?*"

Ganeesh didn't wait for my answer. He lifted the gun and fired.

I was the only one without my fingers in my ears. My brain rang.

"That's the warning line," Missy said after the shooting stopped. "Whenever anyone says 'Do you understand what I'm saying, *white boy?*', they're about to shoot the gun." She frowned. "I thought we told you that."

"Guess I forgot," I said. "I'll remember next time." Then I took another long sip of beer and drained the can. Monica's face flashed in my brain. Time to go. For real. "Sorry to break up the party, but Richard, if you need a ride, we're gonna have to take off soon. I still gotta long drive back to Goose Island."

"How about ten more minutes?" Richard said, standing and exhaling a huge cloud of pot smoke. "My man Ganeesh and I have a couple things we gotta discuss. Have another beer. Maybe Savannah would play a game of pool with you." He pointed into the darkness with the joint in his hand. "Fifteen minutes tops."

I didn't feel like playing pool. Not with my swollen fingers. Definitely didn't need another beer. Just wanted to go home, until Savannah turned on the light over the table with purple felt and racked the balls. Then Missy chalked a cue and I became interested. Because they were gorgeous women bending over and shooting pool.

"I don't know why I even play with her," Missy said to me. "She beats me every time."

"Maybe one of these days you'll get lucky," Savannah said and swatted Missy's ass with the wooden triangle. "You break."

Missy squealed and the three of us laughed. Missy went to the other end of the table. I had a clear view of her as she lined the cue ball up. She wrinkled her nose, closed her left eye, drew her cue back, then unleashed a break that cracked like a gunshot. Instantly, all 15 balls spread across the entire table. Then 14, then 13, as a couple of low balls dropped into the same corner pocket.

"Nice," I said, perched on my stool.

"I don't have many shots," Missy said. "Three in the corner, I guess."

She made it.

"Four in the corner."

She missed.

"Game over," Missy said, shrugging. "Again."

"Maybe not," Savannah said. "You've left a mess out there."

Five minutes later, the game was over. Savannah didn't rush, but she didn't waste time either. She circled the table, lining up shots and sinking them with authority. She specialized in hard angles, multiple banks and rails and complicated combinations. Meanwhile, Missy explained how she'd been born and raised down the road in Irwin. She and Savannah had been best friends forever, since the fifth grade, when Savannah and her family moved to Irwin from New York City. Inseparable ever since. In less than a month, they'd be starting their third year at the University of Maine in Machias. Savannah studied biology and psychology. Missy, an art major, was a photographer and filmmaker.

Just when Savannah made her final shot, Richard and Ganeesh reappeared. I saw a clock. Getting close to six. Felt more like midnight. Despite the fun, I needed to get home.

"Ladies," I said with a slight bow. "It's been an interesting visit."

They both laughed.

"Nice to meet you, Ben." Ganeesh shook my hand. "You're always welcome at the Grange."

"I'll be back. Just wicked tired tonight." I nodded. "Thanks for not shooting me."

"No prob, bro." He patted me on the shoulder. "No problemo."

"Think of all the time you spend behind the wheel, plus gas costing $3.25 a gallon." Richard shook his head as we pulled into the church parking lot. "Waste of time and money. You should just pitch a tent on my land for the rest of the harvest. Won't cost you nothing. That way, you don't have the commute and you can give me and my idiots a ride to the fields. Maybe run me on a couple errands. Seems like a fair trade."

He had a point. Even though I didn't particularly like the guy, staying with Richard would save time, money and eliminate a good chunk of vehicular stress. What would Monica think? Maybe after I was settled, I'd drive back to Goose Island and pick up her and the dogs so they could camp too. She'd enjoy hanging out on Richard's land all day while I was out raking in the fields. And come evening, after we went for dip in the lake, she'd cook dinner over the fire. Such a plan might make the rest of the harvest almost tolerable.

"Sounds good to me," I said. "Let me talk to Monica tonight. I'll let you know tomorrow."

After dropping off Richard, I felt dirty, so I stopped at the boat landing. A quick dip would cleanse and wake me enough to make the drive back to Goose Island. Didn't matter if there was a swimmer's itch outbreak, I'd already been exposed. Just enough water-time to scrub the filth and sweat from my body. A couple minutes later, clean and revived, wearing only my wet boxers and sockless boots, I climbed into Floyd. For a moment, I felt great. I grabbed the steering wheel and noticed my hands were still stained blue.

The Politics of Oral Sex

People are always getting killed Down East because someone crosses the imaginary line on a blind curve on a back road. In Washington County, most roads are back roads. A back road is pot-holed and frost-heaved blacktop, with a foot of gravel or mud shoulder, then a wall of forest. I always worry about other humans, so easily distracted, changing a station on the radio or turning around to yell at the kids, or talking on the phone or texting. All while driving a steel and glass box down a back road. And even if you're lucky enough not to crash into other cars, you still gotta avoid the multitudes of moose and deer who don't look both ways when crossing the street.

I'm a really bad driver. Being behind the wheel results in sweaty palms and stress. I've escaped automotive death a crazy number of times. A moped, two motorcycles, a golf cart, a tractor and a dump truck have all been heavily damaged due to my poor driving skills. A borrowed Porsche, a street sweeper, two run-of-the-mill cars and one station wagon became dented while under my control. I've smashed into underpasses and overpasses, backed into brick walls, trees and lamp posts. At night, every headlight of oncoming traffic blinds me. Regardless of the time of day, I have a tough time judging where the road ends and non-road begins.

"I guess staying at Richard's is a good idea," Monica said while we ate dinner. "I'll miss you a bunch, but it'll save us gas money and I won't be worrying about you crashing the truck."

I took a sip of wine and looked at my beautiful wife. Long, wavy brown hair. Big round eyes. A dusting of freckles on her cheeks. Full lips. A luscious body. Plus a great brain. A gentle bohemian, she was a talented poet and a gifted teacher. It was my lucky night, four years before, when we met in a Portland bar after one of my solo acoustic performances. We've had lots of fun and escapades ever since. Moving Down East was the latest chapter in our adventure. Spending a week away from her would be tough.

"I'd rather not be raking," I said after another sip. "I wish I didn't have to go back."

"I know you don't, babe." She was sympathetic. "But it's our only option until school starts and I get a paycheck. We definitely need the cash. Plus how much would we save on gas?"

"About a hundred bucks a week."

"Three hundred dollars during a three-week harvest is a lot of money for us right now." She sighed. "You'll come home on weekends, right?"

"Yeah."

"Well, I could use some alone time," she said. "I'd love to get the sunset poem done before school starts."

She was working on a book of surrealistic bicycle poems. Her latest effort was re-telling our first weekend on Goose Island when we ate psychedelic mushrooms and took a magical ride on our bikes into the sunset on the long paved runway of the island's tiny airport. When we reached the end of the runway, we turned around and headed back. The full moon rose in front of us, to the east, over Passamaquoddy Bay. We rode and rode, occasionally looking over our shoulders, back into blue sky streaked with pinks, reds and purples.

"Maybe after I get settled up there, you and the dogs can come and camp out," I said. "His land and gardens are wicked nice."

"Let's see how this week goes," she said. "All I ask is that you call me every night. Okay?" She smiled. "Because I'll want to hear your voice."

After dinner, we gathered my gear: Tent, cook stove, two small propane bottles, kettle, thermos, tea and sugar, six pairs of boxers, three pairs of jeans, two pairs of cutoffs, all the socks I owned, my sleeping bag, rain gear and my hand-crank radio because I was addicted to the CBC's dinner time news broadcasts.

Then Monica made sandwiches for the next day's lunch. We took the dogs for a long walk. By ten, we were back home and in bed. Monica climbed atop of me. She moaned and I groaned as she rode me. Just before my orgasm, I squeezed my eyes shut. And then, against all expectations, I visualized both Buffy and Missy.

A little after midnight, the itch awoke me. After a minute or two of intense scratching, I crawled out of bed and staggered to the bathroom. Small white pustules covered both of my inner thighs. Nothing in the medicine cabinet looked helpful. So I fashioned a potion out of tea-tree oil shampoo and aloe vera lotion. Barely made a difference, except the sting of the tea-tree masked some of the itch. Back in bed, I eventually fell asleep because my skin was too slippery to scratch effectively. Several times that night, I awoke and re-applied my greasy mix, then dozed back off.

When the alarm buzzed, I crawled out of bed, exhausted. Took a leak. Rolled and smoked a joint. Made tea. Ate breakfast. Re-scratched both thighs until they were bloody. Googled "swimmer's itch." Turns out the parasite is part of an ecological cycle that links ducks, duck shit, warm lake water, fresh water snails and human beings. According to one web site, the itch, rash and pus-filled bumps lasted from a couple days to a week, depending. Medical attention or drugs weren't recommended, since the bumps disappear on their own. Another Google brought me to a discussion group claiming a non-prescription topical salve called "Corrigan's" provided relief from the itch.

A little before seven, I loaded the truck with my gear, then went back inside and kissed my still-sleeping Monica goodbye. She murmured and I backed out of the room without waking her. The farewell would be too emotional for me to handle. I loved our life together. My time with her was always fun and happy. I'd miss her terribly, even if it was just for five days and nights. I headed out the door and into the truck, hurrying because if I didn't take off right away, I'd never leave. Especially if she woke up and looked at me with her big blue eyes.

I really, really, really didn't want to rake blueberries. Again, I wavered, hand on the ignition, wondering if I should just call the whole thing off. Pain and suffering for 14 cents a pound? I sighed and scratched my inner left thigh. No other options to make cash.

It was a lousy feeling.

Bending over on day three seemed easier. Either I was getting more flexible or just more tolerant of the stretch. Maybe the burning irritation of the swimmer's itch helped distract from my back pain. Or perhaps the relentlessly nibbling bugs attracted to the aroma and taste of my greasy homemade lotion made the rest of my aches seem inconsequential. Muggy as hell, my hands were slippery and on several occasions the rake escaped my grip. Around nine, I took a break to fetch a pair of work gloves from my truck and spotted Jazz and Peggy making out behind the port-a-potty.

Heavy kissing. Aggressive exploring. Explodingly passionate. Then she pulled his head to her breast. Through her tee-shirt, he sucked, leaving, I'm sure, a telltale wet circle. She arched her back, her head pushing against the wall of the plastic outhouse. His mouth still on her nipple, his right hand started to vigorously rub between her legs, maybe a little too hard, through her cutoff jeans. She moaned, loudly.

Their love was obviously a secret. On the fields, they acted liked friends. Laughing and joking, sharing smokes and a water bottle. How did they fall in love? Very confusing, since Jazz, at least visually, appeared to be the epitome of Goth. Peculiar that such a gothy Goth would be entwined with an aging blonde beauty queen. And vice versa. I wished I could go home and sit with my guitar and compose a song about the unlikely couple. But I had to get back to bending over in the field.

I heard other rakers approaching, so I slammed Floyd's door shut as a warning. Jazz and Peggy instantly stopped and separated. She dashed into the port-a-potty and Jazz walked over to the bucket pile just as Little Luke and another teenage boy appeared. They ducked behind the port-a-potty but were still in my line of sight. Little Luke looked around and reached into his huge pockets, pulling out a bag of weed. The buyer handed him a couple bills. Luke tossed the bag in the air, then smoothed out the money and pulled his bankroll out of another huge pocket. The other kid unrolled the bag and sniffed the weed while they both sauntered over to the water jug.

Little Luke was stealing berries off my bushes. The first clue was the patchiness of the berry patches in my strip. Only the fruit on the left side of my six-foot wide lane (the side furthest from neighbor Luke) survived. Also, the white string official border between our strips – usually a taut straight line – was crooked and trampled.

My guess? Seeing blueberries over the line was too tempting for the little thief. Especially since the berries in this section of the fields were plump, juicy and plentiful. He'd just have to make sure I was still a couple hundred feet back, head down, focusing on my own world. A quick extra comb and he'd get every berry within easy reach, leaving me the leftovers and a strip half combed. If Little Fucking Luke crossed the line 60 times, that's a bucket of berries that should have been mine.

It wasn't the three and a half dollars that bothered me. It was the principle. All the berries between the strings of my strip were mine, goddamn it. There would be no justice, though. Impossible to prove his guilt. Not a chance of reimbursement. Or retribution. Or revenge. Spending the morning with itchy legs under the hot sun, besieged by bugs, amplified the injustice of the missing berries.

As I watched Luke drink a cup of water, it took all my self-control not to go over and kick his ass. Instead, I walked back to my strip, muttering and bitching. Bent over with the rake, the pain of the stoop returned.

"Buffy is a terrible mother," Richard said at lunchtime. He showed up minutes before, alone. Standing behind Floyd, we were smoking a fat joint he provided while retelling his latest domestic disaster. "Just after you dropped me off, she sent Jazz out to the camp to get me. Captain was sick. Poor fella had bad diarrhea. All dehydrated." He yawned. "I barely slept at all." He shook his head. "And guess what Buffy was doing while her kid was in agony?"

"I have no idea."

"Sitting next to him on the couch, smoking a cig, watching TV. Then she went to bed and I stayed up half the night with the poor kid."

"No fucking way."

"I hate my sister." He nodded. "Captain's my main man, otherwise I'd call Department of Human Services and report Buffy for being unfit. But they'd take Captain away and put him in foster care and we'd never see him again." He took a long puff of the weed. "He's doing better this morning. I had him drinking lots of water and lots of Tang." He shook his head. "That kid needs Vitamin C. Kid needs to eat more veggies. Less sugar. But Buffy, she don't get it. She's an unfit mother, if I've ever seen one. Unfit person. She would have totally disappointed my mom." He paused. "And I haven't even told you about Buffy killing my buddy Paulie. Captain's dad."

"*What*? She killed him? She murdered him?"

"Yep."

"How?"

"Ran him over in the driveway. They was both drunk. Just had a big fight over something stupid Buffy said. Jazz was there and watched the whole thing. She jumped in the truck, threw it in reverse and run Paulie over. She claimed she didn't see him. But that's a lie."

"How do you know?"

"'Cuz anything Buffy says is a lie. Don't matter with that girl. If it's sunny, she says it's raining. Warm, she says cold. I know what happened. She saw Paul in the mirror and she was mad and she run him over. Killed him instantly. Oh man, it was in all the papers and on TV in Bangor."

"Oh my fucking word." I shook my head. "Did she get arrested?"

"No. She claimed it was an accident. And she cried and cried and acted so sad at the funeral. And everyone felt sorry for her and believed her. Especially since she was eight months preggers with Captain. But she did it on purpose. I know." The look on his face was simultaneously hate and sorrow. "Sucks. Paulie's dead. Never met his own son. And even worse, that means Captain don't have a dad. So it was me that watched him take his first step while Buffy was off drinking and jerking off that loser Eddie French-Fry. And I'm the one who heard Captain speak his first words. And I taught him how to throw a ball. And ride his bike." He took a long puff of the joint and handed it to me. "I'm not complaining, because Captain's the best kid. But he's not my kid and I take care of him more than she does." He shook his head, then smiled. "Don't understand how that ever happened. Luckily, he starts first grade this year. A friend of mine works at the school and will look out for him. Means my job gets easier." He snorted. "Can't trust Buffy to take care of him. But I trust the state even less. That's why I keep an eye on him. Don't want the state to take him away. They do it all the time. Take a kid and the family never sees him again."

"You really believe Buffy ran him over on purpose?"

"Ben, believe me." His stare was dead serious. "I know she killed him as much as I know anything. You gotta understand, I was seven when she was born. I watched her grow up. Tell you three things about my sister Buffy. One, she's evil. Seriously evil. Like Satan. Two, she's a liar. I honestly believe it's impossible for her to tell the truth. And number three, she's got the worst temper I've ever seen. Worse than my old man and he's got a wicked bad temper. Buffy freaks right out. Her eyes get all buggy and her face starts to shake and gets beet red. Hysterical. Sometimes violent, either towards herself or whoever happens to be in her way. I've been on the receiving end many times. Pretty scary." He shook his head. "And that's the truth. I could tell you story after story. She's downright evil."

"That sucks."

"Me and Paulie were tight, but he wasn't the smartest tool in the box." He sighed and shook his head. "Actually he was pretty dumb. I don't know why he put up with her. A million times, I asked him why. He'd just smile that dumb smile and say that he loved her." He snorted. "Love. Paulie was an idiot. She didn't love him. She don't love anyone. She don't even love her own son. That's pretty messed up. You know what's crazy? Look at a photo of Paulie when he was a little kid, you'd think it was Captain. Friggin' nuts. You'd think he was a clone or something."

The joint in his hand had gone out.

"One more hit," he said, re-lighting and taking a long drag. "The rest is for you. I gotta start raking." He handed me the reefer and exhaled. "You know what I wonder? When Captain is 18 years old, and looks just like Paulie, will Buffy freak out? Her son is a replica of the man she killed. Murdered. Comes back like a ghost." He shook his head and smiled. "Maybe, with any luck, she'll be dead by then. I'm serious. I mean, I'd feel bad for Captain, being an orphan and all. But otherwise, I don't care about her. Even if she is my sister." He pointed at me. "Don't believe a friggin' word she says. You can't trust her. 'Round money, drugs, or motor vehicles. Or anything." He shook his head sadly and lit a smoke. "Friggin' Buffy."

"That sucks. Sounds like you're in a tough spot."

"Yeah," he shrugged. "But at least I ain't dead. Now you understand why

I live in my tent." He laughed. "So is your old lady gonna let you camp out?"

"Yes she is," I said. "All my gear's in the truck."

"Good. Good." He nodded and puffed his cigarette. "Make it easier for both of us. How's the raking today?"

"Okay, but it could be better, if it weren't for Little Luke. That bastard is stealing my berries. Crossing the line and stealing my berries. I wanna kick his fucking ass."

"That sucks, but it ain't actually stealing." He shook his head. "Bad manners. Bad behavior. Yes. But stealing means he took something that's yours. The berry ain't yours until it's in your bucket."

"Hmmm. I still hate the little asshole."

"For sure," Richard nodded. "But you just can't go around accusing people of stealing. Stealing, out here, means grabbing someone else's bucket. That's a serious charge. But it wouldn't hurt to let Little Luke know you're on to him." He pointed at me. "I need to rake some money. I'll see you around four." He paused for a sec. "Let's celebrate you staying on the land. How's a nice steak dinner on the fire sound?"

"Really?"

"Got 'em in the freezer." He nodded and sighed and yawned. "Give us something to look forward to."

Again, Richard's sweet weed helped me through the afternoon, but did nothing to quell the swimmer's itch. And I still had the sun, bugs, my lower back and swollen finger to contend with. But like Richard said, at least I wasn't dead. Plus Little Luke left the fields after lunch. Also helping me was the carrot of grilling a steak over a wood fire. And for entertainment, I watched and eavesdropped on Jazz and Peggy. Even though their ardor cooled – because Richard was on the field – I saw clues of their intimacy. The way they shared cigarettes, for instance. And the way they laughed. I knew their love would make a great song. Unfortunately, I didn't have my guitar.

By 3:30, I was done for the day. Richard was still on the other side of the field. After weighing my final buckets (586 pounds for $82), I filled my water jug and was headed to Floyd when I bumped into Larry who'd just come out of the port-a-potty.

"Hey Ben," he said. "How did it go out there? You rake some money?"

"Best day yet, 80 bucks."

"That's not the worst I've ever heard." Larry shook his head. "I'm just glad you stayed as late as you did." He pointed to the fields. Five rakers remained. "Back in the day, there'd still be 20 or 30 people out there, raking money. They'd stay until dark. Hell, up until a couple years ago, my 75-year-old mother would rake after dark. People used to have a work ethic."

"What happened?"

"Hard tellin'." He took off his hat and scratched his head. "Just part of the Washington County problem. Ten, maybe 15, years ago started getting harder to find good workers. Lottsa people moved down state. And all the good workers in Washington County already have full-time jobs and ain't gonna take vacation to break their backs in the fields for 14 cents a pound. Plus, Wal-Mart started hiring kids. Or Burger King or McDonalds or Dunkin' Donuts. Kids can make more money over the course of the summer, working in a grease pit, flipping burgers than three weeks of hard labor in the fields. Inside work is easy compared to raking. But I couldn't do it." He shook his head. "Nope. No thanks. Gotta be outside as much as possible. So these days, I'm stuck with pillheads and slackers. For the most part."

"And floor refinishers," I said.

"Sure. And I've got Peggy and the teachers, the Philpott sisters. They're no trouble and hard working. Jazz and Richard, when they show up. Maybe two or three teenagers are top-notch. But Jesus, most of these other idiots barely make it worthwhile. Always taking bucket breaks. Showing up late. Leaving early. Always bumming smokes." He shook his head. "I should have switched to migrants years ago."

"Why didn't you?"

"Because I'm an idiot."

We both laughed.

"The official answer is that it's a family tradition to hire locals. My grandfather did it. My dad did it. And I've done it." He looked at me. "But who knows the future? The way it's looking, my best bet is to buy a mechanical harvester." He nodded and lit another cigarette. "Yup. Hell, with a good machine, take us a week, ten days, for two of us to do my fields." He nodded. "Shit, I could probably do the whole field by myself. But not hiring locals would disappoint my folks. Feel like I should wait until they die, just to respect them." He shook his head. "Of course, they're both in good shape and will live another ten years. By then, I'd be out of business."

"Why?"

"This is a terrible industry. Dominated by four big processors. Makes it tough for the little guy to survive. Will I break even this year?" He shrugged. "Don't know until the harvest is over. Don't know until the big fellas decide what they want to pay me because I don't have nowhere else to sell the berries. And you gotta sell and freeze 'em right after you rake 'em. I get too many for a roadstand.

And I'm way too small for my own processing and distribution. Plus all you rakers," he said, waving at the field, "make your cash no matter what. I've got bills up the ying yang. And the big boys breathing down my neck."

"Who are these big boys?"

"Down in Cherryfield and Milbridge." He sighed. "Tens of thousands of acres each. The blueberry barrens down there go on forever. Makes my hundred acres look like a backyard patch."

"Really."

"Yep, we're smaller than small. But the big boys are the growers and processors. They set the price per pound for everyone. And they fixed the price so low barely makes growing blueberries worthwhile. Or, some years, less than worthwhile."

"They fixed the price of the berries?"

"Yeah, had secret meetings and everything."

"I thought that kind of stuff was illegal?"

"It is. They got caught and found guilty in court. But the settlement," he shook his head, "the settlement weren't shit. They still made out like bandits." He sighed. "Then when the big guys hear rumors about a little grower struggling, they circle like vultures and one of 'em buys the small fella for almost nothing."

"That's fucking terrible."

"I'd rather sell my land cheap to some rich asshole from out-of-state than to those thieves." He laughed. "Unfortunately, can't see the water from here, so the property isn't worth that much. But luckily, I own all the land outright. Got almost no debt. Plus I got my job at Roosevelt Regional."

"You work at the hospital?"

"Yep, buildings and grounds. Been there almost 32 years. Just after I got out of the Army and the war."

"Nam?"

"Yep. Two tours. But it wasn't so bad." He flicked his cigarette butt toward the fields. "Not so bad for me. Anyway, I take three weeks vacation to run the harvest. Take another week in November to get my deer. Work the farm on weekends and occasional week nights."

"That sounds all right," I said. "If you're making some money."

"The only way to make money is to buy a mechanical harvester."

"How much?"

"Well, the one I got my eye on is about 18 grand. But I'd have to take a loan. Put up some of the land as collateral. I hate dealing with the banks. And a mechanical harvester ain't perfect. Lots of work getting the field stones out of the way. Some places the machine can't even go. Handraking, you can go anywhere.

Ain't that right, Richard?"

"What's that, Lar?" he said, coming up along Floyd. He was shirtless and bronzed. I noticed he was hairless. Chest. Armpits. No sign of hair. Not even stubble.

"Handrakers can go places that harvesters can't."

"That's right," Richard said, taking his smokes out of his pouch. "Right next to the walls and rocks. On the sides of all the steep south facing hills. Them's the best berries. You talking 'bout getting a harvester again?" He turned to me. "Larry is always dreaming. But he knows he ain't gonna buy a harvester. What about all the jobs he creates for the idiots of Washington County?"

"Don't call 'em idiots, Richard," Larry said, pointing at him. "Not all of them are idiots."

"That's right. Me and Ben here." He lit a smoke. "The Philpott sisters. Who else?"

"Some of the high schoolers." Larry thought about it for a second. "Adam, David and Patrick."

"Well, Adam Bradbury and Dave Noyes are good. But Patrick's always taking bucket breaks."

"Well, it's not my fault that today's teenagers are lazy and not as fast and hard working as you."

We all laughed.

"Actually, I'd love to run the harvester," Richard said. "Like I've said a million times, you need a team on the machine and then two or three hand rakers going around getting the edges and tough spots the machine misses." He turned to me. "You'd do that next year, wouldn't you?"

"Ahhh," I paused for a moment. I had no intention of raking blueberries ever again, but revealing that would be in poor taste. "Sure. Probably."

"That's all well and good." Larry removed his ball cap and scratched his head. "You gonna pay for the machine too?"

"Banks," Richard said, "got lots of money to give to fine upstanding tax-paying citizen such as yourself."

"You know how I feel about banks." Larry shook his head. "Not so easy dealing with them."

After work, we hit downtown Irwin, which was a large parking lot with a two pump gas station, a double-wide trailer that was both the post office and town hall, and a metal and glass building named Mary's Market.

Places like Mary's are essential in rural Maine, where the closest full service grocery is often a half-hour, or further, away. Bigger than a convenience store, but smaller than a supermarket, Mary's had a counter for a snack bar, a greasy pizza oven, a small meat cooler and a produce section with orange tomatoes, wrinkled iceberg lettuce, out-of-season shriveled asparagus for five bucks a pound and cucumbers with wax so thick you could use 'em as candles. Mary's also sold booze, smokes, lottery tickets, candles, cough medicine and, miraculously, Corrigan's, the cure for swimmer's itch. I bought a jar of the salve and a case of Budweiser. Which made me cringe, because I generally drink Maine micro-brews like Shipyard or Geary's, Sebago or Gritty's. But budget constraints called for Bud.

When we got back to Richard's, I set up camp while he checked on Captain. I also applied the Corrigan's, which claimed to be a secret blend of camphor, castor oil and wax. Richard returned with two huge frozen t-bones. He lit a fire in the pit. I hand-cranked my radio, picking up the classic rock station in St. John, New Brunswick. We kicked back, drank some beers and smoked a joint.

I was in a pretty great mood, considering the day of hard labor and despite my sweaty, dirty and greasy body. I had a nice buzz from the Bud and herb and knowing I raked $82. Plus, the Corrigan's salve worked wonders. Almost immediately, the itching disappeared, replaced by a slight burning, then numbness. Sitting at the picnic table, not moving, bending or stretching, just watching the fire, I realized my back barely hurt, my knees weren't killing me and the stab wound on my finger just tingled.

Only motion or movement caused pain. So I sat still.

Meanwhile, Richard just kept talking and talking. Unfortunately, he was a dullard with a capital D. Tough to pay attention. He ranted and railed against the high cost of gasoline and the low price of pumpkins. I didn't have to say a word other than the occasional "yup" or "uh-huh." All I wanted was for him to shut up and let me tune in the CBC so I could catch up on the news.

We smoked another joint, then Richard headed to the garden for salad. I followed, curious to see his veggies. Several different types of lettuce. Lots of smallish carrots and big cucumbers. Too early for tomatoes, green on the verge of red. We walked back to the fire and he rubbed salt and pepper into the half-defrosted steaks. He raked the hottest coals into a pile, then put a grate over the pit. A couple minutes later, the steaks started to sizzle. Meanwhile, Richard made a salad. From the cooler marked "FOOD" came a bottle of ranch dressing and a tub of macaroni salad from the Roosevelt IGA. Then steaks were done and we ate.

"Listen Ben, you tired?" Ten minutes after the feeding frenzy, Richard finished a cigarette and started to roll a huge joint. "'Cuz I was thinking we could zip over to Ganeesh's. See what the gang was up to."

"Weird, I wasn't tired until you asked." I yawned. "Unlike some people, I raked blueberries all day."

"Ain't even seven yet." Richard shook his head. "Way too early for bed."

"Maybe you should just take the truck and go by yourself."

"Dude, like I told you, I'm currently unable to drive."

"Really, I don't remember…"

"Well, I can't. Cops see me driving, they're gonna pull me over. And I'll be headed down to Machias, and I don't mean the University."

"Oh."

"C'mon, let's go to Ganeesh's. Have a couple laughs and still be back in time to get a good night's sleep. Didn't you like watching those chicks play pool?"

"No one's gonna shoot me, are they?" I could have gone either way at that point. Sleep would be easy, but seeing the Grange again was appealing. "I don't feel like getting shot."

"No way dude." He laughed. "No one's shooting nobody."

By the time we got to the Grange, it was 8 p.m. Richard decided to bring a 12-pack. Should have protested, saying a late night wasn't possible. But I kept my mouth shut and stared into the sky, a wondrous deep blue, streaked with stretching white and pink tendrils that would soon turn purple, then red, then night. No breeze. Quiet, except for music coming from inside the Grange. The exterior of the building glowed a magic pink. The dusk smelled of grass, flowers and spruce.

We buzzed and the door popped open.

A couple minutes later, six of us were sitting on pillows or leaning on couch cushions in a circle on the floor. The Grange was dark except for a bunch of tall candles sitting on a lazy Susan in the middle of the circle and a few strings of Christmas lights on the ceiling. To my left sat Jenny, who was Richard's second cousin. She was very pretty and emo, reminded me of a half-dozen girls I'd known over the years. Constantly brushing back her jet black hair that hung over her eyes in bangs. Her ears, nose and lower lip were pierced. She wore a tight black tee-shirt, a black miniskirt and fishnet stockings over white leggings. No idea how old she was. Maybe 14. Maybe 22. Hard to tell.

Sitting to my right was Missy, who happened to be Jenny's second cousin on the other side. Missy said she was happy to see me again and gave me a hug after I came through the door, then sat very close to me. I could smell her. Lilac mixed with patchouli. She looked utterly cute in pigtails and a striped cotton peasant dress that went past her knees. Next to her sat Ganeesh, who wore a fez and a long red silk robe, and Savannah, wearing a sari, her blonde hair pulled back tight in a ponytail. A dot on her forehead. A pair of tortoise shell glasses sat perched on her nose. Richard closed the circle.

A Doors album played softly in the background. We smoked a huge blunt. (For the rest of the night, a blunt was in constant motion.) All the girls were drinking wine from a gallon jug of Gallo red. Ganeesh occasionally sipped from a can of Moxie. Richard and I stuck with the Budweiser.

"So Savannah, what sort of psychology do you study?" I knew nothing about these people. And they knew everything about each other. The disadvantage of being the new guy in a small town. The learning curve for growing modern friendships often seems quite steep. Is that why so many people remain friends, even though they've outgrown their pals? Are new friends too much of a hassle?

"Clinical," Savannah said. "Focusing on the psychology of sex..."

"Dude," Ganeesh said. "She's gonna be a sexologist."

"Really?" I said.

"Yeah." Missy smiled in the candlelight. "She's my favorite sexpert."

"And when she gets her PhD, we'll call her 'Doctor'," said Jenny. "Dr. Savannah," she squeaked. "I love the sound of it."

That was the first I heard her speak a full sentence. She had the voice of a little boy, high pitched and almost scratchy. She smiled and handed me the blunt. Again, I wondered her age.

"Interesting," I said, taking a puff. "A sexologist."

"They just like saying 'sexologist'," Savannah said, grinning. "I'll be a psychologist focusing on sexology. Behavior. Roles. The mores, laws and taboos. Plus the culture and subculture..."

"Of sex," Richard interrupted. "Can you friggin' believe it? What a life? You and me, Ben, we break our backs raking berries. And this girl gets to lay on hers. Hah-Hah."

No one laughed and Ganeesh shook his head.

"Listen Little Dick," Missy said. Everyone but Richard giggled. "She wants to find the answers to sexual mysteries."

"Don't call me Little Dick."

"Mysteries like how a loser of an ugly-motherfucker," Missy continued, slightly slurring her words. "Like you can ever get laid, let alone get a girlfriend."

"Frig you, Missy."

"Watch it, Richard," Ganeesh said. "You're talking to my friends. Show respect."

"Ganeesh, don't worry about me, dear." Missy smiled. "I think I can handle a little Dick."

"Frig you!"

"Richard, you better show respect," Ganeesh said again, pointing at him.

The room went silent for a second.

"I'm sorry," Richard said, softly and shook a smoke from his pack of cigarettes. He went to light it.

"Dude," Ganeesh said. "Remember, no smoking in the Grange."

"Oh frig me." Richard shook his head. "I hate going outside. Ruins the whole mood of a drink and a smoke."

"Sorry."

"Dude, that sucks."

"Smoking sucks," Missy said. "We don't want to smell or breathe it, second hand."

"Sorry." Richard put his hands in the air. "I didn't know cigarettes were illegal."

"They are, now," Ganeesh said, "in the Grange."

"Okay, I'm going outside." He stood. "Anyone else?"

The room was quiet again.

"So Savannah," I broke the silence. "What are those sexual mysteries Missy mentioned?"

"Oh, so many," Savannah said. "Many, many mysteries of sexuality. Actually, I have a long list of behaviors I'd like to study. De-mystify." In the flickering light I saw her smile sweetly. "Investigate."

"And no, Little Dick," Missy said. "Investigate doesn't mean laying on her back."

"I didn't say nothing." He shook his head and headed for the door. "Please don't call me Little Dick."

When the door shut behind him, without any perceptive movement, the circle grew tighter, eliminating Richard's spot.

"I don't get why you even let that asshole hang out here," Missy said. "He's such a loser."

"Hey!" Ganeesh said. "We've been pals forever. You know that."

"Anyway, Ben," Savannah said. "I'm studying sex from a scientific, biological and rational perspective."

"Cool," I said, turning back her. "Sounds interesting."

"Especially in light of the current era of New Sexuality."

"The what?"

"New Sexuality, silly," Missy said with a laugh, slapping my forearm and taking the blunt from me. "The New Sexuality."

"Oh," I said. "I wasn't aware..."

"Yeah dude," Ganeesh said. "The New Sexuality is awesome. How old are you?"

"Thirty-seven."

"Whoa! I had no idea you were so old," Missy said. "I thought you were maybe 30. Not 40."

"I'm not 40," I said, smiling at her. "I'm in my mid-30s."

"Nope," She shook her head. "Mid-30s ends at 36. Thirty-seven. That's late 30s. Which is almost 40. Which might as well be 40."

"Depends on how you look at it. Only a number, right?" I half-laughed and looked toward Savannah. "What's the New Sexuality?"

"A different way of considering sex. Not from a Judeo-Christian point of view. A more scientific perspective. And 'New Sexuality' isn't really new. Much of the theory has been around for awhile. Just 'new' compared to the status quo and the canon. Sexology has benefited in the research from the last ten years, which helped us make huge gains, especially looking at biological and psychological reality of sex. Internet's been awesome for that."

"Psychological reality of sex?" I shook my head. "On the Internet?"

"Before the 'Net, researchers doing field work had to trust the research subjects. There was some observational fieldwork, but most of the data came from narratives derived from interviews and diaries of people with spectacular sex lives. Some of these diaries were pretty perverse by almost any standards." She paused for a second. "Lots of pedophilia. Bestiality. But questions arose. Especially reading them fifty years later. How reliable were these narratives? Were the interviewers being told fantasy instead of truth? Desires instead of authentic experiences? How did those falsehoods affect research? How did the flawed research impact society's perspective on sex?"

"Never thought of that," I said.

"She's amazingly brilliant," Ganeesh said. "Tell him about your study."

"Later, maybe," she said, smiling. "The Internet and digital video have changed sex research. Now, thanks to literally countless willing participants, we have more actual data that we can possibly study."

"Wow," was all I could say. It was awesome to hear such revelations from the mouth of a beautiful young woman dressed in a sari rather than a dour, aging white male scientist in a lab coat. I could see her as a media celebrity, leading sex discussions on TV or the Internet. Dr. Ruth had the short cute old lady shtick. Savannah's beauty and brains were a better combo. "That's great."

"At the same time," Savannah continued, "because of the 'Net, people with certain tastes and needs are able to hook up. Brand new opportunities. Makes anonymous and kinky sex experiences much more accessible. Before the

Internet, anonymous sex was mostly a quiet, hit-or-miss sort of affair. Cruising. Porn theaters and bathrooms. Relying on an easily misunderstood series of gestures. Liaisons were often silent and quick. And undocumented. Now, you can have a whole web profile that spells out, in detail, what you like, don't like, want and don't want. And that allows researchers to identify willing study subjects in specific areas of sexual behavior."

"And that's wicked important," Missy said. "We gotta get rid of stereotypes and stop having uptight people decide what sort of sexual behavior is acceptable. Consensual should be the only requirement." She smiled at me. "Do you realize that sensual is part of consensual?"

"Nnnnn, no, I didn't," I answered, surprised by my stammer. I looked at Missy. She was smiling. Grinning. Her eyes seemed so big in the candlelight. "How are you gonna get rid of the stereotypes?"

"I don't know." She shrugged and pointed. "She's the sexologist. I just like having sex."

Everyone laughed.

"Mores are constantly changing." Savannah pushed her glasses up, sipped her wine, cleared her throat, then continued. Without a doubt, she could have a successful career as a college professor, lecturing and molding the minds of nubile young men and women, influencing a whole generation of sexual studies. "A hundred years ago, gay sex was considered abhorrent and abnormal. A form of mental illness. Yet, a hundred years ago, it was perfectly normal for an old man to marry a teenage girl."

"Not even that long ago," Jenny said. "My grandfather was 42 when he married my grandma. She was 15. They were happy. My mom was 17 when she married my dad. He was 35. And they went out for a couple years before they got married." She paused and looked at me. "He's dead."

"Look at society today," Ganeesh said. "If your dad did that now, he'd be in jail."

"My point exactly." Savannah said. "Older men are biologically programmed to be attracted to younger – allegedly more fertile – females. But for some reason, as society progressed, those instincts become illegal."

"You're totally right." I was seven years older than Monica, yet because of her youthful beauty, several people had asked if she was my daughter. And frowned at me when I said we were married. Like I was robbing a cradle. "How did that happen?"

"Pretty convoluted." She shook her head and sighed. "The craziness of modern life. Complicated and contradictory. Society tries to counter nature by making rules. Creating a false dichotomy of sex. Making young females off limits

to older males. Yet at the same time, young females are encouraged to wear pro-
vocative outfits and lots of make-up. So they end up looking more sophisticated
then their actual age. Meanwhile, mature females start dressing in styles best
suited for teenaged bodies. When you really start to study how human society
tries to counter and attack the human sexual response, you see how it gets pretty
strange and misguided..."

"Oh my God," Missy yelped. "You won't believe what I saw Mrs. Grimaldi
wearing the other day when I was in Roosevelt."

"She teaches at the high school," Jenny said, handing me the blunt. "She's
kinda chunky."

"Kinda chunky?" Ganeesh shook his head. "That's being nice."

"She was wearing a mini-mini," Missy said, shaking her head. "Way too
short and way too tight."

"Oh man, that sucks," Ganeesh said. "I'm glad I didn't see it."

"More proof," Savannah said. "She's like, almost 50. And not in the best
shape. Not a good fashion choice for her." She shook her head vehemently. "Fashion is really unhealthy. The fashion industry and magazines are responsible for
some of the problem. Unrealistic and crazy. Thong underwear for seven year-
olds? Seven years old? What kind of parent would let a little girl wear a thong?"

"That's way too young," Missy said. "The way I see it, nature sets the time
for when a girl is ready to mate. Menstruation should be the line. Pre-pubescent,
no sex. But once she gets her period, she should be able to have sex if she wants
too. Especially if her body is telling her to do it."

"I'd agree with that," Jenny nodded. "Makes sense to me."

"Yeah," Ganeesh said. "How old are girls when they start their period?"

"Could be as young as eleven," Savannah said. "But that's only in recent
years. Used to be 12 or 13 years old. No one understands why the age is going
down. Some wonder if it's the saturated fats of our modern diet. Or the hormones
in the chicken and beef we eat. Others theorize it's evolutionary." She shook her
head. "But I don't agree with you guys. Just because a girl menstruates, that
doesn't mean she's ready for sex."

"I was," Missy said. "I was more than ready."

"Baby," Ganeesh said, "you were born ready."

Everyone laughed.

"C'mon," Savannah said. "Maturity is an essential part of sexuality. An
essential part to the experience being pleasurable. If a girl isn't ready, she isn't
ready. And if she's not ready, it's not gonna be fun." She pointed at Missy. "Some
are ready when they're 12." She pointed to herself. "Others, maybe not until 14 or
15 or 16."

"How do we know?" I asked. As much as I'm a total fan of the concept of free love, the idea of 11 and 12 year-olds having sex bothered me. "I mean, how do you tell who is ready?"

"It's pretty easy to spot the mature 12-year-old. She acts totally different than a pre-pubescent. A good parent would be able to tell, and should talk to their daughter. But we shouldn't act surprised by the concept of teen sex. A teenage human is, of course, a biological computer running a program. The real question is how do we handle teen sex? We sweep it into the closet. Call it a crime. It's natural, for goodness sake." Savannah shrugged and sighed. "That's part of the problem. As a society we're so uptight we can't even have a discussion about pre-teens and teens having sex without being labeled a pervert."

"Yeah, I like talking about it," Ganeesh said, "and I'm not a pervert."

"Yes, you are," Missy giggled. "You're a big pervert."

Again, laughter.

"Pre-teens," I said, trying to imagine myself as a sexually active preteen. Couldn't see it. Probably capable, physiologically, but definitely not ready for fatherhood, that's for sure. Not that it mattered, I wasn't getting laid. But my parents and the Catholic school teachers never mentioned the possibility. "That's so crazy."

"Society ignores reality. Twelve year-olds are having sex, that's a fact. Get over it. We're talking about sex, a vital physiological reproductive function of mammals. Sex also provides relaxation. Creates opportunities for intimacy. And it just plain feels good. So why wouldn't teenagers want it?" Savannah shook her head. "We know from surveys and from public health statistics, they're doing it. I just don't want them getting pregnant. Is a 12-year-old female ready for the pill?"

"I hope not," Missy frowned. "The pill is so bad, especially for young girls."

"Will the 12-year-old male use a condom?" Savannah asked.

"Where the hell is a little kid gonna get a condom?" Ganeesh shook his head. "I still get nervous buying 'em if there's an old lady behind the counter."

"Maybe from a friend," Jenny paused. "Or school."

"Right, Jenny," Savannah said. "That's what I think. Offer condoms in every school, from 7th grade up, and teach the kids how to use them. Teach them to turn condoms into part of sexplay. Studies show the obvious: accessible birth control reduces teen pregnancy and disease. Which means reduced health care expenses and social service programs. But we won't have that conversation because school boards fear the conservative Christians."

"*Fucking rednecks!*" Missy yelped.

"Preaching abstinence doesn't work." Savannah shook her head. "Because then 12-year-olds will have unprotected sex. Sometimes they conceive. Then what happens? Do we abort? Put the baby up for adoption? Let the kids raise the baby themselves?"

"No fucking way," Ganeesh shook his head sadly. "Those kids can't handle the responsibility."

"Totally screw up their lives. We've seen it a million times around here," Missy said, looking at me. "I'm never gonna have kids. Too many people on the planet already."

"I want kids," Jenny nodded. "But not until I'm older."

"Not me," Savannah said. "I'm too selfish. To do it right, raising kids takes a lot of work. I'm devoting my energy to sex. Plus, I'm already an aunt." She smiled. "I love being an aunt. The kids go back to my brother's at night and I don't have to worry about them anymore."

"Yeah," Missy said to me. "If you're not gonna be a good parent, then you shouldn't be one. Problem is, anyone can have a baby."

"You're right." Savannah nodded. "These guys are probably sick of hearing me saying this," she gestured to the rest of the circle, "but education needs to start much earlier. Schools need to teach kids the fundamentals of sex. More than just the biology. Teach them the real-world ramifications. The complications. Outcomes. We need to teach them the how-tos and the how-not-tos."

"Do you mean technique?" I asked. "Lessons on how to have sex?"

"Why not?" She paused and shrugged. "Humans think about sex more often than trigonometry." She shook her head. "Kids spend lots of time learning math they will never use in real life."

"There's a great scene in a Monty Python movie," Ganeesh said, taking a puff from the blunt. "John Cleese plays a teacher who fucks his wife in front of the students. Bed comes down from the wall. Pretty fucking funny."

"Teaching technique would make a huge difference," Missy said. "If we taught kids to be better lovers, the world would be much different."

"Yeah, wouldn't be as many wars," Jenny squeaked. " 'Cuz if all the soldiers were more into great sex than killing, they'd probably be too tired to fight."

Everyone laughed.

"What if the women of the world decided to keep their legs shut," Missy said, taking a puff. "And what if all the women in the world said we aren't touching another cock until all war is over. Would it work?"

"Probably not," Savannah said.

"You're right," Missy said. "I don't think Laura Bush touches George W.'s cock anyway." She shook her head. "That asshole. Unfortunately, some women support the war."

"Not many," Jenny said. "Thankfully."

"If men suddenly got shut off from pussy," Ganeesh stroked his chin, then shook his head, "you'd find some would end up raping and pillaging."

Missy jumped up from the circle and grabbed the 9 mil off the coffee table in the center of the room.

"We'll kill 'em," she snarled. " 'Cuz we'll make sure all the pussy is heavily armed."

Everyone laughed.

"I think it's 'all the pussy are heavily armed.' " Savannah giggled. "Anyway, I wish withholding sex could end a war, but I don't think it's possible." She pushed up her glasses and took a long sip of wine. "Our society has vilified sex. Sex is bad. Linked to violence. Linked to drugs and rock and roll. But most sex isn't violent and done without help from drugs or rock and roll." She took a puff off the blunt, then pointed at me. "I've been studying the history of sex and keep asking the same question over and over: when and why did sex become an evil act?" She handed me the reefer. "Do you have any idea why the human sexual response became viewed as evil and sinful? Do you know?"

"Maybe," I said, taking a puff to stall and consider my own upbringing. Felt like I was in a classroom. A very cool classroom. Fun. "Something to do with the Catholics?"

"Exactly," she said. "I blame all the major religions, though. Catholicism, Christianity and Islam all have very strict views on sex."

"That's bullshit!" Ganeesh said. "Why should those fuckers have say over anything? They tell us we're not supposed to have anal sex. Oral sex. Threesomes. Foursomes."

"And moresomes," Missy chimed in.

"Yeah, and moresomes," Ganeesh continued. "Yet for centuries Catholic priests have been fucking and sucking little boys." He shook his head. "I should know. We had some seriously creepy priests on the reservation."

"What drives me crazy," Savannah said, "is the prohibition against birth control. Very anti-woman and another self-serving philosophy. They want their followers to reproduce so their church gets bigger, yet most of the problems on this planet are connected to overpopulation one way or another. For reasons of control and domination," Savannah shook her head, "society and religions put up so many roadblocks to sex. They don't want pleasure to be part of our lives."

"What did Jesus say about sex?" Missy asked. "Absolutely nothing. In fact, I betcha he and Mary Magdalene had something going on. He talks about love. Love often means sex." She shook her head. "The prudes should just face the facts. Humans love to cum. An orgasm feels great!"

"Feels awesome," squeaked Jenny. "I love to cum!"

"Do you know anyone who doesn't enjoy an orgasm?" Savannah asked me.

"Nope."

"And the orgasm is fairly easy to achieve, right. Either by yourself or with the help of one or more other people."

"If you're lucky." Ganeesh said. "Three is the perfect number."

Everyone laughed.

"But society doesn't agree." Savannah pointed at me. "So if you stray or dispute their moral code, you become an outsider."

"Until the revolution," Missy said, raising her wine to the sky. "Viva le revolution!"

"*Viva le revolution,*" Ganeesh boomed. "*Viva le revolution!*"

Ganeesh kissed Savannah. Then he kissed Missy. And then Missy and Savannah kissed each other. This was getting even more interesting. I looked at Jenny. She gazed back at me while puffing on the blunt.

"Zeeez!" the buzzer interrupted. "Zeeez!"

"Fuck me," Missy shook her head. "I forgot that asshole was here. We were having such a good time. Can't we pretend not to hear the buzzer?"

"Yeah, leave him out there." Jenny giggled and handed me the blunt. "Don't buzz him in."

Was this the same blunt? Seemed like we were smoking it for hours. Seemed impolite to turn the weed down. I felt great. Comfortable and happy. Sitting cross-legged on the floor helped with my back pain. New muscles stretched and others relaxed. Maybe it was the weed and the beers.

"Zeeez!" The buzzer buzzed again. "Zeeez!"

Ganeesh stood.

"No! No!" The three females and I chanted. "No! No!"

Ganeesh shook his head and pushed the button. A second later, the door swung open, and the last light of day, orange, for a moment, entered. So did Richard.

"Where's the bathroom?" I asked Missy. She pointed to the door on the other side of the pool table.

"We're on a septic tank," she said. "If it's yellow, let it mellow. We've gotta have rules, right?"

After taking a leak, I walked back into the big room. The CD had stopped and everyone was quiet. I spotted an acoustic guitar leaning against a wall. I picked it up and plucked each string. Not too bad. Tightened the strap and walked back toward the crowd.

"One, two, three, four," I said and started to strum, lightly. "*On a dark desert highway / Cool wind in my hair.*"

My version of the Eagles' classic *Hotel California* was always a hit at parties. I closed my eyes and worked my fingers, sore from the day's harvest, up and down the strings. Occasionally I'd sneak a peek at my audience, especially Missy. They watched, en rapt, despite my swollen fingers' inability to press hard enough and occasionally hitting the wrong note.

When the tune ended, the crowd was silent for a moment, then burst into hearty cheers. Ganeesh, Savannah and Jenny clapped and yelled for more. Richard whistled. Missy nodded and smiled. Grinned straight at me with her wide beautiful grin. I grinned back.

"Play another song," Savannah called out. "That was great."

"Maybe later," I said. "Raking blueberries has messed up my fingers. Who's next? Whose guitar is this?"

"Dude, that's mine," Ganeesh said, shaking his head. "I'd be embarrassed to play after you. I'm serious. That was fucking awesome."

"Thanks," I said, leaning the guitar back against the wall. "Appreciate it."

"My dear." Missy stood and floated toward me, then engulfed me in her embrace. Electrifying me. "That was way better than the Eagles."

"Yeah," Jenny sighed. "Much better. I loved it."

"Thanks," I said, taking a little bow after Missy released me. Moments like this made me miss my old rock 'n roll lifestyle. A big part of the buzz came from chicks digging me. "Thank you very much."

"Oral sex is clean and fun," Missy said. In the hour since I played the guitar, the discussion varied tremendously: from Ganeesh's 9-11 conspiracies alleging an inside job, to Richard's long boring description of a movie he once had seen, but couldn't remember by name. Most interesting, however, was the discussion of oral sex led by the girls. "Very low risk of STDs."

"Oral sex doesn't get you preggers," Jenny said. "And everyone gets to cum."

"Where were you girls when I was in high school?" I asked. "Completely different."

"When did you graduate?" Jenny asked.

"Class of 1986." I lifted my beer can as a toast. "St. John's, in a little town you've never heard of in Western Massachusetts."

"Oh dear," Missy laughed. "I was just a baby."

"I wasn't even born yet," Jenny squeaked. "You are old."

"Did you have lots of sex?" Savannah asked.

"Ahhhh, no."

They laughed.

"Did you get any blowjobs?" she asked. "At all?"

"Well, when I was 14, I sorta got one." I frowned at the uncomfortable memory. Outside the library on the side of a hill with a girl who, to put it politely, wasn't very pretty and didn't know what she was doing. (I had to help finish.) "Then I went four years without it happening again."

"You poor boy," Missy said. "Poor boy."

"Why the dry spell?" Savannah asked.

"I spent most of high school going out with a nice Catholic girl. No sex. Wouldn't even touch me." I shook my head. "Never would have dreamed of putting her mouth on me."

"Man, you must have jerked off a lot. Otherwise you would have exploded." Ganeesh nodded. "I got laid a lot during high school."

"Of course you did," Missy said. "You were so super-cute." She turned to me. "I had a crush on him when he was in high school and I was in the second grade."

"That's when I was a senior." Ganeesh shook his head. "Crazy you still have that memory."

"I was in second grade. Mrs. Hurley's class," she said. "Ganeesh and a couple other guys danced for us."

"My cousins," he said. "I think there was four of us."

"Anyway, they came to our school to demonstrate traditional Passamaquoddy dances. He was this big strong bronzed Indian. To me, a dream." She smiled. "You still are."

Laughter.

"I got a lot of sex during high school," Richard said. "Didn't I, Ganeesh?"

"Yup," Ganeesh said. "You and Peggy would fuck everywhere. In the gym. In the bathroom. In the teacher's lounge."

The room went silent. The music had stopped.

Peggy? Richard and Peggy used to be together? That explained Jazz's secret and made for a different dynamic for the song I'd been thinking about writing. A love triangle. Two brothers. One redneck. One goth. An old flame.

"C'mon Ben, play us another tune," Savannah said. "Break this uncomfortable silence."

"Yes dear," Missy said. "Could you play something by Neil Young?"

I stood and strapped on the guitar. For over a decade, music was the key ingredient of my life. The guitar, an integral part of my body. Every day, practice, a gig or just noodling. But I discarded the rock star dream in favor of the dream of life on the land. At that very moment, however, with Missy's big hopeful eyes staring up at me, I realized I missed the look of an admiring fan. Especially someone like Missy. Farmers rarely experience such adoration. Which is unfortunate because farmers deserve more praise than rock stars. At least some farmers.

So I played Neil Young's *Harvest*, a tune I loved and had strummed a million times. Again, everyone was rapt. Savannah and Ganeesh held hands and smiled. Jenny's eyes were closed and she was slowly nodding her head. Richard's head also slowly bounced to the music. But Missy's reaction was the most intense. A couple tears trickled down her right cheek. She looked as though she was about to start sobbing. Instead, her lips parted into that wide and warm smile.

I liked that smile. A lot.

Song over. More applause. More compliments. But I couldn't hear them. I was staring at Missy. She didn't say a word. Just sat there, looking at me. Shook her head, cheeks wet with tears. She gave a little laugh and rubbed her eyes. I put the guitar back against the wall. She stood and went over the stereo to put on music. I reclaimed my spot on the floor. Missy pressed play and sat down next to me, a little closer than before. Led Zeppelin started playing softly.

"What were we talking about?" Ganeesh asked.

"Blowjobs," Jenny squealed, holding up her wine glass. "Oral sex."

"Excellent topic," he said, opening the fridge for another can of Moxie. "I love blowjobs."

Laughter.

"We were talking about Ben's experience." Savannah again sounded like a professor. Or researcher. She turned to me. "When was your next sexual event, after the side of the hill by the library?"

Everyone laughed.

"When I was 18." A much fonder memory. End of senior year. No longer with the Irish-Catholic girl, I inexplicably ended up having a torrid affair with the beautiful captain of the cheerleading squad. Sex like I had dreamed about. Like I'd read about in the magazines I stole from my brother. "After a four-year dry spell, it was awesome. Amazing."

"You poor dear," Missy said, grabbing my left hand, holding it with both of hers and looked at me with her wide blue eyes. "If we'd gone to high school together, I'd given you lots of oral."

I gulped, absorbing the shock from her electrical touch and her surprising offer.

"Whoa," Richard said. "Ben, too bad we don't have a time machine. Of course, even if we did have a time machine, she would have been a little baby sucking on your penis."

Again, silence. A long silence.

"Because..." he stammered. "Because you're so much older than her."

"Little Dick." Missy turned to look at him, still holding my hand. Her energy pulsed through me. "You're a fucking idiot."

The women I've been attracted to fall into two categories. Some electrocuted me. Some I just wanted to fuck. The purely sexual attractions were acknowledged from the start to be fun with no commitment. One or two night stands. The girls from the rock n' roll days, for instance, are remembered by their faces, not their names.

But the women who've electrocuted me, I remember everything. Forever.

A dozen women have electrocuted me in a way similar to Missy. A voltage that wasn't static. A stronger power. Intense energy flow. A steady current, followed by a rhythmic pulse flowing and flipping through the nervous system. More than a tingle. But not painful. Consciousness raising. A multi-cellular alert system to proclaim the presence of someone special. An internal shout-out.

Not love. The shock didn't mean love. But was more than sex. In fact, in a couple instances, sex never happened. The electric touch, like a Vulcan mind trick, projected a certain willingness to explore each other. Intense. Passion-driven. Unknown and familiar at the same time. Allowing us to bond and exchange. Explain and understand. To have fun and to let go. And for the record, the women of the electric touch have treated me extremely well. Better than I ever deserved.

The electric shock women were eternally embedded in a special section of my brain. The way they looked. Smelled. Sounded. Tasted. Laughed. Thought. Lived. Dreamed. I didn't stay in touch with these women, except for Monica. But on the rare occasion our paths crossed again, the electricity returned immediately. These women had nothing in common, other than their electric touch. They were tall and short. Svelte. Zaftig. Loud. Silent. Rich. Poor. Hippy. Snob. And now Missy joined that list.

"Words are a big part of it," Savannah said and took another long puff from a super-big blunt.

Drunk and tired, I had no idea what time it was. Richard had built a pyramid of empty beer cans. (With a couple Moxie cans mixed in.) As the circle grew tighter, both Missy and Jenny touched me with their legs.

"People are simply afraid of the words connected to sex: Fuck. Cock.

Pussy. Cum. Ass. Cunt."

Richard snickered.

"Richard, you think it's funny for me to say cunt?" Savannah asked him.

"Well, it's a dirty word." Richard looked down. "That's all."

"I like both words," Missy said, looking at me. "Which sounds better? Listen to the options: I want you to fuck my pussy." She paused. "I want you to fuck my cunt. Which would you rather do?"

Luckily the candles were flickering and no one could see me blush. Or see my instant erection. Was this a rhetorical question? Jenny started to giggle.

"Hoo-hah," she said. "That's what my mom insists on calling it."

"I prefer cunt to pussy." Savannah smiled. "A pussy is a cat. What about penis? That's not a sexy word. Too clinical."

"I like cock," Missy said with a grin. My loins stirred, again. "I don't like dick. A dick is a small penis. Guys named Dick," she nodded toward Richard, "are losers. Dickheads."

Richard scowled and stood, drained his beer and added another empty to his pyramid.

"And you can't say any of the other words for penis without laughing," Savannah said. "Phallus? Prick? Pole? Willie?"

"Tube snake," Missy laughed. "Tube steak."

"Trouser trout," Jenny squeaked. "One-eyed wonder mouse."

"Johnson," I said, which turned out to be a conversation-stopper.

"Who?" Savannah asked. "What?"

"Johnson," I said again. "Johnson. Some people call a penis a Johnson."

"Never heard of that." Richard opened a new beer, shook his head and sat back down. "Nobody calls a penis a Johnson."

"Are you sure?" Jenny squeaked. "That's so funny."

"Yes," I nodded. "Hundred percent sure."

Everyone laughed.

"The proof is in the pudding," Missy said, pointing at Richard and trying to hold back her giggles. "We won't call you Little Dick anymore. We're gonna call you Little Dick-Dick."

Everyone but Richard and I were in hysterics. It took a second to figure it out.

"I didn't realize your last name was Johnson," I said to Richard. "Sorry dude."

"Yeah," he was sullen. "So what? You guys are all assholes. My name is Richard. Not Dick. When you all gonna get it through your thick skulls?"

"I gotta admit," Missy said, "I like the sound of Richard Johnson instead of penis." She grinned. "Not meaning you, of course, Little Dick Dick." She sighed and started to groan and moan. "Give it to me, baby. Fill my tight cunt with your rock hard Richard Johnson." She giggled. "Fuck my wet pussy with your rock hard Richard Johnson."

Again, lots of laughs.

"Rock Hard Richard Johnson," Ganeesh said with a smile. "Sounds like a pro wrestler or," he paused for a second, "a gay porn star."

"What's up with that, dude? I thought we were buds." Richard shook his head. "A gay friggin' faggot porn star, what the frig?" He took a long sip of his beer. "You know how I hate faggots."

"Why are you always bashing gay people?" Savannah asked. "I'm curious."

"You know the reason, I've told you," Richard paused. "Don't like faggots. Don't like faggots touching me."

"Oh come on," Missy said, sighing. "How often does that happen?"

"Tell 'em, Ganeesh," Richard said with an air of weariness. "Tell 'em again what happened at the Black Bear."

"Dude," Ganeesh shook his head. "Everyone knows the story. Besides, that was last year."

"Really? Feels like it was yesterday. Ben," he pointed at me, "Ben here, doesn't know this story. So we were at the Black Bear, having a good time and this guy I'm talking to buys me a beer and a shot. Didn't know him. He was from Brewer or Bangor or somewheres. Anyway, he seemed all right. Until he asked if I wanted to go back to the Roosevelt Motor Inn so he could suck me off." He shook his head and reflexively went for his pack of smokes. He had one in his mouth before Missy shouted at him.

"*No smoking!*"

"Oh frig." He put the cigarettes away. "This 'no smoking' is a bunch of bull." He grumbled and shook his head. "So the faggot thought just because he bought me a drink I was his back door boy."

"Lucky you," Missy said sweetly. "Did you let him suck you off?"

"No!" He shook his head violently. "Frig you, Missy. You know I didn't let him."

"Richard, watch it!" Ganeesh pointed at him. "That's no way to speak to a lady."

"C'mon, she knows the story. She knows I ain't no faggot."

"I forgot." Missy giggled. "Sorry."

"What did you do?" I asked Richard. "After he asked you."

"I told him he better forget about it."

"Is that it?" Savannah asked. "Is that all you did?"

In the flickering candlelight, I couldn't see his face, but from the way he held his head, I guessed he was glaring at Savannah.

"What did you do Richard?" Jenny squeaked. "I never heard this."

"Never mind," Richard shook his head. "I'm gonna have a smoke."

"Ganeesh," Missy said. "You were there. Tell Ben what happened."

"Okay. Okay." Richard put his hands up. "I clocked the faggot."

"What?" Even though I already knew Richard was an asshole, punching someone over an offered blowjob surprised me. "You hit him?"

"Right in the nose," Ganeesh said, starting to laugh. "And the guy slugged him right back. I just came out of the bathroom and saw the whole thing. They were just standing at the bar and suddenly both had bloody noses."

"Richard, I've got a question for you," Savannah said. "If an ugly girl offered you a blowjob, would you have punched her?"

"Of course not. I'd never hit a girl."

"But because he was a guy?"

"That's right. I'm no faggot. Not gonna let some guy suck me. No frigging way..."

"What if it was a girl who looked like a guy?" Missy interrupted. "A girl with really small breasts. A girl with short hair and wearing men's clothes? Could she blow you?"

Everyone but Richard laughed.

"How about a transvestite?" I asked. "With a wig and a little make-up. I've seen some guys turn into pretty hot chicks. So if she looked like a woman, but was really a guy, but you thought she was a woman, would it make a difference?"

"What the frig, dude?" He pointed at me. "Whose side you on?"

"Not choosing sides, but I think you getting pissed off about someone offering you a blowjob is crazy. And you shouldn't have punched him. You should have taken it as a compliment."

"A compliment! It's unnatural and gross for a guy to suck another guy's..."

"Richard, another question," Savannah interrupted. "Would you like to watch Missy lick my cunt?"

"Wha...wha...what?" Richard stammered.

"You heard me. Would you like to watch Missy lick my cunt? Would you?"

"Is this a trick question?"

"No." She shook her head. "Just tell the truth."

Richard looked super uncomfortable.

"I already know the answer anyway." She nodded. "You told Ganeesh that you'd like to watch Missy and I 'get it on', right? I do believe that's an exact quote."

"Oh come on." He looked at his buddy. "Why did you say that?"

"Never mind." Savannah pointed at him. "Just answer my question. It doesn't even have to be me and Missy. Do you like watching two girls have sex? Making love?"

"*Fuck and suck, little dick dick*," Missy said. "Lickity split. Licking the clit..."

"Ahha, ahha, well, yeah," Richard stammered. Again, he pulled out his pack of smokes and shook one out. "Everyone likes girl-on-girl."

"*No smoking*," Missy yelled. "So lesbianism should be allowed, but not man-on-man sex. What a double standard! You really are a fucking idiot, aren't you? Ben, what do think about all this?"

"Sex is a personal right guaranteed by both the Constitution and the Declaration of Independence." I wasn't sure if that was true, but it should be. "Freedom of speech. Freedom from religion. Pursuit of happiness. Sex makes people happy. As long as it doesn't hurt anyone, no one should give a damn. People should be able to do what they want in the bedroom."

"Are you crazy?" Richard asked. "It's friggin' nasty to put a penis in your mouth."

"If it's so nasty, why do you love it when Lora gives you a blowjob?" Savannah asked him. "And you kiss her afterwards, don't you?"

Richard looked confused. Nervous. Scared.

"Kissing Lora after she gives you head is almost sucking your own cock," Missy said, laughing. "Interesting. So you're a cocksucker after all. I bet you'd love to suck a nice big black cock, if you had a chance."

"Fuck you, bitch," Richard said.

"Richard swore!" yelped Jenny, turning to me. "Richard swore. I've never heard him swear before."

"Fuck you, Richard." Ganeesh pointed at his buddy. "I'm totally fucking serious. Stop acting like a son-of-a-bitch. Watch the way you talk to her. Otherwise, I'm gonna have to kick your fucking ass."

"Okay." Richard put up his hands. "But it's okay for her to call me a cocksucker?"

"It's just a word, Richard. Let's examine it rationally," Savannah said. "What's the matter with being a cocksucker? Isn't that what all men want? According to most surveys, blowjobs are a number one priority. Men desire blowjobs above all other forms of sex."

"That's right," Ganeesh said. "I love 'em. I'm sure every guy does."

"So that means cocksucking is a desired action." Savannah pointed at Richard. "Yet, for most men, the term cocksucker is construed as an insult. However, they want their cocks sucked, presumably by a woman they love or are at least attracted to. Some men are willing to pay big bucks. Travel long distances. Endure pain and suffering just for an occasional blowjob. Seems to me a," she made air quotes, " 'cocksucker' should be treated with reverence. You'd think cocksucker would be a term of endearment."

"My sweet cocksucker!" Missy exclaimed. "My darling cocksucker?"

"Exactly," Savannah smiled. "But somehow, it became an insult. How did that happen? Interesting research topic for an English major."

"Because," Richard said, pointing at Missy. "The way she was saying it, she was saying that I'm a cocksucker. Meaning a faggot. And I don't think I should have to put up with that sort of bull. I'd rather die than suck a cock."

The room went silent.

"Are you serious?" Savannah said. "You would rather die than suck a cock?"

"Of course." Richard took a long sip from his beer. "Not a chance I'm gonna suck off a man."

"You are a bigger idiot than I thought," Missy said. "You are the biggest fucking moron in all Washington County, Little Dick-Dick. Maybe even the whole state of Maine. Maybe the world."

Jenny giggled.

"So you're telling us," Savannah said, "if someone threatened you with death, you still wouldn't give a blowjob?"

"That's right." Richard pointed at his mouth. "These lips will never do it."

"Ben," Savannah said. "Would you rather suck a cock or die?"

"Of course," I said, "I'd suck a cock to save my life."

"Huh. That means you're a faggot," Richard said with an uneasy laugh. "I wished I knew before inviting you to camp out. You better stay in your own tent."

"What about you, Ganeesh?" Savannah asked. "Would you do it?"

"Ahhh fuck." Ganeesh sounded sheepish. "I was hoping you'd leave me out of it."

"Hah! Not a chance he'd suck one." Richard laughed and nodded vigorously. "Ganeesh would take a bullet to the head before he wrapped his Indian lips around another man's penis."

"Really, Ganeesh?" Missy stood up and took a couple steps away from the circle. "Is that true?"

"Well, I'd rather not have to go around giving guys blowjobs." He sighed and shook his head. "But I don't want to die, so..."

"My friggin' word!" Richard shook his head in disbelief. "I'm surrounded by a bunch of cocksuckers."

"I think you're a cocksucker, Richard," Missy said from the darkness on the edge of the circle near the CD player. "And I want to watch you suck Ganeesh's cock."

"What are you talking about? Ganeesh, you hearing this? Tell Missy to behave herself! Tell her to shut up!"

"You should know by now, Little Dick-Dick." Missy flipped a switch and the floor lamp with three bulbs glowed red. "No one tells me what to do." She took a couple steps forward and pointed the nine mil at Richard. She was six feet away from him, so it took Richard a moment to comprehend the situation.

"*Get that friggin' gun out of my face!*" Richard shouted and started to stand. "*Stop pointing that friggin' gun at me!*"

"Down on your knees, now, Little Dick-Dick," Missy said, her voice calm but slightly slurring. "I've found that's a very efficient place to suck cock. From the cocksucking perspective. Now be a good little cocksucker and wrap your white boy lips around his big Indian rod."

"*Ganeesh!*" Richard – half standing – looked scared. "*Tell her to cut it out!*"

"If you don't want to get shot, you better get busy. Without a doubt, if I did shoot you, everyone here would agree to swear in court that your death was an accident. That you'd been waving the gun around and pointing it at everyone and I grabbed it from you and the gun went off. A terrible mistake. A drinking party gone bad. Just another one of those accidental Washington County gun deaths."

"*Ganeesh!*" he wailed, on the verge of tears. "*Tell her...*"

"*Get on your fucking knees!*" Missy screamed, taking a couple steps closer to Richard. She held the gun correctly. Both hands. Staring down the sight, three feet from his head. That meant Richard was staring into the gun barrel. She was ready to shoot. "*I told you to get on your knees!*"

"*What the frig?*" Richard dropped to his knees, whimpering. She took another step and the gun was an inch, maybe two, from his forehead. Almost touching, but not. "Ganeesh, dude, do something..."

"Listen, Missy." Ganeesh shook his head. "I don't want him sucking my cock. He's not my type. Honestly, I wouldn't be able to get an erection."

"What about you, Ben?" she asked me, gun still pointed at Richard's head. "Interested in a blowjob?"

"Not from him," I said, looking at her. "No thanks."

"Oh well. Here you go, dear," she said, handing the gun to Ganeesh. He put it on the coffee table. "Never mind."

Everyone laughed. Everyone but Richard, still on his knees. Shaking. Shaking in fear or anger? Or both?

"That's bull," Richard whined as he got up from his knees. "Shouldn't be playing with guns. Shouldn't be pointing guns at people."

"*Fuck you*," Missy said. "You're a cocksucker."

"Relax, Richard, she wasn't going to shoot you. The safety was still on." Ganeesh turned to Missy. "Maybe you should stop calling him a cocksucker before he has a fucking heart attack."

"Okay, dear." She took a step towards Richard's beer can pyramid. "I'll stop calling the cocksucker a cocksucker." I'm sure the others knew what was next, but Richard and I didn't see it coming. "Hi-yah!" she shouted and kicked the center of the pyramid. The cans clattered to the floor. Everyone laughed again, except Richard.

"What the frig? Why did ya have to go and do that? You are such a bitch!"

Missy grabbed the gun off the table and made a point of flicking the safety off.

"You're the bitch, bitch," she said. "Do you understand what I'm saying, *white boy?*"

I'd forgotten the warning. She fired three times. By the second shot, I had my fingers in my ears.

After firing the third shot, Missy pointed the gun at Richard.

"You want to know why I kicked over your lousy pyramid?" Missy was almost screaming. "*To teach you a lesson, bitch.* You should be thanking me. If you had finished the pyramid and it was perfect and you went home, that would've been it. Never think of it again. But with me destroying your work, I made it permanent. Memorable. You will never forget that pyramid." She laughed at him. "Just like you won't forget the rest of tonight. This night, as far as I'm concerned, will always be remembered as 'The night Missy almost made Richard suck Ganeesh's cock, then kicked over his beer pyramid'." She smiled. "I know you're mad, but I've got a right to fuck with you. You know it. Payback's a bitch, bitch." She shook her head. "Stop being such an idiot, and maybe, just maybe, someday I might stop fucking with you."

Ganeesh laughed. Richard shot him a look. Pissed. Betrayed. Hurt. Hatred. All of it.

"Dude, she's totally right." Ganeesh shook his head and stood. "If I were you, I'd chill out." He pointed at Missy. "You are nuts. Nuts. But in the best way possible." He picked her up and spun her around and around. She squealed with delight. He put her down. For a couple seconds, dizzy and disorientated, she wobbled. Then they kissed.

"Okay motherfuckers," Ganeesh said. "Anyone not sleeping with me must leave the premises immediately."

"Yeah," Missy laughed, still wobbly, and pointed at us. "Get out of here, you cocksuckers."

On my way out the door, I turned around to bid a final goodbye. Missy ran over, gave me an electric hug and a spark of a kiss on the cheek.

"Thanks for playing those songs," she said, turning and walking back toward Savannah and Ganeesh. "I really love the way you sing," she added, over her shoulder, "my dear."

Walking into the dark night, I was aroused. Richard was having a smoke. Jenny was leaning on Floyd's hood, looking up at the night sky.

I was aroused by Missy's touch and kiss. Aroused by the thought that less than a hundred feet away, she was about to entwine in a ménage of almost epic proportions. I'd never encountered such an open scene before. They were an intriguing threesome. Especially Missy and her electric touch.

By the time I got behind Floyd's steering wheel, I knew I needed to see Missy again. She was special, no doubt. And her use of handguns, while potentially dangerous, made for moments of pure exhilaration and adrenalin rush.

Jenny sat between Richard and I. She needed a ride because she wasn't sleeping with Ganeesh. She didn't speak except to say where to turn. The roads grew darker. No lights. No street signs. No moonglow. No other vehicles or indication of human life. Huge trees were a solid wall along the shoulder.

I was drunk driving, unfortunately. I was a terrible driver when sober, let alone after drinking so many beers and pot smoking. Lucky I didn't crash and kill all three of us. My lame excuse for this behavior: I hadn't planned on getting drunk. So I was driving quite slow. Super paranoid and more nervous than usual, I got the notion of a moose about to run into us. And because of the multiple turns in the rural darkness of a moonless mid-summer night, I was completely lost. Luckily, Richard would know the way home.

Jenny sat as close to me as she possibly could. Her left leg kept rubbing against my right thigh. I considered the two possibilities: Either she liked me or she was just trying to stay as far away from Richard as possible. (He hadn't said a word since climbing in the truck). No matter, I enjoyed her warmth leaning into me as we turned corners and staying there on the straightaways.

Eventually, we ended up somewhere.

"Here," she squeaked. "On the right."

I pulled over.

"I gotta take a leak," Richard said, opening the door. "Back in a second."

"Well," I said, turning to face Jenny in the bright interior light. "It was nice to met you."

Suddenly her slightly open mouth was on my mouth. A wet kiss. For three seconds, her darting tongue surprised and teased mine. Then she licked my upper lip and pulled back just as fast as she came forward. I couldn't even respond.

"Thanks for the ride," she squeaked. "See you around."

I sat, stunned, as she climbed out of the truck and slammed the door shut. For a second, I considered jumping out of the truck, walking her to the front door and kissing her for real under the porch light. My arms could so easily wrap around her, touching and exploring her nubile body.

Was I fucking nuts? What was I thinking? She was probably not even 18. I was more than twice her age. But as Savannah eloquently pointed out, the middle-aged man is biologically programmed to be attracted to young women. Biologically programmed to want a fertile post-pubescent female because she's capable of bearing him many kids to help with the hunt in the forest or chores on the farm. But in the modern world, it's so different. Illegal, almost, and immoral just to talk about the possibility.

Still in a daze due to the unexpected kiss, the beers, weed and drama of the evening, I put Floyd in gear and started to roll forward before hearing a shout and remembering Richard. I hit the brakes.

"What the frig?" he asked, climbing in. "You gonna ditch me out here?"

"No," I said, wishing I could. "Can't do that. I'm lost. Where are we?"

"Pembroke," he said. "Let's go back to my place. I'm ready for bed." He yawned. "Turn this friggin' rig around."

He rolled down his window, lit a smoke and started talking.

"Missy is pretty messed up. Always has been, ever since she was a little girl when her mom died. I totally understand why Ganeesh is banging Savannah. She's got a hot bod, though she's a little too smart for him." He shook his head. "But Missy, I don't get it. She's whacked. When she gets drinking, she gets weird and real mean. Pulling that gun on me wasn't cool. Like I was supposed to know the safety was on?" He took a drag on his cigarette. "I mean, what the frig? No smoking in the Grange? Smoke never bothered Ganeesh until this summer."

"Dude, he's fucking both of them, right?"

"Yeah."

"I think if both those girls were sleeping with me, I'd do whatever they asked me."

"Yeah," he nodded. "But that Missy, she's trouble."

"Why does she hate you so much?"

"Small town stuff." He shook his head. "Everyone's got a grudge against somebody."

"What's her grudge?"

"It's a long friggin' story." He flicked his cigarette butt out the window, sighed and pointed into the darkness. "Take a left here."

I was laying flat on my back atop my sleeping bag, listening to the song of peeping frogs and the faint sawing of Richard's snoring. I took inventory of my physical condition: after re-applying the salve, my swimmer's itch was almost a memory. My feet were sore, but not too terribly. The finger injury was healing well. My lower back, however, was acting up. (Shooting pain with a pulse-like stabbing.) If that was the extent of my hurt, however, I was lucky.

On my back, recounting the day, laying there, drunk, stoned and exhausted, (though strangely awake) I revisited Jenny in my mind's eye. My loins stirred, thinking of her mouth on mine. The way she was so young and soft. The odd squeakiness of her voice. I hardened, remembering the invigorating joyous power of her lips. She kissed, I thought, a lot like Monica.

Fuck, I thought, suddenly remembering my sweet wife.

I never called.

That's all she asked for: a simple phone call. And I blew it.

Regret washed over me. My gut became a hollow pit. Rays of guilt radiated to each and every cell in my body. Every atom of my existence felt remorse. Monica, I was sure, was pissed. Worried. Disappointed. And she didn't even know the worst of it. Forgetting to call her was the least of my misbehavior. The kiss from Jenny, smoking herb and drinking with a trio of attractive underage females hadn't been part of the plan. And, of course, being electrocuted by Missy would clearly be viewed as unacceptable.

Despite the good times, the guilty feelings certainly weren't worth the fleeting pleasure of the party. The remorse would linger while I slept and greet me upon awakening.

Bigger than King-Sized

When Richard yelled for me to wake up on the fourth morning of the blueberry harvest, I immediately remembered the events of the night before. Especially Missy almost making Richard suck Ganeesh's cock and Jenny's lips and tongue on mine and me not calling Monica.

On the floor of my tent, half wrapped in my sleeping bag, I felt like shit. Unable to move. Overcome with guilt and a hangover. Regret and cotton-mouth. Shame and a sore head. Ache inside and out. I promised a phone call and didn't deliver. I knew Monica would be worried and wondering why I hadn't called. I betrayed her. Drinking and smoking weed while Monica thought I was sleeping. Hanging out with a bunch of hot young women. Getting kissed by one of them. Being electrified by another.

"C'mon Ben," Richard yelled again. "We gotta get a move on if we're gonna rake any money today."

First, I had to take a leak and drink copious amounts of water. Second, I had to call Monica. Third, I needed more slumber.

I crawled out of my tent, bladder ready to burst. My eyes floated in their sockets. My skull and brain pounded. Took several seconds to stand firmly on my own two feet on the wet grass, under a cloudy sky. A low damp fog hovered over the garden. The treetops in the distance peeked through the morning mist.

"Wake and bake?" Richard was sitting on a towel on the bench drinking from a can of Bud while rolling a huge joint from the big bag of weed on the table. "Or maybe a little of the dog that bit ya?" He took another swig of beer.

"No beer." Just the thought of booze made me nauseous. "Water." I turned around, my back to Richard. "Water," I pulled my cock out and started to piss. When my bladder was finally emptied, my relief was indescribable. "Water…"

"Beer," he said, "is mostly water."

"No thanks." I spotted my gallon jug on the table. "I need 100 percent water."

While I gulped and gulped, Richard sparked.

"This should help," he said and handed me the joint when I was done guzzling. "Helped me. Supposed to rain. Them clouds looking wet," Richard said, pointing toward the sky. "I sure hope we're able to rake some money today."

"Me too." At that moment, I wasn't ready to comprehend, physically or mentally, the reality of raking. But I could puff on the joint, drink water and think about Monica. Pangs, then pulses, then waves of guilt rolled over me anew. "Listen. I gotta call my wife before we go to the fields. I was supposed to call her last night. Can I use the phone up at the church?"

"Oh man, I was afraid you were gonna need the phone." He sighed, then puffed on the joint. "I gotta warn you, the place is a pigsty. I try not to go in there." He took another sip of beer. "My family lives like a pack of dirty, nasty animals. Could you make it quick? 'Cuz we gotta stop at Mary's Market before hitting the fields."

Even though it was the middle of August, the church foyer was cluttered with shoes, boots and winter coats. Standing in the dim entryway, I got a whiff of rotten. I'd smelled worse, but not in places where people still lived. The stink was old. Putrid blended with dirty. Garbage and more. Old socks. Sour milk. Cat piss. Fresh vomit. Stale smoke. Cheap perfume. Burned TV dinners mixed with wet dog.

There was another door, covered with Red Sox stickers and bumper stickers, that led deeper into the building. I knocked twice and paused for a couple seconds before opening the door.

The living area seemed to be one big room, about 75 by 75 feet, of pandemonium. Giant factory-sized florescent fixtures overhead cast a dull flickering light on the countless piles of junk cluttering the place. Clothes. Magazines. Toys. Trash. Boxes stacked high. Overloaded extension cords crisscrossing the room. Looked like a public service announcement for fire hazards.

In one corner, a fat bald man with a long gray beard lay on a plaid upholstered recliner, sleeping and snoring, in front of a TV tuned to ESPN with the volume turned down. Next to his recliner was one of those tall cylindrical ashtrays found in airports and bus stations, back when smoking in public was still legal. His was overflowing with cigarette butts. The coffee table on the other side of his chair was covered by a shifty pyramid of beer cans. Must be where Richard learned his skill. The floor was cluttered with plates and bowls, presumably licked clean by the huge black dog sleeping in a crate by the fat man's chair.

"Ben Franklin, what the fuck do you want?" Buffy asked from behind me.

I turned around. She was laying on a couch near another TV in another corner, this one showing cartoons. Captain was sprawled on the floor about two feet from the screen. He looked up and waved at me.

"We ain't raking today, are we?" she asked. "TV says big thunderstorms coming our way."

"Richard says we are," I answered. "But first I gotta make a call."

"Fuck," she said. "I was hoping for another day off. I got the cordless here somewhere." She pointed at the coffee table in front of her, piled with junk. McDonald's wrappers. Crushed cigarette packs. A dirty tin from a TV dinner. A full ash tray and an empty beer can she'd been using as an ashtray. Several beauty magazines and supermarket tabloids. A box of crayons. And the phone. "There it is," she pointed. "I don't feel like raking today. At all."

"Me neither." I walked toward her to get the phone. "But Richard says we gotta rake some money."

"Fuck him," she said. "Mother-fucking asshole. He's got plenty of money."

"Hey Captain, how you feeling?" I asked as he slowly got up off the floor. "You gonna rake blueberries?"

"I'm fine, Ben." His nose was stuffed up. "Ben, could you get me 'nother bowl of cwunch, prease?"

He handed me his bowl which was still half full of milk and pointed to a huge box of generic Captain Crunch sitting atop a bureau behind the couch. I filled his bowl and gave it back to him.

"Dank you very much." He sniffled and headed back to his floor seat in front of the cartoons.

"What'd you guys do last night?" Buffy asked, getting up from the couch. All she wore was a Red Sox tee-shirt, barely long enough to cover her ass. She aroused me. Being close to half-naked women did that. "Didn't get back 'til real late."

"Not much," I said, picking up the phone. "Just had some beers."

"Where'd you go? Ganeesh's?"

"Yeah," I said. "Had some beers."

"Smoke some of Richard's good weed?"

"A little."

"Got any? I'm totally jonesing." She stood in front of me, a foot away, and traced her finger across my chest, making a point to touch both of my nipples. "I'd love to get high before raking."

"No. Sorry." Despite my hangover and exhaustion, her touch instantly created a full fledged erection. Dirty girls like Buffy really excited me. Major weakness, I know, but there's nothing I could do about it. "Excuse me for a sec, I gotta call my wife."

"Too bad you don't have a joint," she said, fluttering her eyelashes. "'Cuz we could have some fun..." She interrupted herself with five seconds of phlegmy coughing. "Maybe give you a little show."

She turned around and hiked her nightshirt up high enough so I could see the string of a pink thong nestled between her ass cheeks. She wiggled.

I dialed. Monica answered after one ring and didn't sound pleased. She'd been worried sick. I gave her a lame excuse for not calling. Something about acting as Richard's taxi driver around Washington County and not getting back until late and not being able to get to the phone because of extenuating circumstances. She wasn't happy with my explanation and said so.

I should have turned my back to Buffy. Tough to focus on the conversation with Monica while watching Buffy stretch. Buffy reached for the ceiling, her tee-shirt riding high enough to show off her entire thonged ass, all while keeping her eye on the cartoons. Occasionally, she'd bend down and over, giving me another angle of a glorious view. I told Monica we were late for the fields.

I'd call her later, I promised, when I had time to talk.

We didn't start raking until 9:30. After the conversations with Buffy and Monica, I went back to the camp and Richard sparked another joint. Then we jumped into the truck with Buffy, Captain and Jazz and headed to Mary's Market. Coffee and muffins for them. Filled my thermos with hot tea and my stomach with three donuts. High on weed and sugar, we drove to the fields and parked Floyd near the sani-can and the other vehicles. To the southwest, the clouds were ominously dark.

"What's up, Ben?" Larry asked, eyebrows raised, as I grabbed a couple buckets. "Keeping bankers' hours now?"

"Just running a little late."

"What do you think, Lar," Richard said. "Gonna rain?"

"Yep," the farmer said, taking off his ball cap to scratch his head. "Hopefully blow by quick." He pointed to the fields. "Christ, now that you guys showed up, we got an even dozen rakers." He shook his head. "Not sure if we're ever gonna finish this harvest."

"Sure we are," Richard said. "You say that every year."

"Yeah, but this year's different."

"C'mon bossman, don't give up yet." Richard grinned and pulled on his gloves. "Give us a some nice blue and we'll rake some serious buckets before the rain."

"Okay," Larry said. "Head over to the south of the old stone wall." He pointed. "Looked pretty blue this morning. Watch out for bears. And if there's lightning, you better come in, quick. Don't need no electrocutions this year."

I laughed, but no one else did. It took me a couple seconds to realize, from the look on Larry's face, that he wasn't joking.

"Hey Jazz," Richard called out to his brother, raking in the strip next to him. "If you take them chains off your boots, you might rake faster."

"Screw you, Richard," Jazz said. "Chains don't slow me down."

We weren't racing, but after just a couple minutes, I was in last place. Obviously Richard was raking king of the clan, but Jazz wasn't far behind.

"Hey Ben," Richard said. "You ever wonder how a vampire like Jazz can survive the bright sunlight?"

I didn't know what to say.

"Maybe he's a reverse vampire. Do you believe in reverse vampires?"

"Nope." I was starting to really hate Richard. The night before he was an ass-hole. Plus, I didn't like the way he treated his brother. "I don't believe in vampires."

"Oh, he's a vampire. That's for sure. He had a special set of teeth he ordered off the Internet."

"Richard, screw you," Jazz said, his rake not stopping. He raked and raked. So did Richard. And Captain followed them both, lugging empty buckets. The last thing I heard before they worked their way out of earshot was Jazz whining, "Shouldn't matter to you."

Buffy's style was different. We covered the ground at the same speed even though she raked faster and steadier. Her frequent cigarettes slowed her down, though. Slowed me down too, since she spent her smoke breaks talking to me.

"Richard is a tyrant and a fucking liar," she said. "But I owe him for helping out with Captain. 'Course, he never lets me forget it." She sighed and looked up at the cloudy sky. "I hope it rains so we go home. 'Cuz I hate raking. I mean, I love being outside, but raking really sucks. Though I do like making money. You like making money?"

"Of course," I said. "I need money."

"You sure you don't have a joint?"

"I'm positive."

"Too bad, because I love to party, party, party. If you know what I mean." She sighed and took off her ball cap and ran her fingers through her hair. "You know who I love?"

"Who?"

"Boston Red Sox." She put her hat back on and pumped her right arm up and down. "GO SOX!"

"I like the Sox."

"I love 'em!" she said. "I'd fuck the entire team if I could."

"I wouldn't go that far," I said with a laugh. "Not my types."

"I'd fuck the bat boys. And the guys on the radio. I'd blow Jerry Remy in a heart beat. And don't even get me going on the front office..."

She interrupted herself with a coughing fit.

"Fuckin' cigarettes," she said, when she finally stopped hacking. "Love 'em and hate 'em. Only thing that keeps me going while raking. That and the joint Richard promised we'd smoke later. You sure you don't have any reefer?"

"Yup."

"Tooooo bad." She wiggled and coughed. "Who knows what could happen. You sure?"

"Sorry, no weed. I'm positive. Tell me something. What was up with Larry's warning about lightning?"

"Oh yeah," she said, shaking her head. "That was bad. I mean, I know your name is Ben Franklin and you probably have a kite with you, right? Want to fly it during a storm?" She laughed. "You shouldn't have laughed when Larry was talking. But how could you have known about Jackie? You're the new guy."

"What happened to Jackie?"

"He got struck by lightning. Adam's twin brother. You know Adam?"

"No, I don't think so."

She looked around for a second. "He's over there." She pointed toward the hippie kid with the huge beard who'd been raking like a robot on the first day while I nursed my wasp bites and other wounds. I've watched him several times since. Constantly sweeping and filling bucket after bucket. A machine.

"That's Adam," she said. "He just graduated from Roosevelt High. Number one in his class. Going to Bowdoin. That's why he's raking like a motherfucker. Gotta make some money."

"What happened with the lightning?"

"Him and Jackie were raking right in the middle of the field. Raking some serious money. Berries were fucking awesome last year. Not like this year at all." She shook her head. "This is gonna be a bad harvest. Worst year, evah. Everyone knows it."

"What happened to Jackie?"

"He died. Got struck right in the rake when he was running across the fields. Bad, bad storm. The guys stayed out too long. You're supposed to come in at the first sign of lightning. But they kept going. Damn shame. Berries ain't worth dying for, that's for sure." She laughed. "You better be careful. People say lightning don't strike the same place twice, but they ain't never spent no time in Washington County."

The clouds to the southwest grew darker and darker. Felt like night was approaching, even though it was just before 11 a.m. Rain. No doubt. Which sucked because, despite my hangover and ever-present backache, my mood was great. The strip was the bluest yet. Fat and juicy berries, heavy like grapes, practically fell into the rake. And Buffy amused me while keeping me aroused in her special trashy way.

"You know," she said, "I got a idea on how we could make lots of money without raking. You and me."

"How's that?"

"Okay. Great." She looked around to make sure no one was in earshot. "Here's the deal. You got your truck and I know where a whole bunch of blueberries fields are, right? 'Round here, at least. So we go to each one of them fields and set up a grill and sell hot dogs and hamburgs to the rakers. Tater chips. Soda. Maybe some cookies." She nodded vigorously. "See, no one is running a food cart 'round here. We could do it. And make lots and lots of cash. Lots more than we'd make by raking. You got a gas grill?"

"A little tiny one." I didn't think Monica would endorse this plan. "But it's on Goose Island."

"Hmmm. I wonder if we could borrow a bigger one from someone. Let me think about it." The sky directly above us grew gloomy and sinister. The tree tops danced and bent in the breeze. "I'd pay for the food, you supply the wheels and gasoline. We could start day after tomorrow, when my food stamps come in." She spoke louder and louder because the wind was starting to screech and whistle in our ears. "We'll split the profits 50-50. After expenses. I know we'd make more cash than by raking berries. And none of this bent over in the field shit. Fuck raking."

Her idea reminded me that I was hungry. We hadn't brought lunch. Back at Mary's Market, the food question briefly entered my head, but disappeared with donuts and tea. Temporarily. Now I was starving, wishing for a food cart.

"Let me think about it," I said. To the southwest, the sky went totally black. Clouds swirled and the squall zipped over the rolling acres of blueberries between us and the edge of the forest. Thunder roared. The deluge started. In the distance, successive bursts of lightning. Rain pelted like hail. Right away, we were soaked.

"Let's get to the truck," she yelled. "Where's Captain at?"

Another crack and boom of thunder interrupted her. Lightning flashed closer. Felt real close. Electricity in the wind. Richard, Jazz and Captain came up behind us, empty handed except for their rakes. We all followed Richard as he led the way across the acres of field, stepping over bushes and trying to avoid holes, ruts, rocks, and most importantly, berries.

Five minutes later, we were in Floyd. Shelter from the storm. Richard, Captain and I sat in front. Buffy was in back, along with Jazz, Peggy, Hip-Hop and several young men I recognized but hadn't met. The rain pounded hard on the roof. Thunder clapped. Lightning flashed and struck. Captain was soaked and shivering, so I started the truck and got the heat going, trying to warm him up. Then he began to sneeze. A constant "ah-chew" and a sniffle. Over and over and over. Richard put his arm around his nephew's shoulders. The kid's sneezing fit was interrupted by a knock on the cap window, between us and the gang in the back. I slid it open.

"Hi Ben Franklin." Buffy's face half-filled the window. Someone in back laughed. A cloud of blue smoke entered the cab, sneaking in around her head. "Hey Richard, would you sell us a joint? We got six bucks."

"What the frig are you talking about?" Richard yelped. "I don't sell joints. Especially not to a bunch of young punks."

"Oh c'mon Richard." Buffy's face filled the window. "We got six bucks."

"Buffy, you're an idiot." He shook his head and pulled the window shut. "I can't believe that girl. Thinking I'd sell them a joint." He sighed and took a cigarette out of his pouch. "Hey Captain, you stopped sneezing. That's great."

"Yeah, and I'm not freezing no more," the kid sniffled. "But my shirt is all wet."

"Wish we'd thought to bring him a change of clothes." Richard shook his head, looking at me. "His mother is an idiot." He sighed. "I'm frigging starving to death here. Wish we brought something for lunch."

"Me too."

"I got three apples," he said, looking over his shoulder. "One for me, one for Captain, one for you. Thing is, that window opens, hide the apple. Don't want them scumbuckets begging for bites of apple."

And I had my thermos, still half-full with sweet tea. My little secret. I didn't want to share, either. The truck shuddered in the wind. Rain drummed on the roof and streamed down the windshield, blurring the outside world. Felt like we were in an automatic car wash. Or a submarine. A knock-knock-knock on my door startled me. I rolled the window down halfway.

"You guys aren't taking off, are you?" Larry wore a yellow slicker and sou'wester. He had to yell, almost, to be heard over the rain thumping the truck's roof and hood. "This is gonna blow over. Sky to the south looks bright blue."

"We ain't leaving, boss," Richard said. "Just trying to get Captain warmed up."

Captain sneezed.

"You okay buddy?" Larry asked.

Captain nodded and sneezed again, shivering.

"Hey boss," Richard said. "You got anything dry Captain can put on?"

"Might have a sweatshirt. Lemme check my truck. Where's his momma?"

Richard pointed. Larry took a step back and looked through the side window of the truck cap.

"Jesus Christ, Ben," Larry said, "You got half the crew in the back. Let 'em know as soon as this blows over, we'll get back out there and rake some money."

I rolled up the window and he disappeared into the storm.

"This rain will stop. Always does," Richard said, rolling down his window a couple inches. "I got a love-hate thing with rain during the harvest. Hate waiting around for it to clear off. But the August rain is great for my garden." He nodded. "And the rain's good because wet berries weigh more. Those were some nice friggin' strips over there by the old wall. Sun heats those rocks during the day. At night, the rocks radiate that heat toward the berries. Makes 'em plump and juicy. Gonna weigh up nice."

Captain sneezed several times and the rain stopped. Didn't slow down to a trickle or a sprinkle or a drizzle or mizzle. Stopped completely, like someone turned off a faucet. The clouds vanished. The sun returned, seemingly shining brighter than before.

"Told you the rain was gonna quit. Let's go rake some money." Richard opened his door and turned to his nephew. "Captain, I'm gonna get that sweatshirt. How about you staying in the truck and resting? Maybe take a nap?"

"Yeah Unk." The boy wiped his nose. "Look, I'm not sneezing no more."

"Maybe you're allergic to rain." Richard shook his head and grinned. "Imagine that. Allergic to rain. Would suck big time. Really would."

The rain turned the fields into a muddy bog. A swamp. The mosquitoes and no-see'ums ate me alive. The wet blueberry leaves were as slick as icy sidewalks. I slipped and fell a dozen times. Even Richard, the most graceful of all rakers, landed on his ass at least a couple times that I saw. Despite the shitty working conditions, the berries were plentiful and, apparently, heavy.

A half-hour after re-starting, I was all alone. Buffy was raking with Hip-Hop and his pals. Richard and Captain were a strip ahead of me. I wasn't sure where Jazz was. And I didn't see Peggy either. I was starving. Richard hadn't given me the apple and my thermos of tea was still in the truck. I looked at my heaping bucket of berries. Shiny wet from the heavy rain, they were as beautiful as berries can be. And the rain, I'm sure, rinsed off any residue of pesticide. I grabbed a handful. And then another. And another. Then I lost count. Did I eat a whole bucket? Of course not. A quart? Two quarts? My face was sticky and the fruit sugar gave me enough energy to keep going with the rake.

After raking three more buckets, dark clouds re-appeared. Then came the wind and thunder and lightning. Then another deluge.

Again, we took shelter in the truck, the back filled with people I didn't know. Captain had another sneezing fit. He was dry, at least, wearing Larry's huge New England Patriots sweatshirt, but he sneezed and sneezed. Must have driven the poor kid crazy because he had a meltdown. The fit started quick, like the rain. He wailed and shook. Cried and sneezed. Richard hugged the little guy and held him close, stroked his hair and murmured to him, until he calmed down and his freakout turned into soft sobs.

"Dude, when we get home," Richard said, "I promise we'll have a nice time. Hot bath. Hot cocoa. And I'll read you a story. What do you think of that?"

"Good," Captain said, still a little weepy.

"What story you wanna read?"

"Cure...Cure..." he stuttered. "Curious George!"

"Curious George?" Richard said. "Why, he's my favorite!"

"*Mine too*!" Captain said cheerfully. Then he sneezed.

"Just another thing we got in common," Richard said, giving his nephew a long hug. "We must be related."

We all laughed. The rain continued. A hard drumbeat. Thunder boomed. The truck was running for heat and the windshield wipers going so we could watch the lightning light the clouds, the fields and beyond. Better than man-made fireworks. If it wasn't for the sneeze-a-thon, it might have been fun. After a particularly rapid-fire succession of sneezes, there was a rap on my window.

"Call it a day," Larry said. "Don't matter if it clears off in five minutes." He pointed toward the fields. Captain sneezed. "Gonna be worse out there. Plus the berries will be soaking wet. I don't want to pay you guys for all that water weight, so go on home." He shook his head. "Hope it stops soon, otherwise tomorrow could be a washout."

"That sucks," Richard said. "Give us a call in the morning if we're not gonna rake."

"Will do," Larry nodded and walked away. Captain sneezed.

"What about those jokers in the back?" I asked, rolling up the window.

"Hold on." He opened the slider and a haze of blue smoke drifted into the cab. "Buffy, tell your loser pals to get out of the friggin' truck. Larry is sending us home."

Several people cheered. Captain's sneezes grew fiercer and louder. His eyes bulged.

"Richard, you can't leave these guys out here in the storm. Their ride ain't coming 'til five," Buffy yelled. She said something else, but her words were muffled by a thunder clap.

"Shut up." Richard slid the window closed and locked it. Captain sneezed, his nose swollen and red. Another round of tears seemed imminent.

Buffy rapped on the little window. After ten seconds of knocking, Richard sighed and opened the slider. Smoke again wafted into the truck cab.

 "Frig you," he said. "Get 'em out. We ain't bringing all those losers home."

"I ain't asking you bring 'em home," she yelled. "Just drop 'em at Mary's Market!"

Richard looked at me. I shrugged.

"We gotta stop anyway for grub and beer." Richard sighed. "You okay with that, Ben?"

I nodded.

"Hi Momma," said Captain, kneeling on the seat. He sneezed again.

"Hi Captain," she said. "Richard, you sure you don't have a joint that we can buy from you?"

Richard slammed the little window shut.

"Let's get the frig of here," he said. "Captain, turn around and sit down. And please quit your friggin' sneezing." He rolled down his window halfway, lit a smoke and ignored the rain coming into the truck. "Let's get rid of these knuckleheads."

Me driving, even under the best conditions, was scary enough. But me driving in a blinding rainstorm could be downright terrifying. Even with the wipers going full blast, I could barely see through the windshield due to torrents and heavy gusts of wind. Water flew in every direction. The thunder boomed and the lightning struck the forest on both sides of the rutted dirt road leading back to civilization. When we finally reached pavement, the culverts and ditches rushed like rivers and overflowed onto the roads. I should have stopped because I couldn't see anything other than rain. But I wanted to get rid of the load of passengers riding in the back. And since the afternoon was mine, I intended on having a long nap, followed by a phone call with Monica, a big dinner and then hit the sack for a good night's sleep.

That's what I was thinking when Floyd went into the ditch.

The accident was simultaneously super-fast and mind-numbingly slow. For a millisecond, my brain didn't understand. Had the road disappeared? Nope. My inattention and incompetence put us in the ditch. Nose first. Luckily, Captain was wearing his seat belt and Richard instinctively used his arm to keep Captain's upper body from whiplashing. Those in the back weren't so lucky.

Their long yell, collectively louder than the thunder, sounded like dozens of injuries. I had a horrible image of body parts and blood. Of course, I wasn't thinking rationally. We'd only gone into the ditch. For the carnage in my mind's eye, we needed to collide with a train, plane or logging truck.

"You okay, Captain?" Richard asked, over the chorus of moans from the back.

"I'm fine," the little boy said.

"What the frig, Ben." Richard looked at me. "What happened?"

"I don't..."

"*Ahhhh, my face. My fucking face!*" Buffy screamed. "*Get off me, mother-fucker!*"

I opened my door and jumped out into the rain and the ditch. I made it around to the back of the truck. One of the kids had just opened the cap's rear window and dropped the tailgate. The passengers disembarked into the downpour, like clowns from a circus car. And just as Buffy climbed out of the truck, still swearing and pissed, the rain stopped, again. Turned off like a spigot.

"What the frig, Buffy?" Richard said. He'd left Captain in the cab. "Shut your friggin' trap. You want Captain to get your gutter mouth?"

"Fuck you, Richard," she snapped. "I was at the bottom of the pig pile. And my ciggy butt burned me. Look." She pulled her hair back away from her forehead. "Is it still burning? Fucking feels like it."

There was a dime-sized red mark in the exact center of her forehead. Probably gonna end up a pretty nasty wound.

"What the fuck happened?" she asked me. "Why the fuck did you go off the road?"

"Shut up, Buffy," Richard said. "You're lucky we're even giving you a friggin' ride. Listen," he turned to the rest of the riders, "we're gonna have to use some manpower to get outta the ditch." He pointed at me. "This has happened before. Friggin' culverts around here. In the rain, filled with water, might've seemed like part of the road." He nodded toward the truck. "Ben, get behind the wheel and start her up and put her in 4-wheel drive."

Thanks to the pitch of the roadside, the truck's rear end, just forward of the axle, was bottomed out on the ground. The front bumper sat on the opposite lip of the ditch flowing with rain. The back right tire was lifted slightly in the air. The back left was in the ditch. The driver's side front tire hovered, a half inch above the earth. Luckily, the front right tire was on hard packed ground. Richard directed the teenage boys into position to push the truck. Buffy refused to help. She stood watching, smoking. A couple of the boys complained about the water rushing around their knees as they stood in the ditch, but Richard wouldn't listen. Through brute strength and the front tire's traction, we somehow backed Floyd up and out of the ditch and back on the road.

Everyone but Buffy cheered. She kept touching her forehead and looked like she was about to cry. The passengers climbed back into the back of the truck. As we drove off, Richard lit a smoke and shook his head.

"We got lucky. I've been in the ditch at least a dozen times." He laughed. " 'Bout half the time, I get really stuck. Three times, my buddy Jimmy Tiger had to tow me out with his wrecker."

When we arrived at Mary's Market, the back of the truck cap opened, again reminiscent of a clown car. The teenagers ran across the parking lot and into the store, mobbing the pizza counter and buying all the greasy slices.

"Let's get some peanut butter and grape jelly and bread, you like that? For lunch?" Richard asked. "For dinner, we can have steaks again, on the fire."

"Yeah." At that moment, exhausted and starving, PB and J would do. A nap, then steaks sounded great. "Right on."

"You buy the beer," he said. "I'll grab stuff for sandwiches."

"That girl always assumes someone's gonna take care of Captain," Richard said. We'd just pulled out of the parking lot, headed home. The back of the truck was empty. Just before we left the store, Buffy disappeared. "Probably hiding out in the stockroom. Just so she can get out of watching her own kid. It's the whole family's friggin' fault. When Captain was littler, we were all there for her, whenever. But now, she takes it for granted." He shrugged as we pulled into the church parking lot. "Can't abandon Captain, can we?"

"Nope, Unk," the little boy said. "Hey I'm not sneezing no more."

"Good boy," Richard said, patting Captain on the head. "Ready for a sandwich and a bath?" He pointed at me. "You head up to camp with the food and beer." He nodded. "I gotta chill with Captain for a bit. Give him a bath, read him a story. See if my dad is sober enough to watch him until the world's worst mother gets home."

I ate three sandwiches and guzzled lots and lots of water, then climbed into my tent to lay down for some shuteye. Just before falling asleep, I realized how filthy I was, despite the showers in the rain. Muddy. Sweaty. Greasy because of the Corrigan's. (But grateful the Corrigan's worked.) Drifting off to sleep, my brain was filled with thoughts of Buffy and Missy. Dirty thoughts, some might say, but I enjoyed thinking about both of them.

Woke up an hour later feeling like a new man. Still sore and smelly, but my brain was clear for the first time in days. I needed to ask Richard about taking a shower and calling Monica. Maybe there were some chores around the land we could do. He could teach me how to drive his tractor. Then a fire and steak and back to bed.

I was trying not to think about the mere 25 bucks worth of berries, how that wasn't enough to justify breaking my back in the fields and being away from Monica. Maybe, I thought, laying there in my tent, it was time to go home. Call the whole thing off. Wasn't meant to be a blueberry raker. That's what my body told me.

"Okay Dude, here's the plan," Richard said after returning. "Just talked to Ganeesh. We gotta pick up him and the girls and head into Roosevelt. Got some important errands to run."

"Why don't you just take the truck?" I yawned. Despite my nap, I had no interest in playing Down East taxi-man. "I was hoping to take a shower, call my old lady, then chill out."

"Dude, I can't drive. Don't you remember? I can't drive and all the friggin' pigs in Washington County know it. They see me, they lock me up and throw away the key. They're getting serious about suspended licenses."

I hadn't realized that sleeping on Richard's land meant becoming his full-time chauffeur. The big reason for camping out was to save on gas and wear and tear on both me and Floyd. Where were the savings if I was always driving Richard around?

"Besides, the girls said they hoped you would go. Ganeesh said they thought you were cool. I don't mind Savannah," he shook his head, "but that Missy is out of frigging control."

"They want me to go?" My heart beat faster. "Really?"

"Yeah, they asked for you specifically," Richard said. "I have something to give you a little energy."

"What's that?" I asked.

Richard reached into his fanny pack and pulled out a pill bottle.

"How about speeding things up?" He rattled and shook the bottle for a second. "A little boost?"

"Huh," I paused. Back in the late 1980s, after high school, I served as a sailor in the U.S. Coast Guard. The ship's medic, a pal of mine, gave me a gift of a couple thousand hits of expired amphetamines. When those pills ran out, after a year, I felt pretty bad for five days. Actually, really bad. Ever since, I'd only bumped into real speed on a handful of occasions. "Fill'er up," I said, sticking out my hand.

"How many?" he asked, opening the bottle. "Four?"

"Sounds good."

He shook the little pills into my palm and I took them with a single slug of water. Next, Richard rolled a joint, then drained his beer and opened another. The afternoon, I realized, could turn interesting.

This speed was dangerous for a couple of reasons: it was free and turned me into a chatterbox. The pills apparently had the same impact on Richard. He didn't stop talking the whole way to the Grange to pick up the gang, then on to downtown Roosevelt. He told me stories about people I didn't know and would never meet because they were all dead. His mother had died in a car wreck four years ago. His dad was driving, but found not guilty in court. He told me about his favorite uncle, who weighed 400 pounds and died of kidney failure. Two childhood friends who OD'd on heroin after moving to southern Maine. Three different Washington County pals who – on separate occasions -- took too much methadone then drank too much liquor, overdosed and died. His neighbor whose entire family was killed by a logging truck.

The border town of Roosevelt (population 5,000) felt dreary even on a bright summer day. The sky was blue, spotted low with cotton-white puffy clouds. Difficult to believe the rain came down so hard just a couple hours before. Roosevelt, with two bridges to Canada, across the Levendosky River, is the big city in Washington County. Home to the hospital where Larry worked, a huge grocery, a smaller grocery, a lumber yard, a couple hardware stores, a movie theater, a library, a community college, multiple sandwich joints and two Chinese restaurants. A handful of specialty shops downtown. And a single stop light. Just before we drove by the police station, Richard pulled down his baseball cap and slunk low.

Despite Richard's tales of Washington County woe and death, I felt great. Thanks to the speed and weed. Plus, Missy, Savannah and Ganeesh were in the back. The little window was open. I kept sneaking peaks in the rearview mirror, but couldn't see much. I smelled their sweet scent, though. And from the giggles and laughs, they were high on something. Weed or life. Who could tell?

A debate over the choice of lunch spot began. The girls wanted to go to the Sandwich Man on the other end of town. Richard wanted Chinese. But Ganeesh insisted on Border Subz because it was closer to Furman's Department Store, our next stop. And since Ganeesh was buying for everyone, he was the decider.

After parking, I watched the girls climb out of Floyd. They looked even better in daylight than in the flicker of candles. Both wore black denim mini-skirts and lacy pink and white halter-tops. Both had their hair in pigtails and wore matching big black sunglasses. Their lips were the same hue of bright red. Together, stunning, they strolled arm-in-arm into the sandwich shop like a pair of Hollywood starlets having a leisurely late brunch.

If the girls were starlets, Ganeesh was an action movie star on lunch break. His long black hair in a super-thick ponytail. Black jeans. Leather motor-cycle boots. Tight, clean white cotton tee-shirt. His eyes were hidden behind wrap-around mirrored sunglasses. Sitting at the table, he loomed large. So much bigger than the rest of us.

Richard and I shouldn't have been sitting with them. We were freaks. Greasy, sweaty and jazzed up on speed. Not sure who looked worse. I couldn't remember my last shower. Richard's Budweiser ball cap was faded, ratty and tat-tered. His white tee-shirt, also touting the King of Beers, was stained with blue-berries and mud. His khaki cargo shorts were ripped and filthy. He stunk. Bad. A mix of sweat and locker room. And I couldn't even begin to describe the stench radiating from his ancient skateboarding sneakers.

Inane doesn't begin to describe Richard's and my babbling while waiting for our food. We debated whether Canada was better than America. (I chattered yes, he prattled no.) Luckily, four roast beef sandwiches, a huge bag of BBQ chips and two salads with blue cheese dressing arrived. All conversation ceased and the feeding frenzy began.

My hunger overruled the speed's appetite-suppressant qualities. I tore into the sandwich like a savage. Richard's technique was similar to mine. Mean-while, the more genteel Ganeesh opened the chips and spread the bag flat for the whole gang to share. He also claimed two of the roast beef sandwiches for himself and ate slowly and methodically, chewing with an evenness that seemed slightly mechanical. Was Ganeesh actually a robot?

For a moment, that was a serious thought. The power of the amphet-amine. Of course, he wasn't a robot. As far as I knew, the government was still trying to just get human cloning right, let alone master the technology of android construction enough to create a living, breathing, eating, fucking, good-looking, kind and gentle Native American robot. But when you're hopped up on speed, slowed down on weed and tired and sore after three days bent over raking blue-berries under the hot sun, anything is possible.

After another chomp of my sandwich, I turned my head just in time to see Missy take a long sip from her bottle of water. Her red lips were wet. Glisten-ing. Our eyes met. She smiled. I couldn't smile. My mouth was full of sandwich. Chewed and chewed, but didn't want to swallow yet, for fear of choking. Gave her a closed mouth grin and a little wave with my right hand. She waved back. I felt warm and jittery. After what seemed like both an eternity and a split second (thanks to the amphetamine) she laughed and turned away toward Ganeesh.

I felt his stare. I turned and swallowed my mouthful. He tilted his head, just a little to the left, and looked at me while he chewed his sandwich. I saw my reflection in his sunglasses. He reached for another handful of potato chips and grinned.

We must have been quite the spectacle walking across Furman's parking lot. Half-beautiful. Half bedraggled. Thanks to the speed, I felt like skipping like a kid, but knew it wasn't appropriate considering the circumstances. Needed to be cool. Act cool. Project cool. Needed to suppress my hyperness, though it was bound to get worse. (Or better, depending on my mood.) Already super- jittery, I was waiting for the boost from two more hits of speed Richard gave me after we finished lunch. Popped the pills and washed 'em down with the last of my Coca-Cola.

Furman's is a Maine institution. A family-owned salvaged goods depart-ment store with at least a dozen locations scattered across the state. Roosevelt was lucky, some would say, to have two Furman's. (The second sold furniture and flooring.) Furman's shelves are stocked with bankruptcy liquidations and odd lots. The rows and aisles are a mismatched collection of expired food, ugly new clothes, cheap shoes, lead-painted toys, damaged luggage and candles that smell funny. Tape measures with broken rulers. Hammers with loose handles. Vises that don't grip. Screws with bad heads. Slightly bent nails. Weak batteries. Tackless glue. Most of the stuff is junk, though occasionally you find deals. Right after 9-11, for instance, a whole bunch of dust-covered merchandise from bou-tiques near Ground Zero ended up in Furman's across the state. Clever Mainers bought the chic designer styles and immediately resold the items to grief-stricken, fashion-starved New Yorkers via eBay.

Once inside the store, the gang separated. The threesome (Ganeesh in the middle, holding hands with both girls) headed for the women's clothes depart-ment. Richard said he had to find his buddy Jimmy. I stood alone by the service desk, disorientated by the stuttering fluorescent lights and the prescription speed

racing through my bloodstream. My heart beat so loudly. Could my fellow shop-
pers hear my pulse? What was I doing here? No spare cash to spend on useless
baubles. The free lunch was good, but time to go. I suddenly realized I didn't
want to be traipsing around Roosevelt, acting as chauffeur for these strangers.

I know when I've taken too much speed. From previous experience. In
addition to the paranoia, the pills turned me into an emotional roller coaster. I
would take off happy and crash down sad. Sometimes fast. Other times slow. I'd
get irrational and prone to mood swings. Standing in front of a cabinet next to the
service desk, I felt a crying jag approaching. Tears welled behind my eyes. Hidden, then unhidden. One tear escaped and trickled down my left cheek. I brushed
it aside. Crouched over, pretending to examine the high-priced electronica locked
away behind glass, I cried. For a split second, or two, or three, I cried over my
loneliness and cried for Monica and the dogs. Cried over the physical aches. The
soreness from the harvest, of the stoop and bend. All for what? Fourteen cents a
pound and a campout with Richard-the-loser. But because I was in Furman's, I
hide my tears.

Another mood swing. This time guilt, personified. Guilt said Monica
might not understand why I was hanging out with my new friends, instead of
coming home to spend the rainout with her. Guilt mentioned that a 37-year-old
married man shouldn't be sitting around drinking and smoking herb with underage girls, let alone let himself get tongue-kissed by a hot juvenile emo chick. Guilt
wouldn't understand I hadn't sought out any of this experience. I just wanted
to make it through the harvest and earn some cash. And yet somehow, I found
myself lost in this new gang.

Richard was to blame. All my sins were because of him. Driving drunk.
Driving on speed. Driving in rainstorms with a truckload of minors and going
into the ditch. And something else was bothering me about Richard. Even though
he'd been nothing but nice to me. Free drugs. Great steak. Letting me camp out
on his land. My gut told me this was odd. He was shifty. Untrustworthy. Greasy.
Slimy. Fake. He needed a ride, that's why he was acting cool. Just using me.

My mood shifted again and I made a decision. Standing in Furman's, in
the midst of a speed rush, I decided to abandon ship, sneak out the front door of
the store, jump back into Floyd, drive to Richard's, grab my gear and head back
to Goose Island. Leave the gang behind. Cut my losses before any trouble. Be
done with raking. Done with Richard. Monica and I would figure out another
way to make ends meet. Worst case scenario was me heading back to Portland,
crashing on the couch at my buddy Chicky's house and finding a floor or demoli-
tion gig. Earn enough to tide us over with a little extra until I found some work in

Washington County.

But I didn't want to go back to Portland.

Then I heard a shriek behind me. Missy. I turned around. She and Savannah were 50 feet away, joking and laughing and trying on different hats from a huge rack. Ganeesh stood nearby, talking to an elderly couple, who looked native. I focused on the girls. Even under fluorescent lights, they glowed.

Some might think Savannah was more attractive. Tall, blonde, great body. Movie star hot, plus her love of all things sexual, made her every boy's fantasy.

To me, however, Missy was a dream girl. I was a moth drawn to her flame. And it wasn't only that she looked gorgeous in the mini-skirt, though admittedly, she was super hot. Especially at that moment, laughing and joking and trying on hats. But my attraction ran deeper. First, it was her electro-touch. Then her smile. And aura. But after the events at Ganeesh's, I found myself enchanted with her quick wit, smart attitude and willingness to be a badass. Her assault of Richard was icing on the cake.

Bolting from the store meant leaving Missy behind and never seeing her again. Seemed so awful. So final.

I wanted to see her more, not less. She shrieked again. And Savannah followed with a laugh so loud it could be heard across the store. Only shyness stopped me from sprinting over to the clothing department. I wanted to tag along. Hang out with her. Chuckle at her jokes. Watch her try on clothes. Tell her how great she looked.

Luckily, the last bit of common sense remaining in my brain told me to walk away. Told me I'd make an ass of myself. It wouldn't be cool. The speed would fuck up any conversation because I'd either talk too much or not say a word. Probably ogle. Gaze. Stare. Obsess. Dirty old man. Damn amphetamines.

I headed for the tool department. Faster, faster, the pills ordered. Run through the store. Don't stop. *Tool department*! *Run*! *Run*!

Luckily, I didn't listen to the pills and slammed on the brakes. Forced myself to absorb the scene around me. The store was packed. Pretty people walking with pretty ugly people. Short and tall. Fat and fatter. And sometimes huge. American and Canadian. (Both French-Canadian and English.) Poor and rich, or if not rich, at least not poor. Couldn't believe so many people were actually shopping on such a nice afternoon. And couldn't believe the useless manufactured bullshit they were buying. Multi-packs of camouflage colored jar openers. Simulated wood grain cassette tape racks. Turkey basters the size of your arm. Margarita glasses resembling a prickly cactus with impossible-to-hold stems. Discontinued bulk typewriter ribbon. One-off brands of foodstuffs like "Burger Assistant" and "Blackwell House Instant Coffee." Tall China-made piles of cheap dish tow-els. Damaged boxes of Lipton tea. Left handed garlic grinders. Turnip-shaped veggie peelers. Ten packs of replacement bulbs for old fashioned Christmas lights piled high next to boxes of internally illuminated plastic Jesus doll Christmas tree toppers. I started to examine a pile of plastic cutting boards shaped like differ-ent types of fish. Then I heard Richard's voice, around the corner, asking where Jimmy was. Fabric department today, someone answered, filling in.

I tailed him. Kept a couple aisles between us. Hadn't intended playing detective or ducking behind a bin of mini-basketballs, but the balls provided excel-lent cover and a secret view of the fabric table. For a half minute, Richard stood there, waiting. Jimmy appeared and they exchanged an elaborate hand slap and half hug. Jimmy looked over his shoulder. Felt like he was staring right at me. But he didn't spot my head among the basketballs. He motioned for Richard to follow him, past the bolts of upholstery fabric. They stopped near rolls of lace. Still in my field of vision. Like a movie. All while hidden behind the mini-basketballs.

Thank goodness for the speed. If it weren't for the pills, I wouldn't have been obsessively paying close attention. I'd have missed the handoff between the two while they stood next to the rolls of lace. The fellas started a second round of shakes, slaps and a farewell hug that seemed a little suspicious. Especially for a couple jokers like these guys. But the whole time I focused on their hands. Like trying to see through a magician's trick. That's how I saw the pill bottle end up in Richard's hand and a wad of cash end up in Jimmy's. Done deal. Richard walked away, towards the cash register.

Not wanting to get busted as a spy, I doubled back and crisscrossed the store, past glass water pitchers painted with duck motifs and thermoses shaped like space shuttles. Past the books by-the-pound. Took a left at the groovy floor lamps, ending up in the candle section next to a special display of camping gear. I pretended to check out a new tent while thinking about the scene I just wit-nessed.

Drug deal. Obviously. The pills in my system were still alive and kick-ing. Suddenly, fear and paranoia ruled. Did I want to be driving Richard around, especially when he was known to the cops and was always carrying pills? Not really. Not at all. Time to call it quits and head on home. So I took a deep breath and walked out the front door.

Unfortunately, the whole gang was waiting for me. Ganeesh, wearing a straw hat, was ordering a hot dog from the grill man set up in the parking lot. Savannah and Missy, also in straw hats, were laughing. Richard had on a new pair of shades, outrageously big and brown. Missy waved me over to her.

"We got you a hat," she said, looking up at me, smiling a huge smile. Her eyes were wide and bluer than the nicest patch of berries. She stood on her tip toes, holding the hat. Straw, with a blue band and a funky wide brim. "Scooch down a bit, will yah? Don't want you to get sunstroke."

"Thanks." I swallowed my heart and bent over so she could reach the top of my head. Another electric shock and another mood swing. Warm. Rosy. Feeling great because this hot, sweet woman was thinking of my well being. My desire to escape evaporated. Should have bolted. But I didn't.

Richard stood five feet away. The only one without a straw hat. He was pissed.

"About time," he said, lighting a cigarette. "Ready to go? We got some friggin' errands to run."

Five minutes later, we pulled into the parking lot of another shopping center. Half was taken up by the True Value Hardware and Rental Center. The other half was Roosevelt's second Furman's. The gang went into the hardware store ahead of me, because I was trying to find the posters for my floor refinishing business that had been stashed behind the truck's front seat. Eventually, I found three slightly crumpled flyers and tacked one on the True Value bulletin board. Then I put on my hat and went inside. Ganeesh and the girls – hatless -- were at the gun counter joking with the clerk. (Must have left their hats in the truck. Now I felt goofy wearing mine.) Richard was nowhere to be seen. So I sauntered back to the rental department to check out the condition and price of the Silverline Drum Sander. Back in Portland, if a floor gig was level, I'd rent a Silverline which made the refinishing as easy as mowing a wooden lawn. Nice quick money. Missed those jobs. A million, no, a billion times better than raking berries.

With my hands on the Silverline and my eyes closed, I wished with my whole heart that when I spoke to Monica later, she would tell me someone had just seen one of my posters and called for a refinishing job that needed to be done in a hurry. Wouldn't even need to be a big floor. A kitchen or a small living room would be great. Five or six hundred bucks, including expenses. Enough cash to hold us over until a big job came along. Enough cash to quit raking before the end of the harvest.

I knelt and picked up the Silverline Floor Edger, one of the most cumbersome tools ever invented. It's a big disc sander used to reach the corners and edges of the floor unreachable by a drum sander. I hated the Edger. The Edger weighed 30 pounds and you had to be on your knees to use it. The Edger screamed and howled the most god-awful racket of any power tool. The Edger was a vicious beast. If using the Silverline Drum Sander was like mowing a lawn, the Edger was like wrestling a rabid skunk attacking your dog in your front yard.

So powerful, a single moment of inattention can cause irreparable damage to a floor. Holding the Edger in my hands, I could smell the sawdust left behind from the previous job.

Everything would be different if I had a floor gig and could abandon the harvest. Sure the drugs and hot chicks were nice, but I was unsuited for the rest of the adventure and the labor of raking. Driving people around? No thanks. Spending the day bent over in the field? Nope, too sore and tired. Home with Monica was my dream. Soak in the bathtub while listening to the CBC news, then dinner. Lay on the futon, have sex, then sleep and snuggle with my sweet love.

"I'm warning you, sir," a deep voice said from behind me. "Step away from the sander." I turned around. Richard. "You're a blueberry raker, not a floor sander."

"Yeah." I sighed. Another possible escape thwarted. "Too bad..."

"C'mon. Ganeesh and the girls want to go next door and buy a new bed." He shook his head. "Must be nice to have money."

"Yeah," I said, putting down the Edger. "I need to make some money."

"Oh, don't worry." He patted my left shoulder. "Those berries ain't going nowhere. Still be there tomorrow."

Like a dog, I followed Missy through the front door of the second Furman's. I smelled new couch and was overwhelmed by the rich scent of leather and pleather from an acre of fresh furniture. Rolls of carpet piled high next to towers of vinyl tile. Two huge walls covered with mirrors, floor to ceiling, of all shapes and sizes. The effect was brain-jarring. The lower mirrors doubled the amount of merchandise surrounding me. The higher ones reflected the pale bright shudder of the fluorescent lights. Our gang walked past the wicker and cut through the rows and rows of recliners and ottomans to reach the mattress department.

Missy, Ganeesh and Savannah laid down, side-by-side-by-side on a king-sized bed. Ganeesh was in the center and Missy rolled on top of him and started to simulate sex. Watching her riding him, rolling her pelvis on him, grinding on him in the middle of the store instantly made me hard. I turned away, only to see the same movement replicated in a hundred mirrors. Missy reached for Savannah's hand and held it to her breast and let out a long moan.

Richard seemed embarrassed. He shook his head and looked around. "Glad no one's in here," he said. "You guys are outta control."

"Chill out, Little Dick," Missy said, stopping her simulated sex act. "You are way too uptight...Hey look," she pointed. "There's Ronnie."

"Ronnie," Savannah yelped, sitting up. "Ronnie! Ronnie!"

The excitement was for the pimply kid with bright orange hair, wearing the ubiquitous red Furman's shirt, walking toward us.

"Yo Ronnie," Ganeesh said, getting off the bed. "We need some fucking customer service over here..."

"Hello ladies," said the clerk. "Yo G, what up? How ya'll doing?"

He and Ganeesh exchanged a series of handslaps and bumps that ended in a half-hug.

"Yo Ronnie, this fucking mattress is too small." Ganeesh shook his head and laid back down. "Ain't big enough for a real man. I need something bigger than king-size."

"Sorry G, nuthin' that big in stock." He scratched his crew cut. "But lemme call my cousin Jimmy." He whipped out his cell phone and pressed a key. "He's running that new mattress store in Bangor. See what he can do for us. Hold on...What up, my man?" he said into the phone, then paused. "Right on. Listen Jimmy, my pal G-man needs a bed bigger than king size. And give me the family discount, motherfucka. What you got?"

Again, silence. We were all listening, eagerly awaiting the news. Missy climbed back atop Ganeesh, slowly started moving up and down on his groin. Ronnie and shook his head.

"Uh huh, right. Hold on, bro." He turned to Ganeesh. "Listen, G. He's got a super king by Slumberland. Seven bills, box spring included. Extra c-note gets you a maple headboard."

"No headboard," Ganeesh said, sitting up. Missy fell off him, onto Savannah and kept rolling until she fell off the bed. A slapstick comedian. Everyone laughed. "How much for delivery?"

"Yo, Jimmy. You coming down to see Gram?" He paused. "Oh that sucks. What if your dad takes it on the truck and then brings it by here? Or I meet him somewhere with my truck?" Another pause. "Right on." He turned back to Ganeesh. "No charge. My unk is coming down. You want it?"

"All I got is cash, for this." Ganeesh said, getting up off the bed. "No credit card."

"Cousin," he said into his phone. "How about C.O.D? And your dad brings the cash back home." He nodded. "Right on. Peace out." He snapped the phone shut and holstered it. "No problem, G. $772, includes tax."

"Sold," Ganeesh said, taking a wad of bills from his pocket. "You gonna bring it to the Grange?"

"Right on. Either tonight or tomorrow night. Depends on when my unk shows up."

"How's your Gram?" Ganeesh asked. "She's a great old lady."

"Yeah, she ain't doing so hot. Acting crazy. Dementia." He shook his head. "Almost burned down the farm house last week."

"That's too bad. Me and your brother used visit her for cookies and cocoa after skating on her pond."

"Yeah, that's some good ice. Back there."

"My man, I feel for you and your family," Ganeesh said. The two fellas touched knuckles and Ganeesh gave Ronnie a hug. "Dementia is the toughest." He nodded and sighed. "Thanks so much for the bed..."

"Ronnie, I can't wait for school to start," Missy interrupted. "What about you?"

"I'm so sick of Roosevelt." Ronnie shook his head. "So sick of my mom. Always on my ass about smoking blunts and being on the Playstation. She don't understand I need to relax. Christ, I'm on my feet 50 hours a week selling couches and beds and carpet." He nodded. "Can't wait to get back to the dorms. Then life can be chill and normal and shit."

"Me too," Savannah said. "I mean, I've had a great summer, but I'm looking forward to classes."

Everyone laughed.

"I'm serious," she said. "I miss school."

"I wasn't talking about classes, you geek," Ronnie said and patted her on the head. "I'm talking about the dorms."

Everyone laughed again.

"So, Ben," Missy said from the back of the truck. I turned around to look at her sweet and cute face filling the little window. "What do you do when you're not raking blueberries or driving around a couple losers who don't have licenses?"

"Floor refinisher." Ganeesh and Richard were inside a blue ranch house at the end of a cul de sac on a side street off a side street somewhere near the Wal-Mart. I'd never been on this street before and would have a hard time finding it again. "I sand old floors."

"Like I told you last night, your music was really great," Missy said. "I love your voice."

"Me too," Savannah said, pushing Missy out of the window. "Really great. Great guitar too."

"Thanks."

"Why are you hanging out with little Dick-Dick?" Missy asked, her face again filling the window. "He's such an asshole..."

"Ummm." I agreed with her, but saying so would make me look like a schmuck, dissing him and still hanging with him. I didn't have a good answer.

"Are you a cop?" Savannah's face filled the window. "Are you a law enforcement agent?"

"No, why would I be a cop?"

"Well, you wouldn't tell us if you were anyway." Savannah frowned. "I hope you're not a cop."

"I'm not." I said, suddenly feeling desperate. "I'm not."

"I can give you a lie detector test," Missy said, her face filling the little window. She was closer than before, only her mouth, nose and eyes were visible. Her beautiful mouth, nose and eyes. "You wanna take a lie detector test? Then I'll believe you."

"Yeah," I said, "if it'll convince you I'm not a cop."

"Okay. Stick your hand through the window."

"What?"

"Just put your hand through the window, okay?"

"Then what?"

"I'm gonna administer the test, silly. Just put your arm through the window."

"But..."

"Just do it."

I turned and got on my knees on the front seat and stuck my right arm through the window. She took my hand in both her hands. Again, I felt that electrical charge. And an erection followed immediately.

"Are you in love with anyone?" she asked.

"Yes."

"Who?"

"My wife."

"What's her name?"

"Monica."

"Is she pretty?"

"Yes. Very."

"Do you have a picture of her?"

"I'll need my arm back. It's in my wallet, in the glove box."

Missy let go. I turned around and removed Monica's picture from my wallet. A photo of her on stage, during a poetry slam. She was wearing a sexy dress and pointing toward the ceiling. The image was cool, with groovy lights. I handed the photo to the back.

"That's your wife?" Savannah's face filled the window.

"Yes."

"She's beautiful."

"She sure is."

"When was the picture taken?" Missy asked, replacing Savannah.

"Last year. Down in Portland. She's a poet." It felt strange talking about Monica to these young girls in the back of the truck. Hate to admit it, but I wasn't thinking very much about Monica while in the presence of Missy, whose mere touch gave me an erection.

"Cool," she said. "Okay, give me your arm back."

I reached through the window. She took my hand in hers. The electricity flowed, again. Smoothly. Slowly. Warmly. Pulsing and merging. Very comforting. Comfortable. She leaned against my arm, peering up through the cab at me. The position was uncomfortable, but her touch made the inconvenience worthwhile.

"Are you a cop?" she asked.

"No," I said. "I'm not a cop."

"A state trooper?"

"No!"

"Maine Drug Enforcement Agency. Or are you a Fed?"

"No." I shook my head. "Not D.E.A."

"F.B.I.?"

"No, I'm not a law enforcement agent of any sort."

"Okay," she said. "I believe you."

Savannah pushed Missy aside and her face filled the window. Savannah's chin rested on my bicep, while Missy still held my hand.

"How long is your penis?" Savannah asked.

"What?"

"You heard me," Savannah said. "How long?"

"Oh come on..."

"It's for a scientific study," Savannah said. "Just answer the question."

"Uhhh," for a second I paused. "More than six inches, but a little less than seven."

"Above average," Savannah said. "Good for you."

Just then Richard opened the side door. I'm sure it looked pretty strange, me kneeling, arm sticking into the back of the truck.

"Ben, what the frig are you doing?"

"Nothing," I said as Missy released my hand. Her finger tips gently grazed my wrist and arm as I pulled them back through little window. "Absolutely nothing."

"Then let's get a friggin' move on." Richard said. Through the little window, I saw daylight as Ganeesh opened the back hatch. He was holding a small brown paper bag. "Just a couple more stops and we're all done. That's it."

"So I passed the lie detector test?" I asked, shifting my position in the front seat, leaning against my door in order to have a better view of the window. We were parked in the driveway of a nondescript ranch house in another forgettable neighborhood subdivision near the Milltown border crossing into Canada. Ganeesh and Richard were inside the house.

"I think so." Missy was a couple inches back from the window and I could see her whole beautiful face and her big smile. "Seemed like you were telling the truth. But there's still something a little weird about you."

"I don't know." I shook my head. "Not sure what you mean."

"Like why are you hanging out with Little Dick-Dick?"

"Or like last night," Savannah's face appeared. "When you were talking about how the constitutional right to sexual expression falls under the First Amendment. Sex as speech. Really like that argument. Very New Sexuality. Not very Washington County. "

"Yeah," Missy said, appearing and Savannah disappearing. "And we think it's cool you're willing to admit you're willing to suck cock in order to save your life."

"It was nice to have that whole conversation last night," Savannah said, back in the window. "Gave me a chance to summarize my views. Out of practice, a little bit. Being summer and all."

"You did great," I said. "I was very impressed. You should think about a career in the media. You'd be as popular as Dr. Ruth. More popular."

"No thanks." She shook her head. "I'm interested in research."

"Excuse moi," Missy said, pushing Savannah away gently with her head. "Ben, have you ever read *Think and Grow Rich* by Napoleon Hill?"

"Nope," I said. "Don't think so."

Missy squealed.

"You gotta read it," Savannah said from behind Missy. "We've got an extra copy over at the Grange. I'll give it to you later."

"Read Chapter 11!" Missy yelped. "Chapter 11 rules!"

"Okay, I'll check it out."

"He's all about the power of positive thinking," Savannah said. "He's all about the secrets that guarantee success."

"They're not really secrets," Missy interrupted. "Not secrets at all. Been told and retold all through history."

"That's right," Savannah said. "This isn't some new theory."

"You need to read the book." Missy's pushed her face up against the frame.

"Hey, I think I could fit my head through this window."

"Really?" I said. "Seems like a pretty tight fit."

"If I just turn my head sideways and stick it through." And she did it. Effortlessly, her head entered the truck cab. "Hah, I told you. Like the stocks the Pilgrims used."

"Yeah," I said. Yikes. Crazy. Surreal. A hot and smart chick I barely know, who has the power to electrocute me, sticks her head through the window. So close to me. The sunlight hit the diamond stud in her nose and it sparkled. Twinkled. Like her eyes.

"This isn't very comfortable."

"I bet."

"You know what?" She smiled. "I think I'm gonna head on out of here."

"Probably a good idea." I laughed and watched her turn sideways and extricate herself.

"Bye," she said.

"You understand, Ben, don't you," Savannah's face was in the window, "that she's nuts."

"*C'mon, do it! Do it!*" Missy yelled from behind her. "*It's fun!*"

"No way. It's not fun," Savannah shook her head, then stared me in the eye. "Read Napoleon Hill. He's got some good ideas, provided you can get past his male-centric perspective."

"I can do that," I said. "I'm interested."

"*Chapter 11!*" Missy yelped from the back. She started to pound on the truck cap. "*Chapter 11! Chapter 11!*"

"Anyway," Savannah, "Chapter 11 is the most interesting chapter. The other stuff is fine. You should read the whole book, but Chapter 11 is key. Do you know about 'sex transmutation'?"

"Nope."

"It's using the power of sex, the energy of sex, and funneling it into other endeavors."

"Huh," I said. "I'm not sure I understand."

"The more sexual you are," Missy shouted. "The more powerful you become..."

"Well, that's her version of it," Savannah said with a smile. "I see it in a more scientific way. Understanding your sex drive, enjoying it, but harnessing the powerful energy behind it. I mean, the urge to have sex is the most powerful of all our urges. And the energy of the orgasm is amazing. If you train yourself to re-direct some of the power and use it to expand your intellectual abilities."

"Or artistically," Missy said, pushing her way back into the window. "All the great artists and writers and musicians used sex transmutation. It's really awesome."

"Yes," Savannah said, moving back into the frame, but only halfway, so both of them could talk to me. "And it explains why society frowns upon sexual expression."

" 'Cuz society doesn't want the people to know and enjoy the power of sex." Missy shook her head. "It's terrible, dear. Instead, you got all these people with devotion to their church, praying for this or that. If they just devoted their energy to sex, I bet they'd see bigger benefits than any amount of prayer. Imagine using that sexual energy for good."

"Would solve so many of the world's problems," Savannah said. "Love will save the day, like my mother always says."

"The churches," Missy said, "at least the higher ups, know about this power. That's why they made sex into a sin. And why they believe there's nothing worse than excessive sexuality. They don't want you to accidentally discover the power."

"They want you to have kids," Savannah said, "lots of kids to keep their churches full, but also because they know it takes lots of energy to take care of kids. Especially for women. And that makes parents too tired to have recreational sex."

"Too tired," Missy said, "and too stressed to enjoy the power of sex. That's what the churches want. To prevent parents from discovering the power of sex. It's a part of a grand conspiracy."

"Wow," I said. "I never knew."

"And of course the government is aware of sex transmutation," Savannah said. "Especially the Bush and Cheney gang. Preaching abstinence?" She laughed. "A joke. Might as well encourage societal suicide. Besides, all those politicians know the truth. That's how they get elected in the first place. Politicians get caught in sex scandals because of sex transmutation. They understand they need to have lots of sex in order to maintain their grasp on power. But society says no. And their wives say no. So they have affairs or get prostitutes..."

"Or they end up sexually abusing little boys," Missy interrupted, "if they happen to be bad Catholic priests."

"Napoleon Hill was a scientific researcher," Savannah said. "Worked with Andrew Carnegie back in the early 1900s. Napoleon had the chance to interview lots and lots of powerful people."

"Like Thomas Edison and Alexander Graham Bell," Missy said "Teddy Roosevelt. And my favorite. George Eastman."

"George who?" I asked.

"Founder of Kodak. He invented modern film. A genius." Missy smiled. "Killed himself though." She frowned. "That's so sad. Anyway, the common link between all the guys he interviewed was their attitudes towards sex and their powerful sex drives and how it affected their success."

"Unfortunately," Savannah said, "he didn't interview any women. A sign of the times. I bet if he talked to Madonna or Erica Jong..."

"Or me," Missy said.

"Or Missy." Savannah laughed. "He'd learn the same. Strong sex drive equals power."

"Like Bill Clinton?" I said.

"The power of sex is huge." Savannah nodded. "In all sorts of ways. The power of power. Of domination. Of submission. Of pleasure. Of pain. The power of ecstasy. It's tough for close-minded people to understand."

"It's like trying to explain being high to someone who has never been high," Missy said. "Depending on the words you use and the person's personal history, it can be scary or dreamy."

"That's why churches are successful at making sex a sin." Savannah sighed. "Made sex dirty. Oral. Anal. Group."

"Made all the good stuff off limits," Missy interrupted with a sigh.

"And many religions stress that sex, approved sex," Savannah continued, "is for reproductive reasons only."

I nodded, familiar with the Catholic way.

"They turned feeling good into something bad..." She sounded sad. "If people had better sex lives, they would have better lives. Proven fact. Really does make you wonder if there's a conspiracy."

"Part of the general brainwashing of society. Telling the sheep what to do. What to think," Missy said. "I mean, look how easy it is to brainwash people. How many Americans still think that Iraq had something to do with 9-11?"

"Society is so close-minded." Savannah shook her head. "People refuse to acknowledge the connection between power and sex. It's like a city on a windy hill that won't use windmills. Ignoring all that free energy..."

Out of nowhere, a huge black dog, barking ferociously, jumped onto the passenger side door and clawed at the window. Its gargantuan head and chomping jaw scared the shit out of me. Maybe part Pit Bull, part-Rottweiler and part Devil. He clawed and clawed with his giant paws as I leaned over to roll up the window, fearing the dog would lunge into the truck.

"What the fuck?" I honked on the horn, leaning on it, hoping to get the dog's owner's attention. "This dog is crazy!"

Richard and Ganeesh came out onto the front steps of the ranch house, followed by a small, tired-looking older woman in a frayed pink bathrobe.

"*Zeus!*" The lady screamed, louder, much louder, than you'd ever imagine a person of her age and size could scream. "*Zeus, get the fuck over here!*"

But the dog wasn't listening. Still pawing and scratching at the window. And growling. A guttural growl. Spittle flew, spraying the window. A vicious beast. Willing to tear me from limb to limb for invading his turf.

"*Zeus! Zeus!*" the lady yelled, crossing the yard at a half jog. "*Get the fuck over here you stupid bastard!*"

Zeus ignored her until the lady reached him and grabbed the dog by the collar, yanking him away from the truck. For a second, our eyes met and she stared into me. She was older than I had thought. If it weren't for her dirty pink robe, I might've mistaken her for an old man. Maybe five feet tall with a shock of white hair and stocky frame. Her lined, square face was tough and sad. She dragged Zeus back toward the porch. Struggling, because the dog was bigger than she was. Bigger, but not tougher. I could tell.

When she got close to the steps, Ganeesh came to the rescue and took Zeus by the collar. Apparently he wasn't prepared for the dog's wild strength because Zeus tore loose from Ganeesh's grip. Richard grabbed for the dog, but missed and ended up slapping Zeus in the head. So Zeus snapped at Richard. Instead of getting flesh, his huge mouth caught the corner of the paper bag Richard held in his left hand.

When the bag tore, the contents spilled out onto the walkway. Pill bottles. Three pill bottles. Meanwhile, Richard pivoted, half spun, drew his right leg back and gave the dog the most vicious kick I had ever seen. Zeus' head snapped backwards and the dog dropped to the ground.

For a couple seconds, no one moved. Including Zeus. Had Richard killed the dog with a single kick? Finally, Zeus lifted his head and slowly backed onto his haunches to scooch away from the steps. Tail between his legs, he scampered behind the house.

"Oh my fucking word," I said to the girls, who were looking out the side window of the truck cap. "Did you see that?"

"Yeah," Missy said. "What a fucking asshole. I wish Richard got bit."

"Did he really have to kick that poor dog?" Savannah asked, shaking her head. "Terrible."

"That was brutal," I said. "Wouldn't want him to kick me."

"Yeah," Missy said. "Richard totally used to be into karate or kung fu. I can never remember which one."

I watched Richard bend over and pick up each pill bottle. The woman went inside and got another bag and gave it to Ganeesh, who took the bottles from Richard. They talked to her for another minute, then they both hugged her goodbye and walked toward the truck.

"Man," Richard said after he climbed into Floyd. "That dog was frigging crazy. Nearly bit my head off."

I watched the rearview mirror, waiting for Ganeesh to get in the back. I looked at the old woman again. Standing on her porch, she stared back at me. I'd been too busy chatting with the girls to notice the condition of her house. Unkempt lawn with huge piles of Zeus shit. Dangling gutters. Peeling paint. Crumbling foundation. Bricks missing from the chimney. Storm windows still covered with winter plastic. The house looked dark and cold and tough to heat, even under the bright summer sun.

"So what's the deal?" I asked Richard while backing out of the driveway, waiting until we were on the street before asking the obvious question. "What's with all the pills?"

"Oh, those ain't pills, those are vitamins." He looked at me. "From my aunt. She's my auntie. My mom's sister."

"Oh."

"Ben," Missy said from the back. Gotta admit, just the sound of her voice turned me on. Sent tingles to the right places: Brain and groin. "Two questions: Could we could stop at Shop n' Save? And would you like to come to the Grange for supper tonight? We're making Pad Thai, the house specialty."

I paused as the wave of elation washed over me. Dinner with Missy! Wow. No doubt about it. I was falling for the girl. Her electric touch confirmed it. And the way I felt about the invite for Thai. Felt better than the drugs.

"I love Pad Thai." Our eyes were locked in the rearview mirror. Felt like we were alone and talking to just each other. "One of the few things I miss about Portland. Lots of Thai restaurants. I'm gonna have to get cleaned up..."

"Dude," Richard interrupted, looking pissed. "I thought we were having steaks."

"Couldn't we grill them tomorrow night?"

"Huh," he said. "Don't know."

"Richard, you can come too," Missy sighed. "If you feel it's absolutely necessary."

Richard frowned as if he wasn't sure he wanted to go. "Hey, Ganeesh, you gonna make spring rolls?" he asked. "With special secret spicy sauce?" He said the last words with a bad Chinese accent.

"Of course," said the deep voice in the back. "Special secret spicy sauce will be on the menu."

"Sounds awesome," I said. "What time?"

"What about six or six-thirty?" she said. "We'll play it by ear."

Back at Richard's, I took a shower, scrubbing off the blueberry dirt and mud. The swimmer's itch didn't look good, but was better, thanks to the Corrigan's topical salve.

Considering the condition of the rest of Richard's house, the bathroom was a surprise. A clean, well-lit space with a nice bathtub and shower, lots of hot water and excellent water pressure. The tub had spa jets. For a second, I considered taking a bath. Not enough time, though, because I had to get ready for the party. Relaxed by the heat and steam, my mind drifted back to the girls and the conversations about the power of sex. Couldn't help myself. Arousal arrived. Masturbation began. Third stroke, the shower steam shifted and the curtain was suddenly jerked back. There stood Buffy, looking at me with cock in hand.

"Oh, sorry," she said, after a couple seconds of staring at my erection. "Thought you were Jazz."

"Ahhhh," I was stunned. Why would she open the shower curtain if her teenage brother was showering? "Nope. He's not in here."

"Well," she said, still staring at my cock. Which I was still holding. "If you see him, tell him I'm looking for him."

"Okay," I said.

She closed the shower curtain. I expected to hear the door shutting. Nope. She needed to take a leak. I could hear her, but didn't acknowledge it, so she'd leave. Then she flushed and the shower went super-hot. Scalding. Lucky, only my knees and the tops of my feet got hit because I had just backed away from the stream and was able to scrunch up in the corner of the enclosure.

"What the fuck?" I screeched. "*Buffy!*"

"Sorry," she said, pulling the curtain back again, "I always forget..."

"Is it too much to ask to be left alone?"

"You sure?"

"What?"

"You sure you want to be left alone?"

"Yes."

Buffy fluttered her eyelashes for a couple seconds and shifted her crossed eyes back and forth several times. Looking left and right. Perhaps from a normal person, this may have appeared flirtatious. But she looked like a creepy, broken toy robot. Then she closed the shower curtain.

"I could have grabbed your cock." She opened the bathroom door and the steam moved. Shifted and sucked, drawn out by the new exit. "Just to fuck with you. Give it a little handshake, if you know what I mean." She giggled. "But

I didn't." She closed the door before I could respond.

I jerked off, came instantly and felt guilty because I'd visualized Buffy while masturbating. Not Monica. Not Missy. Buffy. Ugh.

After the shower and a slathering of Corrigan's lotion, Richard and I smoked a joint and then drove to the Grange. Richard seemed kind of jumpy, which I attributed to him popping speed. He didn't offer any more to me, which sucked. I was dragging a little bit and could have used an upper or two. I didn't say much during the drive, but Richard jabbered on and on about how Missy better behave herself, or he'd bend her over his knee and give her the spanking she deserves and probably secretly wanted him to give her.

We pulled up to the Grange and his chatter stopped. I hoped he'd stay shut up when we got inside. Getting sick of his shit. Getting sick of Budweiser. (I had to buy another case while we were at the Shop'n Save.) Only 32 bucks left. And Floyd's big tank was close to empty again.

We got buzzed into the Grange. Felt different this time. The lights in the kitchen corner were on bright. Nice setup, a triangle of steel counters, probably salvaged, and a six burner gas stove. Savannah and Ganeesh, wearing their straw hats and kimonos, were chopping vegetables. Savannah waved at me, took a sip from her glass of wine. Dozens of silk ribbons were attached to the back of her straw hat, like long streams of colored hair.

"Hey dudes," Ganeesh said, a big grin on his face and a can of Moxie by his side. Atop his giant body, the straw hat seemed tiny. This was the first time I saw Ganeesh without his ponytail. His wild mane of black hair was a cape that flowed down his back, almost to his ass. His hat was tipped, slanted, at a rakish angle. Apparently, he had doodled on his straw with a black magic marker, a series of spirals and twirls, lines and loops. "Just getting ready to make the spring rolls."

"Right on, G." Richard walked over to the kitchen with the suitcase of beer. "Hello Savannah." He bowed and stuck his finger in a bowl. "Special secret spicy sauce!" In his fake Chinese accent. No one laughed.

"Where's your hat?" Missy's voice came from behind me. I turned around. "Where is your lovely straw hat?"

"Uhhh, in the truck," I said, as she approached me. For a hug. A long hug. Then she released me and took a step back. She was wearing cut-off overalls with a baby blue tank top. Her feet were bare, her toenails painted bright yellow. Her red hair was in two pigtails, framing her sweet face, which sparkled, because of the glitter on her cheeks. She'd cut the brim off her hat. Daisies, buttercups and little purple wildflowers were woven through the straw.

"Well, that's a silly place for it." She smiled. I melted, entirely, except for the hard bulge trapped in my boxers. "You're supposed to be wearing a straw hat." She laughed. "I mean, it's a straw hat pad thai party and..."

"I don't have a straw hat," Richard interrupted. "Why didn't anyone tell me?"

"Because you're a loser!"

"*Missy!*" Ganeesh said. "C'mon. You promised you wouldn't pick on him."

"Oh all right." She sighed. "Just this once, though." She took me by the arm. "C'mon, let's get your hat."

And we went back outside. She and I. Alone, totally alone, for the first time. We were quiet as we walked to the truck. She broke the silence. "Would you play another song when we get back in there?"

"Sure." I opened the driver's side door and grabbed my hat. "Any requests?"

"*Suzanne?* By Leonard Cohen?"

"That's a great song," I said, putting on my straw hat. "I can play that. For you." I looked at her. "For you," I repeated.

She threw her arms around me. Another long hug. "I'm so glad you're here right now," she said, letting go and looking up at me. "So glad."

I didn't know what to say. Embarrassed again by my seemingly ever present erection. Did she notice?

"It's great to be here," I said, in my rock star voice. "Really great to be here."

She laughed and threw her arms around me again. And squeezed, her electrical energy charging my body.

"Listen," she said. "We gotta do something about that hat. Gotta make it your own. Do something to the hat that no one else could do. Would do."

"Wow," I said. "No pressure."

My straw hat alteration, with Missy's help, looked cool. Some blue paint. (Blue for blueberries, she said). And we added some bright yellow stars when the paint dried. (I should be a rock star, she said). After decorating my hat, I played *Suzanne.*

It's hard to explain how strumming and plucking and singing that song felt. First of all, it's a wonderful tune. Second, I slowed it way down. Each note lingered longer than the note before. Totally immersed in the music, I soared.

When I was in bands, I always sang with my eyes closed, for the added emotional impact. But there, in the Grange, my eyes were wide open, focused on Missy. I was playing for her. Only. Sure, the rest of the gang was there, but the music was for her.

And she was crying.

By the time the song was finished, I was exhausted and spent. The place went wild.

"Those were tears of happiness," she said, a minute later when we stood together in the half dark, near the pool table. "My mom's name was Suzanne," Missy sniffled. "And I never knew this song when she was alive. After she died, I went through her albums and discovered Leonard Cohen." She smiled and wiped tears from her eyes. "He's wicked awesome. I like to think he wrote that song for my mom." She laughed. "Even though I know he didn't." She smiled at me. "And you played it awesomely."

"Thanks," I said. "I played it for you."

She beamed and grabbed both of my hands.

But we were interrupted by the appetizers.

Rice paper spring rolls, deep fried. With Ganeesh's special sauce for dipping. Two spring rolls for each of us. Followed by Pad Thai. The best ever.

After dinner, Missy led me through a doorway into another room in the back corner of the Grange. The lights were brighter, but not too bright. Cool vintage rock posters hung on the walls. Hendrix. Morrison. Grateful Dead. Dylan. Joni Mitchell. A big leather couch and two coffee tables. Three lava lamps. A pair of silver Mac laptops. A huge TV with a video game console.

"Wanna vape?" she asked.

"Sure." The night, so far, was wicked fun, thanks to Missy. I was up for anything. "What's that?"

"You've never vaporized reefer? Dear, you don't know what you've been missing. Sit." She pointed to the couch.

She turned a knob on a small wooden box on the table next to me. The box glowed with a blue light. Then she started messing around with jars of different herbs.

"I like to smoke reefer," she said, opening three jars and tapping a little out of each onto the table. "But I really love to vaporize it. Much better high and so much easier on your lungs. Plus I mix in some sacred tobacco and gingko." She smiled and squeezed a couple drops of liquid out of a tiny bottle. "And a little peppermint oil."

She placed her mix into a glass bowl connected to a three-foot plastic tube with a glass mouthpiece at the other end. She hooked the bowl to the wooden box. "My Uncle Bob invented the vaporizer. He's a wicked cool cat." She shrugged. "Well, I don't know him. Met him when I was little. He's my mom's older brother." She sighed and paused for a second. "This is a Vapor Brothers vaporizer. Bought it on the Internet. Has a thermostat. Halfway is 200 degrees Celsius. The optimum temp for vaporizing. No smoke. Just the essence of the plant via vapor."

"Wow," I said, faintly remembering hearing of this practice. Vogue in Amsterdam or Vancouver perhaps? And I got my introduction Down East. From a beautiful young woman. "Great."

"Push over," she said, squeezing between me and the arm of the couch. "But not too far. Watch. You gotta inhale slowly and evenly." She smiled and put the tube to her lips. She breathed in, then handed me the rig, the mouthpiece glistening, wet from her mouth. "Not like a bong. Don't draw too hard."

I inhaled green bud with hints of peppermint. Another breath and the peppermint tasted stronger. My lungs were full. Exhaled. No smoke. Very strange, especially after a lifetime of smoking weed. Inhaled slowly again and again. And again and again. Then I passed the tube back to Missy.

"What do you think?" she asked. "You like?"

"Yes. Very much."

She removed the bowl and stirred the contents, then hooked me up again. Not sure I needed anymore. Inhaled anyway. Again. And again. Both the room and Missy had taken on a soft glow. The Grateful Dead poster on the wall shook and vibrated.

"Wow," I said, handing the tube back. "Think I'm all set."

This was a different sort of marijuana high. Intense, with a body buzz and shake. I was worried about tipping over on the comfy couch. I decided to stand, to see if my stability would improve. Felt like an amusement park fun house as I struggled to my feet. Wobbly, I walked to the wall of posters just as they stopped vibrating.

"How about some tunes?" she asked.

"Sure." I was real high. "Sure."

"You like Ani DiFranco?" She sprang easily to her feet. "I love her."

"So do I." Totally baked. "She's awesome."

"Cool." She fiddled with the CD player. "I'm kinda surprised. Most guys don't"

"I've seen her live a couple times. Great show," I said. "I love these posters. Wow."

"Yeah, me too. They're Ganeesh's. He likes collecting things." She laughed and nodded. "If you've got a couple days to spare, ask to see his Star Wars collection. His action figures and the spaceships are worth a fortune." She laughed again. "He's a great guy. Very smart and very kind. One of the nicest people you'll ever meet."

"How long have you guys all been," I paused for a second, "together."

"Oh dear." She smiled. "Our story is super complicated and simple at the same time. Savannah and I have been best friends forever, but our sexual relationship with Ganeesh didn't start until last year." She sighed happily. "I love this room. All summer, I've been working in here. Lots and lots accomplished." She pointed at the desk. "I'm gonna miss this place when I go back to university. But Savannah and I will still spend most weekends here since Machias is major Dullsville. In the Grange," she said, picking up a little camera sitting on her desk and turning it on, "we have fun."

She pointed the camera at her own face and posed for a quick self portrait. Then she hopped, like a bunny, a couple steps closer to me and took aim. I gave her a serious rock star stare and she snapped a picture. A second later, her hand was around my neck. Electric shock. She pulled me down to her lips, her tongue darted into my mouth. Just as quickly, she released me and pulled back and took another shot.

"Ahhh, uhhhh," I stammered. "What?"

"I like the way surprise looks on a person's face," she said. "See." She showed me the screen on the back of the camera.

"Interesting perspective," I said.

She put the camera on the table, slipped her arms around me and looked up. She was so goddamn cute. Her mouth grinning the grin I was getting to know and like. A lot. I bent and kissed her. She kissed back. Then she jumped up onto one of the end tables and pulled me towards her. Now we were the same height.

She kissed me intensely. Deeply. I was surprised how quickly her hands wandered, starting with my shoulders and ending up on my ass. Her tongue toyed and tangled with mine until she moved her mouth to bite my left earlobe. She reached for my belt and started to unbuckle.

I remembered my wife back on Goose Island, who thought I was asleep in my tent on Richard's land, recovering from another day of raking blueberries to make the money we desperately needed.

At once, I was awash in guilt. I had to stop Missy. I needed to let her know she was hot and I really, really, really wanted her. But I was married. She would understand, I was sure.

Then she looked up, her eyes smiling.

"Let me know when you're gonna cum," she said softly, getting comfortable, sitting on the edge of the table. Then she engulfed my cock with her mouth.

Twice. She paused and looked up, into my eyes. "It turns me on," she said.

I groaned. Helpless. Not a chance to stop her. Not that I wanted to, really. I could tell by the way she combined her mouth and hand that this blowjob would rank as one of my life's best. Simultaneously, I knew sadness would appear when the blowjob was over. Sadness because it was over and because I knew guilt would arrive soon after. However, Missy's very warm and wet mouth erased that worry. Her flicking and licking tongue removed the doubt. And her luscious lips sealed the deal. Still, in the very back of my brain, I knew that one way or another, I'd pay. Dearly.

I groaned some more. Couldn't believe this was happening. Hadn't expect a blowjob after dinner. Her sexual forwardness was a huge turn on. Plus, I knew she had a sweet body. I wanted her to strip, so I could see the curves I'd felt through her overalls while we were making out like teenagers.

Missy was a man's dream. I wanted to touch her bare flesh. Caress her soft skin. Taste her. Tease her. But she was in charge and it didn't seem appropriate to interrupt those amazing lips. Warm and wet on me. The flicker of a darting and licking tongue. I closed my eyes while Missy used her mouth and her left hand simultaneously, an exhilarating sensory combination of motion and friction.

Any thought of guilt vanished, as the blowjob progressed. There was a bigger distraction, however. The reemergence of the swimmer's itch, amplified by a couple stray locks of Missy's hair. With certain thrusts of her mouth and throat, her hair gently scraped my thigh and the itchy inflammations. The ends of her hair were a butterfly scratching. Torture. Teasing in a sadistic way. Very distracting. Here I was, getting an amazing blowjob from a woman who electrocuted and enthralled me and all I could think about was my itchy inner thighs.

If I didn't scratch, there'd be no orgasm and she would be wasting her time.

"Oh Missy," I cried out. "You gotta stop. I've gotta scratch..."

She pulled her mouth away.

"I'm sorry..." I said.

"What's the matter?" Her big eyes looked up, in disbelief.

"Swimmer's itch," I gasped, using both hands to attack. My erection stared at me, while I scratched both inner thighs almost raw. The scraping brought a sense relief, which turned into embarrassment. "I got it from Sutherland's Lake."

"Oh dear," she said. "Never go swimming in Sutherland's. Pocomoonshine is the best. I like Pleasant Lake, too. There's a secret place to skinny dip. You poor dear. Let me see."

I stopped scratching for a second so she could see.

"Yikes," she said. I looked down. Exposed under the light, post scratch-a-thon, it looked pretty bad. "You probably shouldn't be scratching so hard. Doesn't help it heal."

"I've been using this lotion that I bought at Mary's," I said. "Called Corrigan's. Does the trick, but you gotta keep re-applying it."

"Do you have some?"

"Nope." I shook my head. "Left it back at Richard's."

"That's too bad." She looked up at me with her big blue eyes, not far from my still erect cock. "What are we gonna do now?"

"Ahhh, I'm okay." The itching went away. My vicious scratching did the trick. My erection, thankfully, remained strong. "I think..."

She didn't wait for an answer. Enveloped me again. Her mouth engulfed my cock in her wet oral warmth. Back and forth, sliding and sucking and licking my shaft, all the while gently holding my balls in her left hand. I moaned.

After 30 seconds of activity, she paused to remind me. "Let me know before you're gonna cum."

"Okay." Gasp. Moan. Didn't seem like much of a request, especially since the tingle was quickly quickening its pace. Her left hand and mouth worked together, bringing me closer and closer to the edge. My eyes squeezed shut, trying to hold off as long as possible. To enjoy the magnificent blowjob. To make the blowjob last forever. Impossible, of course. I opened my eyes and whispered a warning. "Very soon..."

Missy pulled her mouth away, but kept stroking with her left hand. With her right hand, she picked up the camera from the table and pointed it at me.

"Beep," the camera sounded three seconds before I shuddered and the explosive eruption raced from within toward the head of my cock. The camera sang a whir. I heard it zoom. In or out. And I came and came. Wave of power. Surge of energy. Spurting forth, all over her left forearm, a stream reaching her elbow.

Her right hand held the camera steady, aimed at me.

Her left hand held my cock until I shuddered and closed my eyes. And she engulfed me again. Soft and warm, but not moving. My hardness resting, relaxing in her mouth.

"Wow," I said, when finally able to speak. "Wow," I said again as she released me and backed away from my groin. Without a doubt, the best blowjob of my life. Not sure if the unexpected camera enhanced or detracted from the experience. "Wow!"

She devilishly licked her lips and plucked several tissues from a box on the table next to the vaporizer. "That was nice," she said, wiping her forearm clean. "I really enjoyed your orgasm."

"You enjoyed it?" I laughed. "Not as much as me."

"Don't be so sure. My experience will last longer than yours."

"What do you mean?" I paused. "Because of the picture?"

"Video, actually. That little camera shoots awesome video. No sound, though."

"Oh," I said. "Really?"

"Part of a long term art project." She grinned. "To film each and every lover's face at the point of orgasm."

"Oh." I went quiet.

The word "lover" triggered the image of Monica. Her lovely face, imprinted on my brain. My wife was my lover. I was devoted to her forever, but in a quick instant, I violated my vow to be true.

I was such a scumbag. Asshole. Guilt arrived and overwhelmed me. Mixed with all the drugs and exhaustion and pain, I felt tears coming.

"You okay?" Missy asked.

"Yeah." I said, though she could tell I wasn't. I should have been in an ecstatic mood in the moments after the best blowjob of my life. No room for this sort of guilt, I imagined, in the world of New Sexuality. "I'm fine."

"Oh dear," she said. "Are you going to cry?"

Thankfully, there was a knock on the door.

"Hey you guys," Savannah called out. "We're gonna do a snort. Interested?"

"Be right out, dear." Missy turned to me. "Listen Ben. Don't feel bad. You shouldn't feel bad. I just wanted to give you oral. To thank you."

"Thank me?"

"For being you. For being a nice guy."

"Hah," I shook my head. Standing there, deflated cock out of my pants. An adulterer. "Yeah, nice guy."

"Seriously, I can tell," she said. "And I wanted you to feel good. You deserve it. You made me feel great, really great, when you sang and played guitar. You have no idea how much your music moved me." She nodded. "Really. And as for the oral, I just wanted you to have a release, 'cuz I feel like I've been teasing you." She smiled. "And I wanted to film your orgasm. Because you're really cute. But there's nothing more than that. I'm not looking for anything from you. I know people think my perspective on sex is unusual. But it's who I am and what I do. We can talk about it more sometime, if you like. I just don't want you to feel guilty. You really shouldn't. Totally ruins the power of the orgasm. I mean, look at you," she pointed at me. "You should be smiling."

For a couple seconds, I remained silent.

"You're right," I said, not believing her.

"You're right," I said, knowing shame would linger, knowing she was wrong. "Thanks a lot."

She wrapped her arms around me. Warm and soft. Despite my heavy sadness and guilt, the electricity flowed between us again. Her embrace was familiar and comfortable. Felt perfect. Was I falling in love?

"Time for a snort." She looked up at me. "Like I said before, I'm so glad you're here. Right now. With me."

Then we went into the other room and snorted what I thought was cocaine, but was actually Oxycontin. Missy and I sat on the couch and talked. A long, slow opium talk. The snort drowned out the pain of raking and the guilt of the blowjob.

At some point, I fell asleep. Or passed out.

The All-You-Can-Eat

"C'mon Ben, wake up! We gotta get the frig out of here." Richard shook me by the shoulder. "It's way past midnight. I wanna sleep in my own friggin' bed. We got a long day tomorrow."

My world: a murky soup of grogginess. Dark room. On a couch. Left cheek wet from a puddle of drool. Eyes open, no clue where I was or who was rousting me. My thoughts a jumble due to the snort, speed, weed and beer. Blink. Blink. Blink. Everything came back. The Grange. The scintillating conversations. The straw hat dinner. All those pills. That blowjob.

I sighed loudly. Missy. Wow. For a moment, I revisited the blowjob. An awesome event. But then, in my mind's eye, I saw Monica crying. Guilt took over. Punched me in the gut, then kicked me in the balls. Slapped my face. Stuck its fingers into my eye sockets and probed my skull. Pierced my brain. Stabbed my soul. Slit my throat. Beat me senseless, but it didn't kill me. No, guilt won't kill you.

Monica wouldn't understand how most guys in my situation would have found Missy impossible to resist. When a woman you find desirable and beautiful puts her lips on your lips, then takes your cock into her warm soft mouth, and strokes it in the way Missy did, instinct makes you helpless by design.

Hurting Monica would be the absolute worst. Monica. Sweet. Generous. Kind. Innocent. Gentle. Understanding. Beautiful inside and out. Understanding. As a husband, I was seriously content. Fulfilled. Intellectually. Philosophically. Sexually. Monica and I shared a marriage of fun and passion. I definitely had no need to cheat. That's what made the blowjob so terrible. Married to a sexually attractive and adventuresome woman, I wasn't desperate for an orgasm.

Simultaneously and incongruously, while laying on the couch in the Grange, my lust for Missy shined through and bypassed the guilt. My brain tried to rationalize a new concept: my desire for Missy didn't diminish my love for my wife. Could I be in love with two people at once? Never happened to me before, but old rules were old. Look at the Missy and Savannah and Ganeesh triad. Seemed to be working.

And if a triad was only temporary or short-lived, so what? Who cares if the third was an occasional? What nefarious schemer crafted these puritanical mores? The rule should be this: As long as no one gets hurt, anything goes.

The problem, obviously, was that Monica and I should have decided up front that our marriage would allow such games. Couldn't make up rules as I went along, could I?

What the fuck had I done?

"C'mon Ben," Richard sounded pissed. "I'm serious. Let's get a friggin' move on."

"Not sure I can drive," I mumbled, wishing I'd never met Richard. Wishing I was home in bed with my wife. "I'm pretty wiped out."

"You can drive." His voice was getting louder and louder. "We'll keep the windows open. The fresh air will wake you up. Drive with your head half outside the truck if you need to." He lit a smoke, breaking the Grange rule. I wanted to scold him, but was too tired. "C'mon. You can do it. Gotta do it. We gotta get home."

I rose from the couch and staggered through the haze of the Grange and outside and into Floyd. Amazingly, I navigated back to Richard's, though I don't remember a single detail from leaving the Grange until Floyd parked himself in the church parking lot.

The walk on the path back to the campsite was etched into my brain forever. The trail was still muddy and the sky was dark and clear, framed by spindly tree tops and dotted with millions of stars. Evidently we were in the center of the galaxy. Or the universe. When we got to the top of the hill, Richard immediately and wordlessly rolled into his tent. For me, for awhile, the picnic table became my couch and I stared into the cosmic light show to remind myself of my own insignificance.

Eventually, my full bladder ended the star-gazing. After pissing, I crawled into the tent. Everything was damp. The nylon walls and floor. The bag and pillow. My small pile of clean clothes. Didn't care, though. Any inconvenience or distraction (even my pain) seemed incidental to my exhaustion. Wiped out, I considered sleeping with my boots on, but summoned enough energy to remove them. Finally, on my back and breathing deeply through the soreness of my whole body, the memory of the blowjob returned. The memory of cheating on Monica reminded me I hadn't called her like I'd promised. Again.

The facts were a bucket of cold water dousing me awake with guilt. Laying there, eyes wide open, shock waves of shame pulsated through my body. Too dehydrated to cry, I sobbed dry tears and wheezed and shook for minutes. Eventually, though, all the pills, booze, herb and hard labor took their toll. Sleep won, trumping guilt. Deep slumber arrived.

Woke a little after seven on the fifth morning of the harvest feeling like shit. The best news: the swimmer's itch seemed to have disappeared. The pustules still lingered, but the inflammation was down dramatically and didn't itch. The other good news: finally, a perfect day for raking. Slightly cloudy with a southwesterly whisper of a breeze. After taking a leak, I headed to the church to use the phone and call Monica. Through the thin walls, I heard the sound of the shower. The old man was asleep in his chair, so I assumed Buffy was in the shower. Which saved me from the torture of the morning before, when she stretched and showed me her thong. So long ago.

I dialed my home number and took a deep breath.

"Hello?" Monica answered.

"Hey babe," I said. "It's me."

Her silence lingered and seemed to last forever.

"Well?"

"Listen, babe, I'm sorry I didn't call. It's real tough to get access to a phone."

"Really?"

She was pissed. I didn't blame her, of course. And from the tone of her voice, she didn't believe me. Which sucked, because I'd never lied to her before. Now, because of the harvest, plus staying at Richard's and the scene with Missy, dishonesty was a necessity.

"I have a hard time believing you couldn't find a telephone to call me and let me know you're alive and okay..."

"Babe..."

"You listen to me," she said, unable to stop. "I'm sure there are pay phones in Irwin. And what about Richard? Doesn't he have a phone?"

"Yeah," I said. "That's where I'm calling from..."

"So you can call today, but not last night? Last night, when I was waiting for your call? I fell asleep around ten o'clock." She paused.

Ten o'clock, I remembered, was the approximate time of my long opiate-fueled conversation with Missy on the couch. "Then woke up at eleven and started worrying and couldn't get back to sleep..."

"Babe, please," I said. "I'm sorry. I totally fucked up."

"Why, Ben?" she sniffled. "Why didn't you call?"

"It's just," I paused. "Just really weird out here. Just wait...Wait until you come out here, you'll see what I mean." There was no way I'd want Monica to camp on Richard's land. Not anymore. That was the plan before Missy. Wouldn't work now. "You'll see what I mean. It's really weird here."

"I don't care how weird it is," she said, "that's no excuse for not calling when you promised you would."

"I'm sorry babe, really I am." I sighed. "These people are freaks."

"Freaks?" she asked. She liked freaks. "What kind of freaks?"

"Hard to explain, over the phone," I said. "Someone might hear me."

"Oh come on," she said, "What kind of freaks?"

"Well," I paused for a second, stalling. "A lot of these people are," another pause. "Crazy. Ummm..." I couldn't tell her about the gun, not yet, because I didn't want her to worry. Of course, Missy was off limits. And I had to say something. "Real rednecks. Like in *Deliverance*."

Monica never saw the film until we got together and was surprised by how much she enjoyed the movie. We watched it twice in one night. Ever since, it had been a constant source of private jokes.

"Oh Ben," her voice finally softened. "They're not making you squeal like a pig are they?"

"No way," I said, relieved to hear her mood lighten. I mean, she had the total right to be super pissed at me. For not calling. And she had the right to hate me, for letting Missy give me a blowjob. "I'll only squeal like a pig for you." As soon as I said it, I realized it was another lie.

"I miss you," she sighed. "If you're gonna camp out, the least you could do is call."

"I know babe, totally." I was such a loser. "It won't happen again."

"Promise?"

"I promise. Listen babe, next time it really rains hard, expect to see me. 'Cuz Larry don't let us rake if it's too wet."

"Are you making money?"

"I made eighty day before yesterday."

"That's great. What about yesterday?"

"Not as good, lots of rain delays." I paused. "I don't even know what my total was. I'll find out and let you know tonight, when I call."

"Okay," she said. "You better."

"I will."

"I love you," she said. "I miss you."

"I love you too," I said. "I'll call you tonight."

"Okay, you better," she said. "Bye."

"Bye," I said and hung up the phone.

"Bye-bye," Buffy cooed, her voice coming from behind me. "I wuv you. Lovey-Dovey. Smoochey-Woochey."

I turned around and Buffy stood in the hallway leading to the bathroom, wearing nothing but a towel around her body, and another as a turban on her head.

"Hi Buffy," I said, wondering how long she'd been standing there. "Just making a quick call."

"Oh, is that what you were doing?"

"Yeah," I said. "Yep."

"Got any weed?"

"Nope," I said. "Do you?"

"Nope. Too bad, 'cuz I feel like getting high. High as a kite, right?"

"Yeah."

"Hey, have you thought anymore about our plan?"

"Our plan?"

"You know, to sell hamburgs and hotdogs instead of raking."

"Oh." I hadn't. "Well..."

" 'Cuz I get my food stamps tomorrow. And we should start as soon as possible, 'cuz I ain't making no money raking berries."

"Me neither."

"Get this, " she sauntered over to me and got real close. "I was thinking that some of the rakers won't have cash on 'em. I never bring any money with me," she laughed, " 'cuz I don't got none."

"Me neither."

"So why don't we set the price for the food in terms of pounds of blueberries?"

"I don't follow."

"Okay, we're getting three seventy five for a bucket." She nodded. "So we charge a bucket for a cheeseburger." She smiled. "Or two hotdogs for a bucket. See what I'm saying?"

"I guess..."

"Except," she said, holding up one finger, "some fields don't use buckets."

"What do they use?"

"Boxes. Plastic boxes. Two of them equal a bucket. So a cheeseburger would cost two boxes. But don't worry. I can keep track of all that."

"What about the money? How would we get the cash. I mean, they're paying us in berries."

"Not really in berries, silly," she laughed. "I would just total 'em, I guess, and ask the blueberry farmer to pay us. With a check, like he pays the rakers."

"They'd do that?"

"Some of 'em," she said, nodding. "We'd have to offer them a deal. Maybe bosses eat free, rakers pay full price."

She seemed so proud of herself, but this was one of the worst business plans I'd ever heard.

"So we gonna start tomorrow?"

"I dunno." I shook my head. "Still don't have a grill. And not sure..."

"Maybe tomorrow we go to your house and get the grill and then stop at the IGA on Goose Island? And then start the next day." She looked at me with her crossed eyes and batted her long lashes. "C'mon. You know it'll be a nice ride." She flicked her tongue at me again.

"Let me think about it," I said, knowing there wasn't a chance in hell I was gonna get into the catering biz with Buffy. Or bring her to my house. "I'll let you know later."

"Really?" she said. "Promise?"

"Yeah," I said. "Promise." Second time in ten minutes I made a promise to a woman I wasn't sure I could keep. "Listen, I better see if Richard is ready to rake."

"If we were working together," she said, "I'd let you watch me get dressed." She laughed. "Or undressed."

"Oh." I was hard again. "Hmmm."

We stood there, staring at each other. Buffy opened the towel wrapped around her body. For one second, maybe two, she exposed herself to me. Long enough to get a good look before she squealed, turned around and ran down the hallway. I heard a door slam. I shook my head, wishing my erection would go away.

A half hour later, on the drive to the fields, Richard told me the bad news. He'd totally spaced and forgotten he had a super-important meeting at one p.m. with his probation officer. If he didn't make it, an arrest warrant would be issued. He was sure of it.

"What the fuck?" I snapped, forgetting I wasn't supposed to swear in front of Captain, who was sitting between us. Buffy and Jazz were in the back. "That fucking sucks."

"Ben said a bad word." The kid wagged his finger at me sternly. His cheeks and hands were covered in powdered sugar. (We'd stopped at Mary's Market for donuts, coffee and a thermos of tea for me. Plus I put twenty bucks of gas into Floyd's tank, leaving me with a ten spot and some change.) "Bad boy."

"I'm sorry." I shook my head. Hated my job as 24-7 chauffeur. And I wanted some actual gas money from Richard, but was sure he'd just mention the free drugs and steaks. "That totally sucks. Totally messes up my day. Dude, I gotta start raking some money. Are you sure you just don't want to take my truck?"

"*Dude*! I've told you this a million friggin' times." He pointed at me with his lit smoke, annunciating each word. "*I-can-not-drive*! Especially not to my probation officer. Anyway, we'll come back and rake late. Rake until dark. Heck, Larry would probably let us stay even later. Too bad it wasn't a full moon. 'Cuz we could rake all night under 'the lantern of the poor'. Actually, going to Roosevelt should work out good, since we'll miss the hottest part of the day."

"What time we gotta leave?"

"Twelve-thirty." He flicked the cigarette out the window. "But lucky for you, Ganeesh wants to take you out for lunch."

"What?"

"Yeah, Chinese. The all-you-can-eat."

"Why?"

"Well, you're gonna need something to do while I'm meeting with the man." He smiled at me. "Plus Ganeesh wanted to talk to you about…the vitamins. That's what he said last night. Don't you remember?"

"No, I was pretty fucked up."

"Ben said another bad word." Captain's mouth was half full with donut. "Bad boy."

"That's right, I'm a bad boy." In more ways than one. "I was pretty messed up. Don't really remember much."

"Don't worry," Richard laughed. "I've seen worse."

"Got any of that speed left?" I needed a boost. Morally and physically. Amphetamines certainly would help. "Make today go much better."

"Yeah, yeah, sure." Richard seemed eager to please. "How many?"

"Four should do it." I felt a twang in my hollow stomach, remembering my Coast Guard problem with speed. Running out and withdrawal from speed wasn't fun, but it was manageable. Because I was aboard a Coast Guard cutter cruising the offshore waters of the Atlantic looking for drug runners. And because I couldn't score any more pills. "Four would be good."

We arrived at the fields a little after nine. Popped the speed and went to work. The uppers helped me rake better. For three hours, I did extremely well. My strips were as blue as blue can be. An ocean of berries. The amphetamine gave me the focus I needed.

Rake. Rake. Comb. Comb. Rake. Rake. Comb. Comb.

Rake. Rake. Comb. Comb. Rake. Rake. Comb. Comb.

Even Larry was surprised by my energy and the 13 buckets I lugged to the scales. Three hundred pounds. A hundred per hour. I was a raking machine! Almost 14 bucks an hour. Maintain this pace for the rest of the harvest, I could earn somewhere between fifteen hundred and two grand. More than enough for Monica and I to survive on until her job started.

Monica. Kept trying to vanquish her image every time it came into my brain. Weird, since usually I loved thinking about her. Never, ever, had I felt such guilt or felt its intense physical manifestation. Worse than any pain from the blueberry harvest. Luckily, for the most part, the speed kept me focused on raking. And when Monica (or Missy) came to mind, I'd take a sip of water and then...

Rake. Rake. Comb. Comb. Rake. Rake. Comb. Comb.
Rake. Rake. Comb. Comb. Rake. Rake. Comb. Comb.

Unfortunately, my record earnings were interrupted by having to play taxi cab. At 12:15 Richard was ready to go. Went to the Grange, picked up Ganeesh and headed into the big city of Roosevelt. Dropped Richard off at the courthouse and then Ganeesh and I drove downtown to the Chinese restaurant.

After finding a parking space, I climbed out of Floyd and had a sudden panic attack, irrationally fearing I'd bump into Monica. Completely ludicrous since I had our only set of wheels. Monica was on Goose Island, a half-hour away. Probably writing poetry or taking the dogs for a walk. But my brain balked at reason. Guilt and speed prevailed. What if we ran into her? How would I explain not being on the fields? How could I face her without the guilt of that blowjob shining through my eyes?

"Hey G," the tiny wrinkled Chinese lady said to Ganeesh. Her restaurant, located on the front street in Roosevelt, had a partial view of the Levendosky River which separated the U.S. from Canada. "How you doing?"

"Fine, Mrs. Wong," he said with a bow. "How are you today?"

"Hey G," came a voice from behind. Ancient Chinese man. "How you doing?"

"What up, G?" asked the cute girl walking by us with a tray of glasses. Also Chinese and maybe 18 years old. "How you doing?"

"Hello, G," said the Chinese busboy carrying a tub of dishes. "What up?"

"Hello, hello, everyone," Ganeesh said, waving with both hands like he was president. Mr. Wong led us to our table, in the far corner of the almost empty dining room. I took a seat while Ganeesh greeted two fellas sitting in a booth in the other corner. When Ganeesh joined me, the old man instantly appeared.

"You want regula, G?" he asked, pen at the ready.

"Yes please, Mr. Wong!"

"You have regula, too?' he asked, pointing at me with his note pad.

I looked toward Ganeesh for help.

"The all-you-can-eat," he said, pointing to the opposite corner toward a buffet table. "It's good. My treat."

"Yes, please," I answered, suddenly hungry. Famished. Hard work overpowered the appetite-suppressing power of the speed drifting through my veins. "The regula."

Ganeesh wanted to eat a plate before we started talking vitamins. Both of us stacked various meats atop a mound of white rice: Boneless red spareribs. Chicken 3-ways. (Deep fried, teriyaki and wings). Butterflied stuffed shrimp. I built a wall of beef on skewers to frame the outer edge of my food pile and keep the whole mess on the plate. We rushed back to the table and ate like men in a hurry. Obviously, the restaurant would lose money on our feast.

"Gotta take a breather," Ganeesh said, opening his second can of Moxie. Both of our plates were empty. "Gotta pace myself to take full advantage of the-all-you-can-eat."

"That's for sure," I said, swallowing the last piece of rib. "This is great."

"Listen." He leaned forward and pointed at me. "Let me cut through all the bullshit. I hate the fact we even gotta talk about this, but that fucking Zeus really fucked up the entire plan." He looked around. The restaurant was still empty except for the other booth. "I know you're not an idiot so I'm not gonna lie to you. Unfortunately, you saw those pill bottles."

I nodded.

"Those weren't vitamins. I imagine you already figured that out. Especially after last night's snort. Well," he looked around, "we're the middlemen in a new operation that is possibly very lucrative."

"Really?" I smiled. "Lucrative."

"Yeah." He pointed at me. "Listen, I like you, Ben. And the girls like you. And Missy." He stared at me. Intently. "Really likes you."

"Oh." I sighed. Ganeesh knew what happened with Missy. I could see it in his eyes. "Well, I ..."

"And I know you ain't a cop, because no fucking pig would have a floor refinishing business as a cover."

"Dude," I said, pointing my fork at him. "I am not a cop."

"I just said that. That's why I decided to let you in on our little secret. Here's the problem. We need a driver because Richard and I can't legally drive. If the cops 'round here see either one of us behind the wheel, it's a guaranteed trip to the Washington County jail," he said, sighing before continuing. "When we set up this deal, we hadn't counted on Richard totaling his truck and getting arrested for driving with a suspended license. Plus, he refused to take the Breathalyzer and the state doesn't like that. Besides, he's already on probation." Ganeesh shook his head. "And I can't drive because," he squinted, "they took away my license because of my eyes. And there's no way I'm gonna get Missy or Savannah mixed up in this. So it makes getting the pills really complicated, because our sources are all over Washington County." He took another swig of the Moxie. "We can't trust people from around here to drive because we don't trust nobody from around here." He looked across the dining room. "Because everyone talks. And since you don't know anybody, I'm counting on you not blabbing."

"I won't."

"I know," he said, looking me hard in the eyes, "because we checked you out. Got your phone number, thanks to the floor refinishing poster. In fact, I already programmed 853-2763 into my cell phone. Then did a reverse search on the Internet."

"What?" I couldn't believe they looked me up. "What the hell?"

"Monica Franklin, 12 Key Street, Goose Island, Maine. Right? Asked one of my cousins to drive by your house. He said your wife was hot."

"Dude," I interrupted. No idea where he was headed, but I didn't like his tone. "What the fuck are you talking about?"

"My cousin said you've got little dogs. I like little dogs." Ganeesh pointed at me. "Get this. We know your phone number. Where you live. Makes it simple from here on out. You rat or rip us off, we tell your wife about a certain web site with a short film of her husband ejaculating. I'm pretty sure she'd recognize you. That's a way to keep you from blabbing. Right?" Ganeesh finished his Moxie with a long swig, then looked into my eyes.

"Yeah," I gulped. My stomach turned. A wave of terror. Horror and anger. Betrayed. Set up by Missy! Never would have predicted it. I really believed she liked me. I thought our electrical connection was genuine. "I can't fucking believe Missy!"

"*Ha-hah*!" Ganeesh laughed and slammed the empty soda can on the table. "Gotcha! She didn't say shit. She's a nice girl. Wouldn't do nuthin' like that. I was just bluffing, but you fell for it. Confirmed my suspicions. You guys were in the back room for awhile, so I guessed something happened and since Missy films everything..."

"Oh, great." Now I was doubly-fucked, plagued by guilt and the fear of possible exposure. How did raking blueberries so quickly disintegrate? "Fuck.

This really sucks."

"Doesn't have to suck. If nothing goes wrong. Your wife never needs to know. I don't want to ruin your life. That's not what this is about. You've got wheels and I've got dirt on you, which makes me think I can trust you. A little insurance."

"Dude, I wouldn't say anything to anyone."

"Funny," Ganeesh paused and popped open another can of Moxie. "I usually don't trust white men. And now I'm stuck with you and Richard. And I gotta trust you guys, because there's no one else. And the trust I have in you," he smiled and shook his head ruefully, "comes from me being able to blackmail you." He sighed. "All very confusing. Morally." He took another long sip of Moxie and nodded at me. "Am I right?"

"Yeah." All I wanted to do was rake blueberries and earn enough to tide us over until Monica started work. "You can trust me."

"Well, I'm not asking for you to do much. Just drive us around so we can run errands."

"Drive you around? That's it?

"Yup." He picked up his plate and licked it clean. "Time for round two. I'm starving."

I followed him back to the buffet table and we focused on a surprisingly good salad bar, piling lettuce, tomatoes, cukes, carrots and sprouts high with a generous pouring of dressing. Ranch for him. Blue cheese for me. This time, I used four egg rolls as a wall to keep the greens on the plate. Back at the table, the feeding frenzy resumed.

While munching on my salad, I considered the situation. Did driving for these guys make me a drug runner? If we got busted, could I plead ignorance? An unknowing accomplice? Or would I be accessory to the crime? Probably. Risk meant compensation. In cash money, which I needed desperately. So in a strange way, this was a lucky opportunity. A temporary part-time job, Down East style. By the time I took my first bite of egg roll dipped in duck sauce, I was 100 percent on board.

I wondered what Monica would think of my drug running. She didn't need to know. Besides, this was the only way I could keep my adultery secret from her. Desperation, plus greed, were the strongest motivators I'd ever experienced.

And maybe, now that I was part of a pill operation, I could get more pills. In the last couple of days, I'd ingested two different types that really helped. Uppers and downers. Obviously, the speed helped me rake faster and made hard labor pass quicker. I was looking forward to another Oxy crushed and shaped into a long sliver, then snorted up my nose to make my backache disappear. No wonder Washington County had a pill problem, since so many people were either in pain or working a shitty job. Or both.

"All I have to do is drive? That's it?" I asked, swallowing egg roll. "For how long?"

"Couple or three more days. Four at the most." He wiped duck sauce from his chin with his napkin, then took a long sip of water. "This is short-term. A quick gig. One time only."

"What's the pay?"

"Hmmm." Ganeesh stared across the table. His face was a blank. "Hadn't really thought about it. See, transportation expenses weren't part of the business plan."

"Business plan?"

"Dude, you think we're amateurs?" He gave me a reckoning look. "We're not. I learned a lot from the classes I took."

"Classes?"

"Yeah, through Washington County Community College."

"The college has classes on drug dealing?"

"Dude, keep it down," he said. "Don't be screaming shit out loud like that. And no, the classes weren't about drugs, they were about small business."

"Really."

"It's all applicable, no matter if you're running pills, weed or running a health food store. Use sound business principles. Consider risk, liability and market conditions. Supply and demand and," he looked up at the ceiling, "something else. Ahhhh, a willing and available consumer."

"Uh-huh."

"Why reinvent the wheel? I mean people have been buying and selling goods and services for thousands of years. Hell, they've been buying and selling drugs for thousands of years. Know what I mean?"

"I guess so." If this was a business, then there had to be some wiggle room in the budget. "So what are you gonna pay me?"

"What about a couple hundred bucks?"

"Three hundred." Pretty damn cheap, considering the risk of a hassle with the cops and possible jail time. Definitely worth three bills, I thought, since the fellas were in a bind and I was doing them a big favor. Of course, if they wanted to be assholes, they could say no money and threaten to tell Monica about Missy. "Could you swing $300?"

"Dude," he looked incredulous. "This job is probably two or three hours for three or four days." He did the numbers in his head. "That's forty or fifty bucks an hour."

"Yeah, but includes the truck rental, wear and tear, plus gas."

He sighed and I sensed an opening.

"Plus I'd need half up front." That was a stroke of genius, since I was flat broke. "If you could, please."

He stared at me across the table.

"Just like the white man," he pointed with his fork, "always trying to screw us natives." He sighed. "If I pay you three bills and then you fuck with me, I will have you killed." He nodded. "You understand? I have militant cousins who would love to get some revenge." He took a sip of his Moxie. "Payback on the white man. Dude, they would tie you up in the basement of some abandoned house on the reserve and torture the fuck out of you and your old lady."

"*All right*," I said, my voice louder than it should have been. "Leave my wife out of this. Besides, I'm not gonna fuck with you."

"I know. I know." He reached to offer me his hand, across the table. "Dude, I know."

We shook hands. Then he laughed.

"How about another plate?" he asked. "I'm still starving. Round three?"

"Yeah," I sighed. "Sure."

The restaurant was filling up. A late lunch crowd, many of whom wanted to say hey to Ganeesh. So I continued on to the buffet which had been reloaded since our last visit. Steamed veggies – carrots and beans -- on top of brown rice. Plus broccoli chicken with cashews. A new stack of boneless red ribs. More wings. More skewers of meat. Two egg rolls.

"I was wondering where these were," Ganeesh said, coming up behind me, pointing to a fresh tray of Crab Rangoon. He put three on his plate. "My favorite. Love 'em."

"Man, I could totally take a nap now," Ganeesh yawned and stretched his long arms. He twisted his neck to the left and right, then tilted it side to side. His bones cracked and popped. "Fucking-A."

We were sitting in the truck, sweating, in the Wal-Mart parking lot, across the street from the courthouse, waiting for Richard to return. Two reasons for the sweat. Bright sun pounded the hot blacktop, radiating and baking us. Secondly, I was reacting to the MSG from our lunch. Could taste the food chemical in my saliva. Felt my cheeks tremble. Watched my forearms shake. I've had this feeling many times before, especially back in the rock' n roll days, eating shitty manufactured industrial food re-heated in small town diners and highway rest stops across the country. Garbage saturated with preservatives. The diet of the road and the lazy.

I couldn't wait until Monica and I got our land. Grow our own veggies. Raise our cow, goats, pigs and chickens. Root cellar shelves lined with jars of tomatoes, salsa and pickles. Bins heaped with potatoes, carrots, onions and garlic. A deep freezer filled with corn and broccoli, beef and pork. I'd feast on my own harvest, and not get the shakes from the "natural flavors" used to make factory food edible.

Of course, if Monica learned about Missy, then all plans would be cancelled. She'd take off. I'd be left alone, without a partner to homestead and grow old with. And that's the real reason I was sitting in my truck with Ganeesh, waiting for a knucklehead.

That, and 300 bucks.

"When I get back to the Grange, gonna totally sack out. On my new bed. Ronnie was gonna drop it off by two." Ganeesh looked at his wrist watch. "What the fuck is taking Richard so fucking long? We got shit to do. People to see, pills to pick up."

"Oh," I said. "I thought we were going back to rake berries."

"Dude, didn't you just sign on to drive us around?"

"Yeah, but..."

"No buts. We got places to be." He looked at his watch again. "In less than an hour."

"Where we going?"

"Back to your neck of the woods. Gonna meet someone."

"We're not going to Goose Island, are we?" Panic struck. My mind raced and shook. Speed, MSG or paranoia? Not a chance I could risk running into Monica. "Are we?"

"Relax," he said. "Pleasant Point, then Pembroke, then Perry. Then back to the Grange."

"Whew." Relief. I looked at him. "I can't go to Goose Island. Sure you understand."

"Sure thing, bro." He lifted up his sunglasses. "Don't want to explain to your old lady why you're driving around a redneck and a redskin." He smiled and dropped his shades. "Right?"

"Something like that."

We both laughed. I liked hanging out with Ganeesh. A million times cooler than Richard.

"Can I ask you a serious question?" I looked at him. Hands folded on his broad chest, relaxed. "About Richard and the pill operation?"

"Maybe." He paused. "What's the question?"

"If you guys stand to make a bunch of cash on the pills, then why is Richard wasting time raking blueberries?"

"Hey," he pointed at me. "In Washington County, you can never have too much money or too much work. Better remember that. If you're gonna survive, gotta work hard when there's work and play hard, when there's play. Around here, seasonal work is the best chance you've got to make money. Look, Richard rakes like a motherfucker, so he does well. Plus he's making cash from his garden. And maybe this year, his pumpkins will pay off. And in November, he'll spend a month in the woods getting balsam boughs for the wreath makers. Other than that, not many opportunities for him to make cash. Unless the new truck he gets has a snowplow. And then he's dependant on the weather. And 'round here, with global warming and all, how long will it take to pay off a plow? Years."

"Well, you guys gotta be making tons of money off the weed operation," I said. My turn to bluff. Richard's generosity with reefer had been bothering me. He acted like ganja was free, so it must be. Especially considering his green thumb. They had to be involved with the weed trade. If not, they were idiots. And Ganeesh wasn't an idiot. "I mean, that's a cash crop."

"Yeah, well," Ganeesh yawned, then let out a long burp. "Compared to pills, the weed business is more work and less profit. Weed is seasonal. Bulky, with limited payoff. Gotta worry about slugs, snails and the weather. And you gotta hide your garden because all sorts of losers around here go for walks in the woods just to see if they can stumble upon someone's grow op. Then they wait until a week before the plants need to be harvested and they steal 'em. Bastards." He shook his head. "Plus trimming green bud is real labor, when you're talking about pounds. With pills, we're just the middlemen, not dealing with real customers. Plus you gotta grow the weed to begin with, which Richard, luckily, is able to do quite well. But it's a lot of work. With pills, the pharmaceutical companies do the work for you."

"Much easier."

"That's right." Ganeesh yawned again. "I don't know how much Richard told you about the weed, but the pills is a totally different game."

"Hah-hah." I laughed gleefully, unable to contain myself. "I was bluffing. He didn't tell me anything. Figured since he's so generous with the reefer, he had to be growing and selling."

"Fuck you," Ganeesh said, pulling off his shades. "I just got suckered. Hey, I told you not fuck with me, whitey."

"Dude, I just wanted to make sure you weren't a cop setting me up."

"Me a cop? Are you fucking crazy?"

"Wouldn't be the first time cops have impersonated pill dealers."

"Dealers? Dealers?" Ganeesh opened his eyes wide and stared at me. "We ain't no fuckin' pill dealers. Get that straight." He shook his head vigorously. "Don't fucking insult me. We're the fucking middleman. The bridge between people with extra pills and the guy who wants to sell 'em to pillheads in Southern Maine."

"Southern Maine?"

"Yeah, well, I probably shouldn't tell you any of this."

"C'mon dude. I'm not gonna rat. Just curious."

"You know," he pointed at me, "curiosity killed the cat."

I didn't answer.

"And," he paused. "Curiosity could kill the rat." He sighed. "We're not dealers. Middlemen. Just like with the weed. We're not selling dime bags. We're selling pounds of manicured high quality Washington County marijuana. Bulk sales only. We've never dealt directly with the users. Way too much risk."

"I understand."

"Plus, I don't want people coming by the Grange. Very few people are allowed inside," he looked at me. "Hope you understand and appreciate that."

"Sure."

"That's why I've got the obvious security system and cameras at the Grange. To scare away the junkies and scumbags." He shook his head and sighed. "Pillheads are friggin' zombie thieves. They'd steal their grandma's prescription in order to get pills. Or steal her jewelry to sell to get money for pills. Used to be, when I was growing up, no one locked their doors around here. Now, everyone does. With deadbolts, too. Even if you're home. If a pillhead thinks there's a chance there's pills or money inside your place, he'll kick down doors. Smash windows. Do whatever is takes."

"That sucks. Really sucks." I shook my head. "So, if you're so against pills then why are we running," I paused for a sec, "these errands?"

"Hey, I'm not against pills, just pillheads. Used correctly, either for pain or for pleasure, the shit is great. Besides, like I said, we're the middle man. Listen," he looked around the almost empty parking lot, "I got a guy from Lewiston, a pal of my cousin, who is interested in buying as many Oxycontins as he can get his hands on. And I mean, as many as he can."

"A guy from Lewiston?" That surprised me. Lewiston was a small city, a former milltown struggling to find a new identity, 45 minutes from Portland.

"Yeah." Ganeesh took another sip of Moxie. "But he's got connections all over southern Maine."

"Hmmm..."

"There's a real pill shortage down there. Especially for the Oxycontin.

You know that, don't you? I mean, you lived in Portland. You heard about the pharmacy robberies and shit."

"Oh yeah." He was right. In my last couple years in Portland, there were dozens of pharmacy break-ins and strong-arm heists. Which the cops said were the first signs of an epidemic. I knew an idiot who tried to rip off a Rite Aid in downtown Portland. Caught and jailed.

"They've totally changed the way Oxy is dispensed. Some pharmacies aren't even carrying it anymore. All of the drug stores go into lock-down mode at night. Pillheads would have an easier time breaking into a bank. And the newest twist is for the pharmacist to give fake pills to a hold-up man. The pills look legit, I hear. Just a tiny difference in weight. Pillheads can't tell until they get 'em home and crack 'em and grind 'em and snort 'em and nothing happens." He frowned. "Poor sucker, strung out and trying to get right on a sugar pill." Ganeesh shook his head. "And don't even think about going doctor shopping because except for the Emergency Room, takes two or three months to get an appointment and if you don't have insurance, the price of an office visit is crazy. And then the doc isn't likely to write a script because he doesn't write for people that come in off the street because the cops are coming down hard on doctors caught writing scripts for cash. Not like it used to be around here. I blame the doctors for starting this," he looked at me, "the Washington County epidemic."

"Really?"

"Yeah, fucking bastard doctors, for the longest time, they were over-prescribing for relatively minor accidents or injuries. Lots of people got hooked because of it. Turned junkie. Then the doc cancels the script and the junkie freaks out and needs pills and buys 'em from whomever. So supply is low and demand is high, because both the junkies and the kids like pills more than heroin."

"Kids prefer pills to heroin?" That surprised me. Most of my Portland pals smoked lots of pot and drank heavily. But I had junkie friends. Some shot up. Others snorted. I stayed away from heroin because I was worried I'd like it too much, get hooked and overdose, turning into another wannabe rock star cliché. "That's crazy. All my pals who had a heroin habit complained about how expensive it was. "

"Heroin's dirt cheap, compared to Oxycontin." He nodded. "And there's so much stigma attached to the needle. Plus, shooting up is work. Chewing or snorting a pill is easy." He shook his head. "Most kids these days don't think I-V drugs are cool. Especially if you want to fuck and suck." He smiled. "And for the recreational user, even if the pills cost more, they enjoy the crazy ride that comes in a familiar package. The pill. Not scary like a needle. Easier to handle. Know what I mean?" He leaned toward me and opened his eyes wide. "You liked that snort, right?"

"Yes."

"Why?"

"Well," I paused for a second. Snorting the pills made the night super-fun. "Felt great. Floating. Pain free, which was a good thing since raking is fucking killing me."

"Makes you feel great. That's the irony of drugs." He shrugged. "The effects of them are awesome, but to use them recreationally is considered bad. For some reason, society doesn't want us to feel good. It's like Savannah says about morality and sex. They don't want you to have fun. Part of the grand conspiracy." He sighed. "If you hurt your back raking blueberries and you know that snorting a cracked Oxycontin would help, you should be able to go to Mary's Market and get some."

"Yeah, I agree." I nodded. "But what about abuse?"

"Let abusers pay the price. That's what we do with booze. You get busted drunk driving, you go to jail. If you start ripping people off to pay for the drugs, you're eventually gonna get caught. And you'll go to jail. But a couple of bad apples shouldn't ruin pain relief for the masses, that's the fact. Wish Richard would hurry the fuck up. I fucking hate sitting around, waiting for that little motherfucker. We got shit to do."

"Yep." Better than raking blueberries for cash, especially since I was gonna make three hundred bucks. "What the fuck is taking him so long?"

A police car pulled into the Wal-Mart parking lot and made a slow loop around the perimeter. For a second, as he drove behind us, I thought we were busted. Even though we weren't doing anything. I took a deep breath and held it, hoping I was invisible. A mix of nerves and shakes. Even though innocent (or maybe not guilty), just the appearance of the cops was enough to trigger panic.

Until I saw him pull back out onto North Street and drive away.

"For a long time, around here, the doctors treated pills like candy," Ganeesh broke the silence. "Shit, they used to prescribe Oxy for a hangnail, almost. When I got hurt working on the fish farm, you wouldn't believe how many pills they gave me. Huge bottles. All I could eat. More than I could eat. Shared with anyone who wanted 'em. That was just a couple years ago. These days, the pills, by weight, are more valuable than gold."

"More than gold?"

"Dude," he looked at me. "Gold goes for 700 per ounce. An 80 milligram oxy is worth 80 bucks on the street. Sometimes a hundred. Do the math."

"Wow. Never thought of it like that."

"That's the reality. So what we're doing is buying bottles of pills from a bunch of different people and moving 'em down the road to Lewiston. Voila, everyone's happy."

"Everyone?"

"The ones in the operation, at least. Plus we pump cash into the local economy."

"Really?"

"Yeah dude. Who do you think our independent contractors are, anyways? Mostly old people on fixed incomes who can really use the help."

"What about that fella at Furman's? He's not old."

"Jimmy? That's one of Richard's cousins who lives in Canada. Since he works at Furman's, he walks across the border almost every day. Border guards don't ever search him, so he smuggled a bottle of 50 Oxycontins. Those pills came from another one of Richard's Canadian cousins. She's real broke."

"Oh."

"Like Richard's auntie, like many of the people we're getting pills from, collecting a disability check or welfare. Which don't hardly amount to much. Especially with the price of everything going up." He shook his head and sighed. "Gonna be tough for some of these people next winter, that's for sure. But if we can get a deal going, monthly, that would help out a lot of people. Five hundred bucks goes a long way in Washington County, especially if you're used to being poor."

"Whoa." I didn't know what to say. Things were so bad in Washington County that old people were selling their painkillers just to survive? "Yikes."

"Now Richard's auntie, she'll go and spend that money, or most of it, at the slots in Bangor. She calls it 'investing.'" He made quotation marks in the air and laughed. "I'm not judging her. Lots of times, she comes home with a couple thousand bucks."

"Wow."

"In the long run, she's winning. On slots. I know that it sounds strange when I say we're really helping these people. But it's true. It's money, right? They need money and have never had it. Never will, unless something freaky happens like they win the lottery." He sighed. "Or get a settlement like I did. Lots of people round here think I'm lucky." He looked at me. "And I am. Lucky to be alive. Lucky to have the Grange. Lucky to be chilling with Savannah and Missy. Dude," he looked at me. "I am one lucky man. I credit the power of positive thinking."

"Great."

"But some people around here think I'm lucky because I got the settlement. They say the injury and time in the hospital was worth it. And if there is pain, they say, there are some pills to fix it."

"Do you get pills for your pain?"

"Not anymore," he said, nodding. "But I used to. Wish I still did, 'cuz I'd move 'em all down to Southern Maine and make loads of extra cash." He twisted and cracked his neck again. "No pain, these days, thanks to two things. Yoga and trigger points. You know about it?"

"I know about yoga." Monica did yoga every day. In my mind's eye, I saw her stretching and reaching on the blue mat. Then my brain picture shifted to Buffy doing her x-rated stretches in front of the TV. Then Missy's cute smile popped into my head. Then back to Monica. I felt terribly guilty again. Had to get Missy out of my mind. "What's the other stuff?"

"Trigger point therapy."

"Nope, never heard of it."

"Well, it's a way of massaging pain away. Trigger points are predictable spots in your muscles that get tense and freeze up after an injury or trauma. You massage the knots out so your muscle fibers return to normal and stop causing the pain. This is hard medical science, not mumbo jumbo. You should look it up. Especially if you're in pain."

"Raking blueberries is killing my fucking back..."

"Remind me when we get back to the Grange. I've got a good book that might help you get better."

"Really?"

"Yep. Teaches you how to work on yourself using a tennis ball. Great book. Changed my life."

"Yeah, I'd love to borrow it."

"Borrow it? Dude, you can look at it and get your own copy. That's my own personal copy."

"Sorry," I said and remained silent for a minute. "But you still snort pills?"

"Yeah, that's recreational use. Not a daily event. Last night was a special occasion. Makes a difference. Not like a pillhead. Some pillheads snort a dozen or more pills day. Imagine that. I mean, how do they ever get anything done?"

"I don't know."

"You don't know what?" Richard asked, coming up along my side of the truck, stealthy as a cat and surprising both Ganeesh and me. "What are you losers talking about?"

"Wondering why it was taking you so fucking long, motherfucker," Ganeesh said, leaning across the front seat. "Don't you realize we got work to do?"

"Yeah, well I couldn't figure out a way to tell my probation officer to stop talking 'cuz I gotta hook up with my homeboys and get some," he looked at me, "vitamins."

"Ben is on-board," Ganeesh said. "He's officially our driver, on the payroll and everything." He pointed at Richard. "You gotta take care of half his salary."

"How much?" Richard asked.

"One-fifty each," Ganeesh said. "This white man drives a hard bargain. C'mon, get your ass in the back of the fuckin' truck. We got errands to run."

Hours later, I was alone back at the campsite. The errands were uneventful. From what I could tell, Ganeesh's money paid for the pills and most of the suppliers were related to Richard. I also observed that Ganeesh was the boss and Richard was the bitch. I dropped them off at the Grange because they said they had some work to do. Savannah would give Richard a ride home. My services wouldn't be needed.

Finally, some time on my own. As I built the fire that would become the coals that cooked my steak dinner, I made a mental to-do list. Call Monica. Shower. Smoke the huge joint Richard had given me. Chill out, alone, and consider the events of the day. Get a good night's sleep so I could rake some serious money on Saturday.

I grabbed my towel and last change of clean clothes from the tent and headed down the path, praying the church was empty. Stopped in the vestibule and put my ear up against the little glass window in the center of the front door and heard the blare of television. No matter. I had to call Monica and I needed a shower. After taking a final deep breath of clean country air, I knocked three times loudly, paused, then opened the door.

Richard's father's recliner was empty, but his TV broadcasted a baseball game at full volume, competing with Buffy's TV in the other corner playing the operatic soundtrack of an old Bugs Bunny cartoon. The stench of cigarettes, spilled beer, burned food, rotten garbage and the distinct odor of urine, pet or otherwise, wafted across the big room. The fetid air, pushed by the slow, lazy, ceiling fan, enveloped me as I entered.

No sign of life. No Captain or Buffy or Jazz. No dog or old man. Coast clear, I headed for the phone and dialed my home number without being discovered. With the first ring, a strange noise blasted from the other side of the rear dividing wall of the church. Sounded like a mix of squeal and grunts, interrupted by the flush of a toilet. Ring-ring. Another flush. Ring-ring. Answering machine. Hearing Monica's voice made me sad, lonely and guilty. She and the dogs were probably walking on the shore path. How I wished the harvest was over and I was home with them. The answering machine beeped.

"Hey babe. It's me. Sorry, I missed you. I miss you so much. Everything's fine out here. Hope your poem is going well." I paused for a second. "I just want you to know that I love you very much..."

"*Who the fuck are you?*" Boomed a voice from behind me. Richard's dad appeared in the doorway leading to the bathroom. Fat, old and bald, dressed in pin-stripped pajamas and using a cane, his beard was like Santa's, only longer, food-stained and matted. "*What the fuck are you doing in my house?*"

"Uhh, uhh," I covered the phone's mouthpiece with my hand, trying to protect Monica from the shouting. "I'm a pal of Richard's. I'm, ah, raking berries and camping out..."

"*Are you one of those cocksucking hippies?*" He pointed his cane at me. "*Are you? Are you?*"

"Everything's fine," I repeated into the phone, trying to ignore the old man. "I'll give you a call tomorrow. Gotta go. We'll talk tomorrow..."

"*Who the fuck do you think you are? You fucking commie bastard!*" the old man screamed. "*Get out! Out! Out!*"

"*Love you,*" I yelled into the phone and hung up.

"*Who the fuck are you?*" The old man took a couple steps more towards me, swinging his cane like a baseball bat. "*Get the fuck out of my house before I kill you!*"

Drunk and feeble, he normally wouldn't be considered a threat. But he had me cornered. If he connected with the cane, I'd be hurting for days.

"*Pa!*" Buffy screamed from the front door and raced across the room. "*He's a friend of ours!!!!*"

"*Fucking hippie!*" the old man hollered. "*Hippie!*"

"*Pa.*" She grabbed the lapels of his robe. "*Leave him alone!*"

Buffy's touch distracted her father and gave me the opportunity to escape. By the time Buffy called out to me, I was halfway across the room.

"*Ben!*" she hollered. "*Wait for me!*"

I waited on the other side of the vestibule door. I needed fresh air, badly. Never would have expected such an attack. Ten seconds later, Buffy came outside.

"There you are," she said. "You okay? The old man didn't get you with his cane?" She grinned and the burn on her forehead oozed yellow pus. "Looks like he missed yah." She touched my arm. "No blood, far as I can see."

"I'm all right," I said, wishing I had a cigarette even though I hadn't smoked cigs in years. "I'm fine."

"Good," she said. "Where's Richard? I seen you come back, alone."

"Over at the Grange," I said. "I think Savannah is gonna give him a ride home."

"Listen, sorry about my dad going all crazy and shit on you." She sighed.

"He's bad most of the time, but some days are worse than others." She shook her head. "Thanks to 35 years of non-stop drinking. He's either drunk, asleep or crazy. Pick one. Or all three. Don't matter, they're all bad."

"Even sleeping?"

"Oh yeah, he can be an asshole. Sleeptalking. Hah." She pulled a cigarette from her pack. Took all my willpower not to beg for one. "Sleep-yelling is more like it. Sometimes the stuff he says is mean. And I wonder whether he's just being an asshole and faking it. But Richard's convinced it's real. Says it's Pa's 'unconscious' talking to us."

"Oh."

"I don't give a fuck." She lit her smoke. "Just wish he wasn't so mean."

"I'm sure. That sucks." I shook my head. "I feel sorry for you."

"Don't feel sorry for me, Ben Franklin." She laughed bitterly. "I'm all set."

"Good." I remembered the fire back at the campsite. "Well, I'll see you later."

"Where you going?"

"Back up to the campsite. Got to cook my dinner."

"Really?" She blinked her eyes up at me. Hopefully. Flirtatiously. "Aren't you gonna invite moi? I mean, I just saved your life. Besides, you abandoned me on the fields. I thought you guys were coming back to pick us up."

"Oh yeah. Well, Richard had a change in plans. Uhh." I didn't want her coming to the campsite. I wanted to be alone and enjoy my steak. "I really don't have that much food."

"That's okay," she said. "I just want to hang out with you."

"Where's Captain?"

"Off with Jazz somewhere." She gestured to the other side of the property that I hadn't even visited, yet. "He's all right." She laughed. "Sounds like you're afraid to be alone with me. Don't worry, I won't bite." She laughed again. "Unless you like being bitten."

She stared at me hopefully.

An hour later, Buffy had eaten a quarter of my steak and half of the potato salad from Richard's cooler marked "Food." We both drank a couple Buds out of the "Beer" cooler. Against my better judgment, I shared the joint with her and laughed at more of her funny stories about people and places I didn't know and didn't have a desire to see. Despite a warning in my brain, as dusk approached, I didn't tell her to leave.

In the fire light, she looked great. The flickering shadows danced on her face, hiding her crossed eyes and forehead burn. Her outfit: short shorts and a tight tee-shirt. Pert nipples and no bra. Bare legs and bare feet. In the semi-darkness, she was hot. And she knew I was checking her out.

"Ben," she said, taking a step closer and putting her hand over my heart. "I know you want to fuck me and I know you've got a nice cock."

"How do you know that?" I didn't step back from her touch. I should have, but I didn't.

"In the shower, silly. Remember?"

"Yeah."

"So you want to fuck me?"

I moved away to stoke the campfire. To avoid answering her, I added a couple of logs, then two more. The dry wood caught quick. The blaze roared higher. I poked the coals with a long stick. She took a couple steps closer and grabbed my wrist. Through the wood smoke, I could smell her fragrance.

"After the other day, when I saw you in the shower, I wondered how you'd fuck me with your big cock." She gave a quick laugh. "If I let you, that is. Would it be from behind?" She turned around and in the glow and spark of the fire, she shook her little ass, then bent over and like a stripper stared at me from between her ankles. "Or," she said, turning and grabbing my right wrist, this time with both hands. "Would you want me to ride on top? Riding you so you can play with my nice titties while I rub my clit. Your huge cock in my tight cunt." She let out a tiny moan and lightly scratched my forearm. "Don't that sound like fun?"

"Yup," I squeaked, harder than a rock. She was a well-written letter to a porn magazine. "Yes, it does."

"Or I could suck you off and let you cum all over my face. Or my titties. Or in my mouth. I'd swallow all your cum, if that's what you wanted." She nodded and licked her lips. "C'mon, baby."

"Okay." I'm embarrassed and ashamed to admit I wanted Buffy so much, at that particular moment, slightly drunk and very high, sitting atop a small hill in Washington County in the flickering shadows of a roaring blaze. On the verge of exploding, I desperately needed relief. From Buffy. I reached for her. "Let me fuck you from behind."

"Oh, not so fast, you dirty old man." She took a step away from me. "Get me a couple Oxys and I'll do anything you want."

"What?" I asked, incredulous. "A couple what?"

"A couple Oxys." She nodded vigorously. "You can't expect a girl to give away her body. For nuthin'. I want a couple pills. Two forty migs or one 80. Then you can do anything you want."

"I don't have any pills," I said, suddenly very confused. "I can't..."

"Oh come on Ben," she sneered. "You and I both know Richard and Ganeesh have something going. Word's out across Washington County that those boys are on the prowl. Buying up all the Oxy that's out there."

"I don't know what you're talking about."

"Come off it, Ben. I'm not a fucking idiot. Those boys can't drive and yet somehow they're buying pills from people all over the county. My auntie told me a guy with a big blue truck brought Richard by her house so he could buy her pills. Can't keep a secret, no way, not 'round here."

"Really Buffy, I don't know what you're talking about." My erection softened.

"Ben, don't lie to me. Get me the pills and I'll bring you around the world." She leaned forward, kissed me and pushed her tongue into my mouth, then pulled back just as quick. My hardness fully returned. "Oh, baby," she said, "I'll make you feel so good."

"OK! OK!" I blurted out. Desperate. Re-aroused. Weak. "I'll get you two pills tomorrow. Tomorrow I'll get you two pills." I reached for her. "But let me fuck you..."

"No way." She slapped my hand away with a giggle. "I don't front nobody." She pointed at me. "Ben Franklin, get me a couple pills and you can do anything you want. Anything at all."

She turned around, walked over to the cooler and helped herself to another beer. She opened the can and took a tiny sip, considering me across the distance.

"I'd really like to fuck you. You're cute," she said, almost timidly. "But if a girl like me gave it away, I'd get a reputation." She took another sip from the can. "Thanks for the beer and the pot. Get me the two pills and tomorrow night," she giggled softly, "we'll go around the world. And back." She smiled. "Okay?"

Not waiting for my answer, she turned and started down the path. I exhaled. Fuck, I thought, deciding to rake blueberries was a big mistake.

Buffy was gone, but my erection remained. I grabbed another can of beer, took a sip and put it on the picnic table. Reached overhead, stretched, then tried to touch the earth with my palms. Then stood straight. I couldn't stop thinking about Buffy, about what she promised. Around the world. And back. My erection, unbelievably, got harder and harder.

What was the chance I could score a couple pills? Tell Richard I needed 'em so I could fuck his sister? Or was there something I could say to Ganeesh? Or was there a way I could steal them? What the fuck was I thinking? Stealing from drug dealers who threatened to kill me if I misbehaved. I shook my head. Who was I turning into?

Didn't matter. I needed those pills. I needed to fuck Buffy. I looked into the darkening woods around me, unzipped my jeans and began to masturbate. Closed my eyes and thought of that dirty girl, bent over, offering her sweet ass. I arched my back and my feet, then came. Quick. Like a shot.

And just as quickly, the post-ejaculation remorse began and my feet grew incredibly sensitive. Walking on the earth felt like walking on a bed of nails. I was overcome with waves of disgust. Ugliness and revulsion. Guilt and regret. Sorrow. Why was I sinking so low and acting so depraved? And why did my feet suddenly hurt so much?

At the Movies

My slumber was full of nightmares. The bad dreams awoke me three times with baths of cold sweat. All were variations of a theme: my sexual antics. All ended with Monica discovering my bad behavior. With each session of sleep, I cheated on her again. Which left me exhausted and sullen when I woke for the final time around seven.

My feet hurt like a son-of-a-bitch. Shooting pain. Stabbing. Specifically, the soles, which throbbed. For a minute or two before getting up, I rubbed them gently, then stood and felt an intense shock jolt my ankles, shins and calves. Overwhelming pain, almost. I let out a long moan.

The events of the night before were enough to make me wish I had never signed up for the blueberry harvest. Made me wish I never moved Down East, even. My remorseful behavior filled me with shame. Number one problem, of course, was the betrayal of the woman I loved. Number two problem was Missy and Buffy, plus the unacknowledged trouble that lurked within my new part-time job as a drug mule. Under the light of the new day, the deal didn't look so great. I felt like a fucking idiot. Risking so much for three hundred bucks. And yet the only other legit way for me to make cash, not connected to the drugs, was the back-bending labor of the harvest, which resulted in endless pain.

Not many options, that's for sure. Definitely not what I imagined after leaving Portland. And as my list of sins grew longer and longer, my angst grew. Especially troubling was my behavior with Buffy. Had I actually promised her two pills in exchange for sex? What was wrong with me?

We didn't get to the fields until nine because everyone moved in slow motion. Took awhile for Richard to get going. Rounding up Buffy, Jazz and Captain took even longer. Mary's Market, for coffee and donuts, also took forever because it was Saturday morning and the place was packed. I put six dollars in the tank, leaving me with less than a buck and a heavy sense of dread. I probably had enough gas to get back and forth from Richard's to the fields for another couple days, but not enough fuel to get back to Goose Island. I needed cash, quick.

When we finally arrived at the bucket pile, Larry was waiting and looked pissed.

"What the hell?" He scowled at me and pointed at Richard. "I thought you guys were coming back yesterday and were gonna rake until dark. Listen, I get enough trouble from pillheads and crybabies to take any shit from you fellas." He removed his hat. "You're acting like slacker high school boys. Yesterday was a great day for raking and you blew it. And today, you shoulda been here at dawn. But you weren't. And if I wasn't so goddamn desperate, I'd send you home to teach you a lesson." He let out a long sigh and lit a smoke. "Should just hire me some Mexicans and wouldn't have to worry about nothing."

"No way Lar," Richard said, patting the boss on the back. "No worries. We're raking all day. And we're gonna get you more berries than you can sell. Sorry about yesterday, things got all fouled up. You know how stupid the state is. By the time I was finished at probation and the courthouse," he shook his head, "seemed like a waste of fuel to come back. And don't blame Ben. Ain't his fault. I totally screwed him over. He didn't know what to do. He wasn't gonna abandon me in Roosevelt."

"Yeah, well, please, no more fucking around. We gotta get these berries raked." He sighed deeply. "All right, you all go to the other side of that ledge." He pointed to a section beyond the trucks. "There's enough strips for everyone, all day. Real blue, too. So you better rake like machines, 'cuz we gotta make up for lost time. All that rain," he shook his head, "and all your time off."

"Yes, sir," Richard said with a mock salute with his rake. "We'll get some blue."

"I hope so," Larry said, walking toward the port-a-potty. "Gotta talk to a man about a horse."

"This is definitely my last blueberry harvest," Richard said, lighting a cigarette, after we'd been raking for 15 minutes. "Gonna use the money I make from the pills for a down payment on that land I told you about."

He wasn't raking very fast, either because of a hangover or because he wanted to talk with me. When he stopped for a smoke, I was just ten feet behind him. He'd raked a bucket and a half to my one, but I was doing okay for a newbie plagued by pain and suffering. Buffy and Captain, 50 feet behind us, were raking in a strip next to Hip-Hop. On the other side of us, Jazz and Peggy and some fella I didn't recognize took up three strips. They were at least 75 feet behind us. Was I faster and better than the rest of the gang? Or did they let us get ahead so they wouldn't have to put up with Richard? Didn't bother me, I didn't even want to see

Buffy, let alone talk to her.

"Great." Obviously, I wasn't returning next year either, no matter what. Not even considering the ill effects of my sins, the job sucked. My feet were killing me. And even though the strips were getting bluer and raking was getting easier, the potential to earn 12 to 15 bucks an hour, tops, for hard labor just wasn't worth it. Unless, of course, I had a buzz on. "Got any more of that speed?"

He reached into his fanny pack, then tossed me a small bottle. "You can have 'em," he said, "I'm all set."

"Thanks." Twisting off the lid, I counted at least a dozen tiny pills. Felt a rush of relief and a little bump of fear. Enough speed for a couple days, at least. And just enough, probably, to get me believing speed was a necessary part of this harvest. A scary thought, but not enough to stop me from shaking three pills out of the bottle. Into the mouth, quick, chased by a long sip of water. "Now I'm ready to rake some money."

We raked with no break for lunch. Normally, I would have collapsed due to starvation, but every time hunger pangs struck, I'd eat a little pill, and several handfuls of freshly raked blueberries, chased with lots and lots of water. Around two, Richard sparked a joint. Buffy, a hundred feet away, noticed and practically sprinted across the field in order to get in on the puffing.

"I swear, that girl's got a nose like a friggin' drug dog," Richard said, shaking his head and watching as his sister got closer. "But at least she's out here raking some money." He sighed and handed me the joint. "Suppose that alone is worth getting her high, just so she keeps on raking."

"This our lunch break?" Buffy asked, panting, out of breath from her dash across the strips. "Because I'm fucking starving. What's for lunch?" She looked at me. "Oh, I see you've already eaten." She laughed. "Ben Blue-Mouth, that's what we should call you."

"Hah," Richard laughed. "That's kinda of funny, Buffy. For you."

"How about Old Blue Face?" She smiled her crooked, toothy smile and reached for the joint. "Man, you are looking blue."

Richard laughed again.

"Old Blue Face," he laughed. "That's friggin' hilarious. Like they called Frank Sinatra 'Old Blue Eyes', they call you 'Old Blue Mouth'."

"Blue Face," Buffy said with a giggle and snort. Then she took another long hit off the joint. "His whole friggin' face is blue."

"What are you talking about?" Suddenly I was pissed. Hated being the butt of a joke, especially one I didn't understand. "What the fuck?"

"Dude," Richard said, "You've got the worst case of blue mouth I've ever seen. All over your cheeks. How many berries did you eat? A whole bucket?"

"Your forehead," Buffy said, laughing harder and pointing with the joint. "Your forehead is blue."

"Don't bogart the friggin' marijuana," Richard said, grabbing it. He puffed and puffed.

Buffy, seeing Richard was busy, held up two fingers and mouthed the words silently, "Two pills!" Then she stuck out her tongue and started licking her fingertips provocatively. She took three steps backwards and put the two fingers in her mouth and sucked them like a cock.

I turned away and grabbed the joint from Richard. Took a deep drag, trying to ignore Buffy. Didn't work. Fear and arousal, simultaneously. I looked at her again, watching as she thrust her fingers, in and out of her mouth while staring at me with her crossed eyes. My erection grew hard for her, all while wondering just how I was gonna be able to get two Oxycontin.

I cursed myself for being so weak. The answer was simple. Don't play her game. I slowly shook my head. Not gonna get her the pills. She'd have to find them somewhere else.

She uncrossed her eyes and pulled her fingers out of her mouth. I turned around. Richard was watching her.

"Buffy," Richard said, pointing at her. "What the frig are you doing?"

"Nothing," she said. "Just having a little fun with my fingers."

"You disgust me," he said, taking the joint back from me, intentionally skipping Buffy. "If Mom could see what a...what a," he stuttered, "skank you turned out to be, she would be so friggin' disappointed."

"Well Mom ain't here, so don't be getting all moral majority and shit." She looked at me. "He gets this way whenever anything sexual comes up. I think he's jealous. Jealous of the fact I slept with his girlfriend before he did."

"Shut up, Buffy." Richard shook his head. "You know what? No more weed. This joint is for me and Ben and you can't have any."

"Oh come on!" she whined. "Richard!"

He ignored her and puffed repeatedly. She stuck her tongue out at him and wiggled it for me. She sneered, held up two fingers, and walked away, slowly, back toward Captain and Hip-Hop, still a hundred feet behind, taking a bucket break.

Richard watched her and shook his head. "That girl is bad news. Just be aware of that. And I wish Captain wouldn't hang out with that Hip-Hop punk." He handed me the joint. About a third was left. "Finish it. I've had enough. I gotta get back to raking. Wouldn't want to set a bad example for the rest of these losers."

He bent over, grabbed his rake and started to sweep his strip with amazing speed and grace. I took a puff and looked around. Including myself and Captain, there were eight people visible in this section of field. And Richard was the only one actually bent over raking. Hip-Hop was sitting on a bucket listening to Buffy, probably bitching about us. Jazz and his pals were taking a smoke break and sharing a joint. No wonder Larry wanted to replace the locals with migrant workers.

After a long drink of water, I stretched toward the sky, then bent with my rake and swiped at the berries. Immediately felt the familiar stabbing in my back. Followed a second later by sharp pulses, starting from the soles of my feet, working up the shinbones and calves, and pulsating in both knees. From there, the pain radiated upwards, through my thighs, until it crashed into the pain descending from my lower back.

I stood up straight and maybe a quarter of the pain stopped. But then my right arm, my raking arm, began to throb and pulse. Then my fingers, on the right hand, went numb and I dropped the rake. For a second, I wondered if a stroke or heart attack was approaching, right there on the fields.

What if I died while raking? Monica would definitely learn of my sins. She'd have to deal with Richard and Buffy to get my stuff back. Probably meet Ganeesh. And what if Missy came to the funeral?

If I died and Monica learned the truth about my infidelity, she would forget we were kindred spirits. She'd ignore the fact that were cut from the same cloth, with the same hopeful dream of living off the land, with pigs, chickens and goats. She'd remember me as a no-good philanderer and druggie. A failure at music, a failure at raking blueberries and a failure as a husband.

Obviously, the potential pain and suffering wasn't worth the lousy 14 cents a pound. The potential 300 bucks was not worth the gamble of being a drug courier. All the bullshit with the ladies wasn't worth the stress. Standing there, high and alone in the middle of my strip, I decided I was done and finished with the harvest. Done with Richard. No one could stop me. Not like I owed anyone an explanation. Except Monica.

So here was my new plan, conceived and hatched in a millisecond. I'd pretend I needed to use the port-a-potty. Instead, I'd drop my rake into the back of Larry's truck, jump into Floyd, rush back to Goose Island and tell Monica the truth. Explain how the situation disintegrated so quickly. Let her know there was some involvement with some, for lack of a better word, shady people. I'd explain Ganeesh and the Grange and the girls. Of course, I couldn't, wouldn't, tell her about Missy and the blowjob. Or how Buffy thought I was gonna give her a couple pills in exchange for cheap casual sex. But I'd tell the truth about everything else and then we'd plan a way to survive the next month or two without starving.

This felt better. A weight was lifted from my shoulders. For a second or two, my back didn't hurt. Escape was the right decision. The only move. The situation, unchanged, would get worse. A quick exit was the only way back to normality. I'd soak and stretch, in my own bathtub, to get rid of the pain, then figure out a way to rebuild my marriage. And never cheat again. My devotion to Monica would grow stronger and stronger and someday, eventually, the guilt would disappear.

"Hey Ben," Richard called to me. He was already 20 feet ahead and had filled a bucket. "You are not gonna believe how blue your strip is." He pointed down and across the field to the distant treeline. "And it gets bluer and bluer. It's friggin' awesome. Gonna finally start raking some real money."

"Oh," I said. Not me. I was so outta there. In my mind, I was already on the road, hoping Floyd had enough gas to get home. "That's good."

"Oh yeah," Richard said, walking back towards me. "I forgot to tell you. Ganeesh said we're invited over for pizza night. Should be a blast, especially if we bring an icy cold case of beer. The girls really want you to come. Especially Missy. Gonna be a P-A-R-T-Y, if you know what I mean." He stood about ten feet away. Big grin on his face. Did he know about Missy and me? He lit a smoke. "A real party 'cuz it's Saturday night. We'll probably even take a snort or two."

"Yeah?" Who was I kidding? I wasn't going back to Goose Island. Floyd didn't have enough gas. And less than a buck in my pocket, no way near enough to buy the fuel to get home. Pathetically, I was counting on the three hundred from Ganeesh and Richard. Plus, the fields were suddenly looking blue, the color of real money. I could see it.

"Not to change the subject," I said, "but I'm almost broke. Ganeesh said you guys were gonna pay me for driving. What's the chance I could get some of that cash today?"

"No problemo," Richard said. "Tonight, at Ganeesh's. How much we paying you? Two hundred?"

"Not two." My mood shifted. Happy and glad, knowing I'd see Missy again. I took the pill bottle from my pocket and popped two more. "Three hundred. One-fifty from each of you."

We arrived at the Grange a little after five p.m. My feet were killing me. A constant pain, almost unbearable, except for knowing I made about a hundred bucks raking. My best day yet, though my feet hurt more now that I was sitting on the couch, feet up on a hassock, drinking a beer and smoking a joint with Ganeesh and Richard.

The girls were nowhere to be seen. Richard was telling us a story about fucking his old lady the night before she went to jail and how he couldn't wait until she got out. And how he hoped jail didn't turn her from bisexual to full-fledged lesbian man-hater.

"What's the matter, bro?" Ganeesh asked, handing me the joint. "Something wrong?"

"My feet hurt like a son-of-a-bitch." I moaned. "Don't know how I made it through the day."

"Sheer will and stupidity," Richard said. "And because you're friggin' desperate."

"I'm not desperate."

"Dude," Richard pointed at me. "You've said it a million times already. That you are desperate. And you're always complaining. 'Bout this or that." His voice went high, like a girl's. "My feet hurt. My back hurts. My vagina hurts."

Ganeesh started to laugh. I laughed too. Richard wasn't funny, but laughing was easier than acting pissed. By now, I despised Richard, but my current situation was so dependent upon him. For weed. For a place to stay. For money. Couldn't tell the idiot to fuck himself. Not if I wanted to get paid for driving. Not if I wanted to rake some money and finish the harvest. And not if I wanted to visit the Grange.

"Seriously Ben," Ganeesh said, after he stopped laughing. "Where exactly does it hurt the worst?"

"On the bottom."

"You said that already. Where on the bottom?" Ganeesh walked over to the bookcase near the kitchen. "Because maybe we can cure you."

"With a snort?" I asked, almost too hopefully. "Would that help my feet?"

"Not a snort." Ganeesh shook his head. "I told you. Pills only mask the pain. Doesn't get to the root of the problem. Pills for party use only." He laughed. "Dude, I'm talking trigger point therapy."

He stood in front of me, holding a book. "You gotta buy your own copy." He nodded. "*The Trigger Point Therapy Workbook: Your Self-Treatment Guide for Pain Relief*," he read the title aloud. "By Clair Davies." He flipped through the pages. "This book saved my life." He paused. "This book, plus my daily yoga workout has made it so I'm relatively pain free." He shook his head. "Dude, if you only knew how much pain I was in." He sighed. "The fact is, I'm cured. Right, Richard?"

"That's right. He was crushed between two pens being towed to a salmon cage site. Would have killed a lesser man."

"Or paralyzed me," Ganeesh said. "Ugh! Paralyzed. Must fuckin' suck."

"Or paralyzed," Richard nodded, "a lesser man."

"My muscles had all sorts of injuries and the white doctor in his white lab coat didn't solve my problems." He grinned. "This book did."

So I sat on the floor. Ganeesh told me to take off my shoes and socks. When I did, he grimaced and backed away.

"Dude," he said, "you fucking reek. You ever wash your feet?"

"Yeah."

"Well, you never would know it." He shook his head. "Man, they stink. Maybe you should take a shower."

"I'd love to," I said especially embarrassed, knowing Missy would be showing up. "That would be great."

"Okay. You gotta show me where, exactly, your feet hurt."

"Everywhere."

"They can't hurt everywhere."

"They do."

"Seriously," Ganeesh said. "You need to be more specific. Top, bottom? Right, left? Arch or heel?"

I thought for a moment.

"Well," I said, after focusing on my feet for a moment. "I'd have to say that they hurt the most," I grabbed my right foot and pointed, "here, here and there."

Ganeesh looked at a chart in the book and then started flipping though the pages.

"A-hah," he said. "The Flexor Digitorum Longus. Totally makes sense. Says here can be caused by strenuous walking on uneven terrain." He put the book down. "Like blueberry fields, right? Okay, relax your leg."

I did as told and with his huge fingers, he started to poke and prod the flesh of my right calf, almost under my knee. Then he pressed hard.

"*Ahhhhhhhh*!" I screamed. "*Owwwwwwwwwww.*"

"Gotcha!" he said, smiling. "That's the spot, isn't it."

I nodded, unable to speak, tears cascading down my cheeks. The spot he touched fucking hurt. I mean, really fucking hurt. Incredible anguish. Bolts of pain shot down my leg and throughout my entire foot.

"See," he grabbed the book and showed me a chart on one of the pages. "Totally predictable locations of 'trigger points' when you can pin-point the muscular pain." He smiled. "Your muscle fiber is all knotted up. You gotta get the fibers to relax. To repair themselves. And you do that by massaging that spot on the back of your leg."

"But the pain is in my feet."

"Don't matter. Dude, remember anatomy class? It's all connected."

"So you're saying that spot you pressed is causing the pain in my foot?"

"Yup. So watch." He wrapped his huge hands around my lower leg and using his giant thumbs started to rub the painful spot on my flesh, slowly and deeply, toward my ankle. "Notice that I'm not rubbing back and forth. Just down and out then back to the top. You gotta massage in the direction of the fiber."

After the first half dozen strokes, the pain in my legs seemed to subside. Then like magic, it seemed, my foot didn't hurt. The relief I felt, though, was only in my right foot.

"What about my left foot?"

"Does it hurt in the same place?"

"Yeah, I guess so."

"Dude, I told you, you gotta know the exact spot." He pressed his fingers into my other leg.

"Owwww!" I screeched. "Motherfucker!"

"That's the ticket," Ganeesh said. "I'm gonna show you how to use your knee to massage that trigger point."

At this point, I was laying on my back, Ganeesh was on the floor, Richard kneeling next to us. Ganeesh lifted my left leg and placed the hurting spot of my left calf -- the trigger point -- on top of my right knee. Then the front door opened and the girls walked in. Missy saw us first.

"Oh my God, Savannah," she yelped. "Looks like the boys are gonna get it on. A three-way. Let me grab my camera so I can film this suck and fuck."

"Oh yeah," Savannah said. "Three boys. That's wicked hot."

"Too bad Richard's in it. Maybe I can shoot the film so his face doesn't show up." Missy paused. "Or his little dick."

"Screw you, Missy," Richard said, standing quickly. "Ganeesh was just teaching us some trigger point therapy."

"Sexy," Missy said, walking toward us. Then she stopped in her tracks. "What's that smell?"

"I don't smell nuthin'," Richard said.

"That's because you're an idiot," Missy said. "Smells like rotting flesh."

"That's Ben's feet," Ganeesh said. "Something awful, isn't it."

"Ganeesh," I said, struggling to get on my feet. "Please let me take a shower."

"Sure thing, dude," he said. "I'll lend you some clean socks and sweats if you want."

"Yeah, that would be good."

"And I'm gonna throw your socks in the burn barrel," he said. "The stench is ruining my appetite."

A couple minutes into the shower, while scrubbing and scouring my feet, there was a knock on the door and it opened.

"It's me," Missy said. "I gotta pee."

"Okay," I said. The sound of her voice stirred me. "How ya doing?"

"I'm fine," she said. "How are your poor feet?"

"Oh, okay, I guess. Hurt like a son-of-a-bitch."

"Trigger point therapy really works," she said, "so do what Ganeesh told you to do."

Over the sound of the shower, I could hear her pissing. The sudden intimacy surprised me. But Missy's presence was different than Buffy's invasion a couple days before. (Seemed like a month ago.) And I thought it was cool that a beautiful and smart female like Missy felt relaxed enough with me to urinate in my presence. Of course, two nights earlier, we'd been much more intimate.

Standing in the shower, I wondered if she was gonna try something. I'd have to resist. Even though I was totally attracted to her, the pain and suffering of the guilt hadn't been worth the fleeting pleasure of the orgasm she'd given me. Standing under the cleansing hot water, I experienced a rare moment of mental clarity: Missy and I could flirt and joke, but not have sex. That would be as much (or almost as much) fun without betraying Monica again. Once was enough.

"Thanks," she said. "I really had to go. Okay, I'll leave you alone now."

And she left the room.

I let out a long sigh. My erection was automatic. Insistent. Had to be dealt with. So I started to masturbate and, initially, conjured up Missy. Or I had wanted to. But instead, Buffy's tongue entered my mind. I squinted and shook my head, hoping her face would disappear and be erased, replaced by Monica or Missy. No such luck. The image of Buffy's tongue licking her two fingers made me cum. I shuddered and moaned as my ejaculate made its way down the drain. Immediately, I felt dirty and scrubbed myself, again, from head to toe.

When I got out of the shower, the Grange smelled of pizza with pepperoni. Everyone was hanging around the kitchen eating cheese and crackers and drinking red wine from a gallon of Gallo. The B-52s blasted from the stereo. Jenny, who'd kissed me three nights before, had arrived with another teenage girl while I was in the shower.

"Hi Ben," she said. "This is my friend Maggie."

"Hi Maggie." Another Goth girl. What was it with all the Goth kids in Washington County? "Nice to meet you."

"Hi," she squeaked. "I hear you play guitar real good. Do you know any of the Furs?"

"The Psychedelic Furs?"

"Yep."

"Maybe later." I smiled at her.

"Oh c'mon, Ben," Missy came over to me and wrapped her arm around my waist. "Will you play something now? Before dinner?"

"Please?" Jenny said. "Pretty please?"

"Oh all right." I smiled, loving the attention from this bevy. Made me feel special. "If you insist."

Heaven was the only song I knew by the Furs. I think it was from the movie *Pretty in Pink*, but I'm not sure. Regardless, I picked up the guitar and turned it into my own song, singing and making eye contact with each person in the room, even Richard. Everyone except for Missy. Then, when I was almost done, I stared at her. Intently.

And she mouthed, silently, "Thank you."

When I finished, the crowd went wild.

"Encore!" they shouted, "Encore!"

"Maybe later," I said. "My fingers are fat and sore from raking."

Just then, the oven timer buzzed.

"Pizza time," Ganeesh announced.

On the counter was a stack of mismatched plates, a huge bowl of salad and three huge pizzas. Self-service. One veggie. One pepperoni. One with everything. There was joking and laughing, but soon all mouths were focused on the food. Delicious. Ganeesh made the dough, he said, three days before, using his bread machine. And the sauce was from scratch.

"I use canned tomatoes," he said. "But everything else is fresh."

Missy sat next to me, real close, at the big table. Could feel her heat. Halfway through the meal, her leg touched mine. Electricity. Despite masturbating 20 minutes earlier, I was aroused. My brain vowed not to fool around with Missy. Flirt, yes. Sex, no. No sex. No matter what.

My body, however, had a different plan. And my borrowed sweat pants made my erection stand out. Literally. Luckily, no one was sitting under the table.

After a couple glasses of wine and two huge blunts, Ganeesh and Richard started playing *Grand Theft Auto* on the Nintendo. Jenny and Maggie were painting intricate designs on Savannah's arms with a henna paste. I watched for a couple minutes until Missy grabbed my hand and led me to the back room. Again, we vaporized marijuana until the walls shook.

"Listen," Missy said. She was so beautiful and cool. Her red hair was tied back in a ponytail. She wore a *Clash* tee-shirt and a pair of faded and holey jeans. No shoes. Toenails painted bright yellow. Cute and sexy. Yet innocent. "I need some help. From you."

"From me?"

She nodded.

"Sure. Anything."

"Well, you don't know what I want you to do."

"I'd do anything for you." At that moment, I would have. High as a kite. Showered and well-fed. I was hers. Her wish was my command. Provided Monica never found out. "Seriously."

"You can't tell anyone what I'm about to tell you." She looked me in the eyes. "Especially Richard." She paused. "This is super top secret."

"I'd never tell him anything," I said. "Not a chance. I fucking hate him."

"Okay. I'm serious about how top secret this is. It's pretty hard for me to even to bring it up. I mean, we barely know each other," She sighed. "This is very sensitive information." She stopped to inhale from the vaporizer. "I'm about to launch a web site."

"Really? Cool." A top secret web site? "What kind?"

"Erotica," she said, matter-of-factly. "Short films. Three to five minutes. Just long enough for the viewer to achieve orgasm."

For several seconds, I was quiet. Surprised silence.

"We're calling it Philter Films. Philter with a P-H."

"Oh."

"Do you know what 'philter' means?"

"I guess not. I mean, I know filter with an F."

"A philter is a magical potion." She grinned. "A potion that causes a person to fall in love."

"Really? Didn't know that." Was I in love with Missy? Felt like it, especially sitting next to her on the couch, feeling the glow of her body, as she described her secret. "Cool."

"Philter Films is dedicated to making classy erotica, not the run-of-the-mill 'cum on the girl's face' movies." She laughed. "Not that there's anything wrong with that."

"Right." I laughed, shifting my position on the couch, trying to cover up my erection. Damn sweat pants. "Interesting."

"We'll probably launch in November." She nodded. "Just getting the details worked out on the servers and all the technical mumbo jumbo. The site design is almost finished. And I've got eight films done. Probably have two or three more by the time we launch."

"Wow, never would have guessed it."

"We'll release one film a week. That gives us a couple months buffer for providing the content. I've got a whole bunch of girls who like making these movies. Members, of course, can watch each one as many times as they like for a monthly fee. And we'll release trailers to the free sites. Dangle the carrot, so to speak. But there's one problem. Soundtrack."

"Soundtrack?"

"Yes, the soundtrack." She nodded. "See, I was hoping to use certain songs with the movies. But I was pretty naïve. Turns out licensing fees for the Internet would have cost way too much. If they'd even license the music for erotica." She sighed. "So then I thought one of my pals from school who is an excellent musician would do it for me. But during last semester, right around finals, she had some sort of religious experience." Missy shook her head. "Became a hardcore Christian. Big surprise. Because the year before, she was all sexed up and fucked and sucked everyone. But when I showed her one of the movies and asked her to create some music for it, she was absolutely horrified. She won't tell anyone, though, because she thinks I'd tell people about her secret Adderal addiction. I wouldn't, of course, but I'm letting her think it, just so she doesn't blab that I'm making 'dirty pornos.'" She moaned and shook her head. "I hate that word. 'Pornos.' So lame."

She put her hand on my knee and looked into my eyes.

"That's why I was so excited to hear you sing and play guitar. Obviously, you're a real musician." She smiled. "I was like, 'Ben could do the soundtrack, no problem.' Savannah thinks so, too."

"Thanks." I shook my head. "Really, I'm at a loss for words."

"Don't need any words. Just music." She laughed. "Seriously, I already know the type of song I want. I'd show you a movie and tell you the music I was thinking of, then you do whatever you want. You play keyboards?"

"Yeah, I know my way around 'em."

"Drums?"

"I've got this cool little jembe."

"Hmm, that might work." She got up from the couch. "Can I show you one of the movies?"

"Yes. Please."

Over at the Mac, she clicked on a file. The words "MASSAGE WITH HAPPY ENDING" filled the full screen. She gestured to me.

"Come closer," she said. "All of these films are intended to be viewed on the computer."

The first shot was of an all-white room, empty except for a massage table covered in a black sheet. Interesting overhead angle. Shot from either a tall ladder or a camera mounted on the ceiling. Like a security camera, almost, but crisp digital clarity and excellent composition.

A door opened and a guy walked in. Huge. Muscular. Brown. Took me a couple seconds, because you couldn't see his face or hair, but I could tell it was Ganeesh. The lighting was natural and from above. The camera work was awesome. Slow and steady, the tight frame showed his feet, then his lower leg. The camera moved to his ass and lingered for a second or three, until the shot shifted, backed away to capture him climbing onto the massage table, stomach down. Door opened again. A tall woman with jet black hair entered, dressed in white like a nurse. A very sexy nurse. Again, no face, but interesting details. Legs, in white fish net, that seemed to go on forever. The camera focused on her cleavage, then a close-up of her lips. So far, 30 seconds, no sex, and I was aroused. Doubly so when I realized the nurse was Savannah. Viewers couldn't be 100 percent positive, though. The arty shots, the black wig and close editing protected her identity.

The lens followed her oiled hands as they slowly stroked the man's neck, then kneaded his shoulders. Unhurriedly, her hands snaked their way down his bronzed back and spine. Camera zoomed in on her index finger touching a star-shaped scar on his lower back. She traced it, gently, with her fingertip, then pressed. Hard. The frame jumped to the man's quivering lips. Back to the female lips. No sound, but her message was clear. Turn over.

Until this point, the pace was quite slow. Measured. Too slow, almost. But when he flipped over, everything went high-speed. Her hands. His cock, juxtaposed to shots of innocuous body parts. His fingers clenched the table. Her knees, slightly bent. A vein in his neck pulsed. Her ankle, pivoted. Mixed with shots of lips. Balls. Bare skin. Ears. A blue eye. A brown eye. Suddenly, the pace went even more frenetic. A quick series of shots, flashing most of the body parts we saw earlier mixed with the handjob. Then the film slowed for his orgasm. A geyser in slow motion. A pause, and then she rubbed the ejaculate into his skin, like lotion, massaging and stroking his cum into the flesh of his quaking hips and pulsing thighs.

Random shots again. Perspiration wet his upper lip. Her ached brow. He climbed off the table and the camera focused on his knees, then his feet. Slightly unsteady, he walked to the door and left. Back to the woman's lips. The camera lingered, until her head turned quickly. The camera jumped back. The door opened again. Feet again. Small feet. Tiny feet. Bright yellow nail polish. I turned and looked at Missy. She smiled and pointed at the screen. Now the camera was behind her. Her green robe, short and silky, fell to the floor as she hopped up onto the table. The camera shot from the side, the new woman laid on her back, head and face outside the frame. Invisible. Her body was perfection. My eyes were drawn, as the camera slowly zoomed, to her breasts. The masseuse's fingertips drew slow, leisurely circles around both alert nipples, then vanished. A spurt of white lotion creamed her breasts. And the masseuse's hands returned, slowly, gently, rubbing the line of ivory. The screen went black and a "Philter Films" logo – a simple heart with an arrow through it – appeared.

"Wow," I exhaled, finally remembering to breathe. My cock was rock hard. All alone, watching the film, I would have masturbated and not lasted the entire five minutes. "That was great."

"Thanks," she said. "Can you see why the soundtrack is important? Silent, the pacing is way, way off. But a soundtrack would tie it together. In my head, I hear the music."

"Really?"

"Yeah, the beginning is really slow, intentionally, you know, to set up a sense of the unknown. Of possible conflict." She closed her eyes. "I hear gentle and sparse guitar. A little piano. Almost random notes. Like some sort of avant garde new age music. But as soon as she orders him to flip over, it's almost like a dance beat. Hypno-trance. Something like 'Air' meets 'Fantastic Plastic'. Maybe with some of that jembe giving a back beat. Speed up the beat until he cums. Then silence, a beat then, a variation on the beginning theme, but maybe with some strings. Violin would be sweet." She opened her eyes. "Can you play violin?"

"I did when I was kid."

"Maybe the violin setting on the keyboards? Or would that be too cheesy?"

"Ahhh, not sure."

"So what do you think?"

"Ahhh," I paused. "About what?"

"All of this." She pointed at the computer monitor. "The films. The soundtrack. All of this."

"Love it," I said, grabbing her hand. "Really great. Real professional."

"Could you please do the soundtracks? I can pay you. Not a lot. A hundred bucks per film? Maybe more when the site takes off."

"Sure," I said, easily. "Sure. A hundred is fine."

Great. I'd committed to my second top secret project in two days. Now, instead of just being a blueberry raker, I was driving for a pill operation while writing and recording scores for porn. Erotica, I mean. Between the two gigs, that was $1,300. Not bad for Washington County. Under the table, too. Tax-free.

Of course, how would I explain either new job to Monica? The pill money was from the blueberries, I'd say. But the soundtrack work would be tough to keep secret. Would Monica understand that my watching these movies over and over and over was the only way to perfect the soundtrack? And what kind of lies would I have to spin in order for her not to suspect that Missy and I had been intimate?

"Would you like to see another film?"

"Sure."

"See why we want to keep this project a secret? Spent lots of energy figuring out ways to protect our identities without making it too apparent that's what we were doing. If word ever got out that we were making erotica, I don't know what would happen. Not good."

"I don't think anyone would be able to figure it out. I mean, only because I know about those two could I tell it was them." I pointed toward the door leading back into the big room. "But you're putting this on the World Wide Web." I paused for a second. "Besides, the regular viewer will be so enthralled, they probably won't even realize they don't know what the actors look like. And that's cool. If you were wondering about their identities, then maybe you'd think the actors were famous or something."

"Great. Some of that comes from the editing, but since I visualize the whole piece beforehand, the shots are pretty clean to begin with."

"Visualize?"

"Yup." She smiled. "Or fantasize it. Same difference." She touched my arm. "I watched the whole movie in my head before I even talked to anyone about making it. Long before I even picked up the camera to shoot the film, I've seen it. Came out exactly like I planned."

"Wow. Exactly? That's amazing."

"Well, when I saw it in my brain, I hadn't slowed down the cum shot. But once I had the actual shot and started fooling around with it, I couldn't resist. She pulled away just in time. And slowed down, his cock looks like a volcano." She giggled. "And behaves like one, too."

"I'll say."

"Would you jerk off to that movie?" she asked.

"Right now?" I asked, panic-stricken.

"No silly, not now." She slapped my forearm playfully. "If you were alone, at home, and you found yourself at the Philter Films web site."

"Oh yes, definitely."

"Great," she said. "Because guys like you are the target audience."

"Guys like me? Whaddya mean?"

"Middle-aged or older," she said. "Or almost middle-aged."

"Thanks a lot. I'm not even close to middle age."

"I'm not insulting you." She leaned against me. "I love older men. More dignified. Much more interesting and smart. More sophisticated than guys my own age. Without a doubt. Much more interesting. I thought I demonstrated that the other night?"

"Well, I don't consider myself middle-aged."

"I'm sorry, dear. It's a silly label, I know. How are old you, again?"

"Thirty-seven."

"Do you think you'll live until you're, let's say, 76 years old."

"If I make it to 76, I'd be psyched."

"Not to ruin your day, but you're halfway there. I guess that means you're in the middle of your life. Middle-aged."

I was quiet. Hadn't thought about it like that.

"Nothing wrong with getting older, dear. Better than not getting older."

"What do you mean?"

"Dying, silly."

"Yeah, I guess you're right."

"Don't let it bother you."

"Okay." But it did. Aging wasn't something rock n' rollers enjoyed contemplating because it always led to bouts of depressive self-doubt. "I won't."

"Think about it this way. I think you're wicked cool. And cute. If you were just some schmuck that Richard brought over, I'd barely give you the time of day." She smiled sweetly. "Let alone give you oral."

"Gotcha," I said. That lifted my mood immediately. "Thanks."

"Want to watch another film?" she asked. "Old man."

"Yes, please," I answered. "Young lady."

"For this film, I was thinking of horror movie music. Like a theremin. Do you have a theremin?"

"Ahh, nope. But a pal of mine down in Portland does. Maybe I could borrow it."

"That would be awesome. I love the theremin. Totally scary sounding. Foreboding." She smiled and bent over the keyboard, double clicking on another file. The screen went black. "Scary music until she starts masturbating. Or just before. Then something techno-punk. But I don't want to give anything away."

A thunderclap boomed from the computer and interrupted her.

The words "I'D BEEN HERE BEFORE" appeared on the screen.

"I've already added a handful of sound effects, plus a little natural sound. There's no dialogue in this one, either. So I thought the music could push the mood a little bit.

"Okay."

The first shot was a 15-second close-up of an attractive woman, looking vaguely Asian, with a bob of bleached blonde hair. Couldn't tell what she was doing, but there was a slight band of sweat on her brow, so you could assume she was doing something physical. Something sexual. The camera pulled back and revealed her rowing a white wooden rowboat. The sea was choppy, but she was getting closer to shore. In the next shot, she hauled the boat onto the beach and tied it to a tree, which allowed us to see her whole body. She wore high boots, a red mini-skirt and a white halter top. She was cold. The camera drew to a close up of her nipples strained against fabric. She looked up. The sky was looking dark and stormy.

In my head, I heard the theremin. From the computer, a boom of thunder blasted. On the screen, a long flash of lightning filled the frame.

"Wow," I said, looking at Missy. "That's awesome."

"Thanks." She smiled. "Watch the film, please."

The woman climbed the rocky path as the sea crashed against ledges below. At the crest of the hill, the camera jumped far, far back, to a mansion perched on the cliff. From this new distance, we watched the heroine walk towards house. The camera zoomed in carefully, slowly, so the frame was close-up when the woman knocked on the front door. So close we could see her fingernails, painted black and white. A beat, then thunder. She tried the doorknob. Unlocked. She entered the darkness within. More lightning. She lit a candle, yet the entryway was still dark. She climbed a winding stairway and the lightning flashed through a window. For a second, we saw her face. Not scared. At all. At the top of the stairs, she paused, then turned left and opened the first door. She entered the room and lit another candle. Then another. And another. A billiard room. She grabbed a bottle of booze off a side table, glanced at the label and took a tentative sip. Then a longer sip. She put the bottle down and racked the balls. The storm continued. She broke and shot. Various close-ups focused on her eye, aiming. To the bend of her back. The cue hitting a ball. Side view of her hot body. All bathed in the blue flash of lightning mixed with the flicker of candlelight.

"Wow," I said. "The lightning is great."

The clatter of the ball surprised me as it jumped off the table, landed on the floor and rolled away. The woman shrugged. With her empty hand, she grabbed the bottle and accidentally spilled booze on her hand that held the cue. She licked her fingers, slowly, with a long, luscious tongue. She licked the shaft of the pool cue. Suddenly, my cock was rock hard from those simple licks.

"Here's where the music changes." Missy grabbed my arm. "Techno meets hip hop and trance meets punk. I can hear it."

I nodded.

The frame switched to a different scene. Same girl. Broad daylight, but topless and sitting on the same pool table. A large black penis filled her mouth as she stroked her cunt. Her dark pubic hair was trimmed into a narrow line. Suddenly, another cock entered the frame. Took a couple seconds, but I recognized it, thanks to the earlier film. The Brown Volcano. Ganeesh. But then the frame jumped back to the stormy scene. Our heroine on the table, fingers glistening wet. The frame went back to broad daylight. The action grew hotter and hotter. I heard music in my head. Felt the beat as the pace grew faster. Close ups, juxtaposed between the solo and the threesome scenes. Her fingers probed herself. Rubbed her clit frantically, occasionally sliding into her sweet hole. Her tongue licked her lips. Her mouth sucked the boys. The camera worked from above. From below. From the side. Until they ejaculated, one after another, onto her breasts, turning her nipples white. Slick and dripping, she rubbed the cum into her skin, then licked her fingers.

Missy let out a short, approving moan.

"That still gets me," she said. "Every time."

Got me too. But I was unable to speak. Wouldn't have wanted to, anyway. Didn't want to miss the woman's orgasm. She came and came. The camera focused on her mouth. Her lips pursed, then opened widely. The camera jumped all around. Each erect nipple. Her pierced belly button. Her thigh. Her knees. Her fingers rubbed and brushed, back and forth across her glistening wet cunt. Quicker and quicker. Faster and faster on her clit, under the stripe of jet black pubic hair.

Then, the camera pulled back. Her spine arched and a solid stream of fluid came forth. Squirted from within her. Her moans, I could tell, were real. She panted. Moaned. Cried, almost. Louder and louder, just this side of screaming. I was confused. Was this urine? No matter. Turned me on. Big time.

"She's ejaculating. Squirting. That's female ejaculation. The secret nectar." Missy spoke in hushed tones. Almost reverent. "And I got it from three angles. Three cameras."

The frame finally rested on the woman's face. Rested on her smile.

The screen went black and the words "The Secret Nectar" appeared, lingered, then faded, replaced by the Philter Films logo.

"Wow," I said. "Wow. Wow. Don't know what else I can say."

"You don't have to say anything." She gently pressed her soft palm against my erection protruding hard, stretching against the borrowed sweatpants. "Enough proof for me. You liked it, I can tell."

"Loved it." I nodded. "I've never seen anything like it. Very, very hot."

"How about the music?"

"I could hear it. I know what to do." And I did. The film had its own pacing, a visual song. "I can hear the theremin. Even at the end."

"Really, Ben?" She clapped her hands together. "This is really great. The music will make all the films complete." She hugged and held me tight. "Dear, you are a lifesaver. Really and truly."

"Glad to help," I said. "Really glad."

"When?" she asked. "When can you have them done?"

"Uhhh." I had no idea. Suddenly, reality struck. Honestly, I had no idea when I was gonna return to Goose Island. No idea what I'd say to Monica to explain my new project. No idea how long it would take for me to write and record the music. "Jeez," I shook my head. This was the craziest situation. "I really don't know. Let me think about it."

"Okay," she released me from her hug and looked up at my face. "Can you give me a ballpark? A month? Two months?"

"Definitely within two months."

"All eight films?" she asked. Persistent. "Is that realistic?"

"If not eight, close to it." That was false confidence. A lie, perhaps. Really had no idea. "Damn close."

"OK," she said. "I can live with damn close." She hugged me tight again and looked up to me. Her lips pursed. Ready to be kissed. Needed to be kissed. I could not resist. All previous memories of guilt vanished. Fear of future retribution was non-existent. We kissed. Just for a couple seconds. Then she pulled back.

"Which film did you like better?"

"Jeez, I don't know. Both were really awesome. The first one was super-erotic and sexy. But the second one had more of a story. And great setting. Whose house was that?"

"A summer person's down in Roque Bluffs. We only shot the exteriors there. They didn't know, of course. They weren't home. The billiard room was here. Just moved the table into the corner. And the staircase is in a friend's house down the road. Separate locations, but I bring 'em all together during editing."

"Of course." I nodded. Had me fooled, though. "Came out really seamless. Excellent. And the actress, I gotta say, was wicked hot."

"You know who she is?"

"No," I shook my head. "Why would I?"

"Well, you've hung out with her a couple times."

"That's not Savannah." I was confused. "And it's not you."

"You gave her a ride home the other night." She pointed to the door back into the big room. "And ate dinner with her tonight."

"Jenny?" I gasped. "Jenny? Never in a million years. Never would have guessed."

"Amazing what a little eye makeup and wig can do, isn't it? Really fun for us, too. Everybody loves playing dress-up. Luckily, since costumes help protect our identities. Remember when you came over the other night and Ganeesh was wearing the fez and Savannah wearing a sari?"

"Yeah."

"Dress rehearsal and film test for our next movie. Checking on how the costumes will look on film. See if the disguise is good enough. I want these stories to be believable and unique. That's why Savannah is getting hennaed. When the sari comes off, her beautiful body will be covered with lines and squiggles and circles. Lovingly drawn by Jenny. *Oh my god*!" She suddenly yelped. "Damn-it!"

"*What?*"

"I should have made another film. A lesbian one. Jenny applying the henna and they end up getting it on. That would be so hot. Don't you think?"

"Yes," I said. "Yes." I was such a dirty middle-aged man. "Jenny. Wow. Isn't she just 16?"

"Seventeen, and she'll be 18 just after the movie appears on the 'Net. But no one is gonna know because she looks much older. Doesn't she?"

"I'll say. Didn't look like her at all."

"That's the point." She smiled. "I'm glad you think so."

"Fantastic. Everything was fantastic. The lightning was awesome. How did you get those shots?"

"I shot a lot of film during a storm last summer that I used for the sky shots of lightning. But the lightning in the house was from a photographer's strobe."

"Wow. Looked really cool."

"Thanks. The blue lights and candles and the off-camera lighting are tough to pull off, but once you know the tricks." She shrugged. "Just part of the wonder of digital filmmaking."

"You know," I said, "you're every guy's wet dream. Beautiful young pornographer."

"I'm not a pornographer," she said, indignantly, hands on her hips. "I'm an eroticist." She sighed. "I know it's only semantics, but a pornographer is a fat greasy guy with lottsa gold, smokes cigarettes and exploits the actors." She smiled and laughed. "I create erotica. Much much different. I tell stories intended to arouse and stimulate. I'm showing more than just the sex act. I'm creating the context for the sex act."

"Okay. Okay." I put my hands up. By this point, I knew I was in love with her. With her attitude. Her talent. Her beauty. And her sexual energy. "You're every guy's wet dream. Beautiful young creator of erotica."

"Thank you," she said wrapping her arms around me again. I hugged her back. "That's very kind of you to say."

We both laughed.

"Making movies isn't as exciting as it may look." She gazed up at me with her blue eyes wide. "I've got to stop the actors whenever I want to switch cameras or the angle. For instance, in Jenny's movie, I must have shot close to 30 minutes – with three cameras -- of her cock-sucking the boys. But in the movie, there's only a minute and half of blowjobs. Plus the cum shot. Which was tough to shoot, by the way. The boys wanted to cum. They both thought a 30 minute erection was too long. But shooting that much film meant every millisecond of the minute and a half blowjob is red hot. I think. And Jenny was exhausted. Her lips and mouth were wicked sore."

"I bet."

"But you'd never know it, because she's a great actor."

"Oh yes," I said, wondering what Missy thought of my erection pushing against her. "You're gonna be huge. The movies were awesome. Really sexy."

"Well, I think my timing is good. Perfect time to be in the business. The industry is totally changing."

"How?"

"Well, I bet you'll see the big studios suffering. There's so much free porn on the 'Net, consumers aren't gonna be buying DVDs. Not if they can get enough on-line jerk-off movies for free."

"Oh."

"I'm focused on the niche of female-produced erotica. Which isn't as widely available on the web. Plus, I'm in charge of my own empire. If it weren't for digital video and streaming Internet, I'd never be able to generate and distribute original content. Traditional filmmaking costs would have killed me. Thanks to the 'Net, very little advertising. Mostly through word of mouth. Let consumers know about us through erotic blogs and e-zines and the content we put up on the free sites. You haven't even seen any of the fetish films yet."

"Fetish?"

"The one I'm most proud of is practically innocent."

"How?"

"Very original. No sex, just young-looking females, naked, using hula hoops and pogo-sticks and trampolines."

"Hmmm..."

"I bet that film is gonna be a hit. In fact, if we get as popular as I think we're gonna be, we'll probably even generate revenue through selling ad space on our site."

"Good idea."

"This girl Lana, a friend of mine who grew up in Perry, has her own web site. She lives in Bangor now and she's making big bucks. Thank goodness for PayPal. She has less than a thousand subscribers, but they're paying 10 bucks a month, so she's rich. She makes videos that cater to her clients' likes. On her web site, she posts possible scenarios and everyone votes. Then she films the most popular ones."

"Cool."

"They're okay. Not narrative-based. More of the bright lights, jerk-off porn variety. Her blowing five guys. Fisting. Public sex. Extreme dildos." She nodded. "I prefer hot sex with a narrative."

"Me too."

"But Lana showed me how the 'Net is the best distribution network ever. Plus, she's gonna let all her subscribers know about our launch. So I know we're gonna succeed. Since we'll be selling the films via download, no duplication costs. And the consumer is happy with the one-click shopping. Like Amazon. com. Instant grat." She smiled up at me. We'd been holding each other for awhile. "I love gratification, instant or otherwise."

"Me too."

For a second, we just stared. Then, kissed. And kissed. Harder. And harder. Until she stopped and took a couple steps backwards. We both needed to catch our breath.

"I'm really excited about you doing the music. I hope you don't get bored."

"Not likely." I wondered how many times I'd have to watch each film in order to complete the soundtrack. "Can I ask you a question?"

"Sure."

"Do the films still turn you on?"

"Only certain shots," she nodded. "But for the most part, I've seen the footage way too many times during editing to get aroused. But I do get turned on by watching people watching the film. Like when you were watching. I could tell you liked it. From your face and your bulge," she said, touching my crotch again with her right hand. "There is one film that always turns me on." She laughed. "A private picture, not a 'Philter Film. Not gonna share this with the general public."

She walked over to the keyboard and clicked on a folder.

"Orgasa-pic." She scrunched her nose. "The name is corny, but don't blame me. That's what Savannah called an early version of this and it stuck. The film just gets longer and longer. This version is just under four minutes. Added some new stuff," she smiled at me, "yesterday."

The screen was black. A slow beat of a bass drum came from the laptop

"Since I'm not planning to release this commercially, I'm using *Where Did Our Love Go* by 'Soft Cell' as the soundtrack."

Then pictures appeared. Still shots of many, many humans. The focus was on the mouth. Male mouths. Female mouths. Various colors and lighting. Some looked like they'd been altered by Andy Warhol. Some with the soft Vaseline lens of a Penthouse photo shoot. Others with the crisp focus of an Avedon portrait. Each image flickered on screen for three or four or five seconds, before another appeared.

Worked really well with the music. The beat of a drum, the rattle of the high hat and tambourine. A set of keys playing a smooth baseline. Then a second keyboard joined the party, going up and down the scale with a techno tempo. Simultaneously, a still shot of Missy appeared and lingered. The second keyboard started another set of scales and the image went to movement. Turned into a motion picture. Her mouth moved. Her lips parted and formed an "o". Her tongue flickered. And then the screen turned into a kaleidoscope of sex. Four, six, eight images, all in motion, of different mouths, faces, eyes, breasts, nipples, cocks, cunts, toes, all at the point of erectness or orgasm. A cornucopia of sex. Then full frame shots of males and females in obvious states of ecstasy. Hot. Hot. Hot.

When the words "burning yearning" came around for the second time, my own face startled me. My own mouth, on screen, was wide and tall. A vertical hole. Looked like I was screaming. Looked like I'd just been punched in the stomach. The camera zoomed out, but stopped, above my waist. And since my shirt had stayed on during the filming, it would have been tough to know I'd just orgasmed. Seeing myself, without the proper context, I appeared to be either in pain or frightened. Didn't look like I had just experienced the best blowjob of my life.

Then it was another slideshow of mouths, until the music started to fade and Missy appeared on the screen, again. Cumming. Her face almost filled the frame. Seemed to be laying on her bed and holding the camera with one hand. When the lens zoomed in and focused on her eye, she blinked and the screen went black.

For several moments, neither of us spoke. The film was so unstaged. Vulnerable. Erotic. Sexy. Real. To say my cock was hard is an understatement. Missy was also aroused. Her lips were wet and her eyes were soft and wide as she took my hand.

"Wow!" I said. "That was intense."

"C'mon dear. On the couch," she said, pulling me toward her. "And I promise I won't bring the camera."

We laughed. Five seconds later we were horizontally entwined. She atop of me, her lips on mine. Kissing. Touching. Exploring. Her tongue teased and probed my mouth. Then, she pulled back and rolled off, but was still sitting on the couch.

"I like you," she said.

"I like you, too," I answered. Though the truth, I think, was that I loved her. "A lot."

"Are you sure you want to do this?" she asked. "I mean, for me, this is casual. I don't want you to get upset."

"I won't," I said, successfully burying the guilt trying to surface. "I'm fine."

"Great," she said as she peeled off her Clash tee-shirt, showing me the beautiful, firm breasts I'd recently seen on film. "Please remove your shirt. I want to feel your skin on mine."

I half sat up and did as told. Then she was on me, again. Forcefully, pushing her body against mine. Her skin was hot, almost on fire. Her nipples were hard points, like bullets, pressing into my chest. Simultaneously, we rolled over and I was on top. My mouth traveled south, down her neck, giving her a gentle bite. She moaned.

My mouth went to her right nipple, my left hand on her other breast. She moaned again as I traced her areola with my tongue, licking, followed by a nibble. Her hands grabbed my head and pulled me closer while she pushed her pelvis against me, grinding.

My tongue continued down her stomach, stopping to bite and gently pull the piercing in her navel. Another moan and grind from her. My right hand went between her legs and pushed against the blue denim. My other hand went to her ass. Lifting her into me. My head followed. Even through the thick fabric, I smelled her sweet musk.

I looked up. Her eyes were closed, her tongue curled against her upper lip. With a quick motion, I undid her belt and the snap of her jeans. With my teeth, I pulled down her zipper.

She arched her back, obliging me as I pulled her pants down, stopping at her knees. Her panties were ivory cotton and moist. I pressed my mouth against her cunt, nuzzling her engorged lips. She moaned again. I pulled and tugged the jeans, until they came off. Her legs spread wide, I returned to her cunt. I slipped a finger past the cotton and into her. Wet, soaking wet, she took my finger, pulsed and clenched it. With my thumb, I teased her clit, still hidden by her panties. My mouth gently kissed her cunt, through the fabric. She bucked and rocked against me. Her entire body shuddered.

I desired her so badly. More than anyone I'd ever lusted after before. I wanted to put my cock inside her. Slip in, for an instant, then pull out. I couldn't fuck her, because even in the height of this passion, Monica loomed in the back of my brain. But in her once, twice, thrice, that wasn't cheating. I'd finish in her mouth.

Who was I kidding? Once inside her, I'd cum and cum.

I was about to pull down those ivory panties, about to betray my wife, about to further break my vows, when someone knocked on the door.

"Go away!!" Missy shouted. "This room is occupied!!"

But the door swung open. It was Savannah.

"Bad news," she said. "Buffy is here and she's wicked drunk. Ben, you better get out here. Quick."

My erection disappeared. I tried to sit up. Missy pushed me back down on the couch.

"What's the rush, dear?" she said. "Who cares about Buffy?"

"She wants to speak to Ben," Savannah said. "Says you two had a date planned. And she's talking about pills. I have a feeling this is about to get pretty messy."

It was another one of those moments when my instincts told me to flee. Told me to dash through the big room, out the front door and into the truck before anyone realized what was happening. Drive back to Richard's to sprint up the path, rip down my tent, grab my gear and rush back to Goose Island. Surprise Monica and tell her the whole story. Or, most of the story.

"*Ben*!" I heard Ganeesh boom as I grabbed my shirt. "Get your fucking ass out here!!"

Back in the big room, *Hollywood Nights* by Bob Segar blasted from the stereo. Jenny and her pal Maggie sat at the kitchen table. Ganeesh stood behind the sectional couch. Richard and Buffy were squared off in the middle of the room. Half in the shadows, leaning against the door, was Hip-Hop. What was he doing there?

"Gonna ask you one more time, Buffy. Who the frig is watching Captain?" Richard asked. "Answer me."

"Dad," she sighed, taking a long swig from the bottle of Allen's Coffee

Brandy she held in her left hand. She wore a yellow mini-skirt and matching tank top with a brandy stain down the middle. She puffed the cig in her right hand.

"*Dad?*" Richard shook his head. "He's probably passed out by now. What if the kid needs something?"

"No smoking in the Grange," Missy interrupted, her voice authoritative and precise. "What the fuck is she doing in here?"

"She was yelling something about Captain being sick," Richard said, "so we let her in."

"Sorry 'bout the smoke," Buffy said, taking another puff before dropping the cigarette on the floor. She ground out the smoldering butt with her shoe. "Didn't know there were rules in the Grange. Never used to be. Not when I was hanging out here."

"Oh my God," Missy said, pointing. "What happened to your forehead? That looks like an oozing sore."

"It's a burn," Buffy moaned and shook her head. "Not a sore." She turned to me. "Hi Ben! Where are my two pills, honey? You promised me two. I was gonna let you cum all over my tits." She took another long swig of the brandy. "Remember?" she said, slurring.

"Buffy, you are a friggin' pill whore." Richard spoke more with sorrow than anger. "I'm gonna call the state and tell them you're an unfit mother. I'll miss the little guy, but this has been going on way too long."

"Fuck you, Richard." Buffy smiled. "You call the state and I'll call the cops. Tell 'em where your secret garden is..." A coughing fit interrupted her. "And I'll tell them you and Ganeesh are buying up all the Oxycontin in Washington County. You guys are making it tough on those trying to score on their own. Supply," she burped. "Excuse me." She belched again. "Coffee brandy, gotta love it... Supply and demand is all fucked up because of you guys." She pointed at me. "And you, you're breaking my fucking heart. Promise a girl something, you should deliver. You told me two pills." She nodded and turned to Missy. "I was gonna let him cum all over my tits." She grabbed a hold of each one, like a stripper, giving them a little shake and squeeze. "My pretty titties. He was gonna cum all over my titties."

Everyone was staring at me. I looked from face to face. They were waiting for me to respond. What could I say?

"She's a fucking liar," I said and turned to Ganeesh. He and Missy were the only ones I needed to convince. "I have no idea what the hell she is talking about! Pills? *What the fuck?*" I turned to Richard. "You told me yourself. Can't trust the bitch. You said she's been lying since the day she was born."

"*I'm a liar? Fuck you,*" Buffy said indignantly. "You told me you were gonna get me two pills, then I was gonna let you cum on my tits."

"You're such a liar." I shook my head. "Biggest liar I've ever met."

"Oh yeah?" she sneered. "Hip-Hop, gimme my cell phone."

The kid crossed the room and pulled the phone out of his pocket. She took the phone and gave him the booze. He just stood there, holding the bottle.

"C'mon," she said. "Drink up."

"No thanks. I'm driving, remember."

"That's okay. More for me," she laughed and grabbed the bottle. "More for me."

Hip-Hop turned to the girls in the kitchen and gave them a half-hearted wave. "Hi Jenny. Hi Maggie."

"Hi Hip-Hop," they said in unison.

"C'mon, drink up!" Buffy let out a hoot. "Let's party!!" She turned to Hip-Hop. "Sure you don't want a little sippy-sippy?"

"I really can't," he said. "Gotta be super careful with my mom's van."

"Oh real great, Buffy," Richard said. "Contributing to the delinquency of a minor. Good job. Can't wait until I tell D.H.S about that."

"Fuck you, Richard. Each one of these girls," she pointed around the room, "is under 21. And you dirty old men feed 'em as much booze as they want. Then have your way with them." She shook her head. "That's fucking worse, you old perverts. And you, you fucking liar." She pointed at me. "You fucking fuckface, I have a video of you jerking off into the campfire."

"What the fuck are you talking about? *What the fuck?*"

"After I got you all hot and bothered last night and you promised me pills, I left the campsite." She opened her phone. "You thought I was gonna check on Captain, but I was hidin' in the woods. Filming you with my camera phone."

My heart dropped into my stomach. What was it with dirty girls in Washington County and their cameras?

"See here," Buffy said to the rest of the crowd. "Kind of hard to make it out. I mean, it's a lousy camera phone, but you can see his whaddya call it?" She stumbled. "Outline?"

"Silhouette," Hip-Hop yelped. "I seen it. You can tell it's him, choking his chicken!"

"Fuck you," I said. "You're a fucking idiot."

"Look here," Buffy said. "Anyone wanna see Ben beating his meat?"

"Show me," Missy said.

I wanted to grab the phone and smash it against the wall. That, of course, would confirm my guilt. Instead, I stepped forward to watch another film with Missy. This one wouldn't end well. That's for sure.

Luckily, the footage was grainy and pixilated and dark.

"I don't see nothing," Richard said, watching over my shoulder. "Just flames."

"Look here." Buffy pointed. "Right in the middle."

I thought for sure that only Buffy and I would know the truth. The others wouldn't, couldn't, identify the figure as me. Definitely not able to see what I had been doing. Time for more aggressive maneuvers.

"My fucking word," I said. "I don't think I've ever met a bigger liar. If that's a guy jerking off, I bet it's that fucking punk." I pointed at Hip-Hop.

"Fuck you," laughed the kid. "That's you pulling your pud."

"Bunch of friggin' bull." Richard shook his head and backed away. "I don't think that was Ben."

"Thanks man," I said. A wave of relief washed me. "She's a fucking lying pill whore."

"Buffy," he said, "You've been lying since the day you were born. You and I both know it. Now get the frig out of here and take your little friggin' boyfriend with you."

"Fuck you, Richard." She gave him the finger. "I don't have to listen to you!"

"C'mon Buffy," Hip-Hop said. "Let's get out of here. I'll give you a ride home."

"You don't have a driver's license," Missy said, taking a couple steps back. I tried to gauge her reaction to the movie, but she avoided looking at me. "You can't drive."

"I stole my Mom's van," he said. "She's in Bangor until tomorrow."

"I don't give a frig!" Richard said. "I hope you crash into a tree and both of you die! Now get the frig out of here."

"I told you, Richard, call me Hip-Hop."

"Little Luke. Little Lukey Frigface. Friggin' retard."

"Richard," Hip-Hop said. "I'm warning you."

"Whaddya gonna do?" Richard asked. "Kill me so you can chill out with your dad? In prison?"

"Fuck you. Don't be an asshole," he said.

"Did you just call me an asshole?" Richard pointed toward the kid. "Did you?"

"No," Hip-Hop said. "I said, 'don't be an asshole.'"

"Frig you, you little punk," Richard said, taking a couple steps closer. "I'm gonna teach you a lesson."

"Richard," Ganeesh said. "Don't teach him a lesson."

"Ganeesh, this little punk needs to be disciplined." Richard took another couple steps towards Hip-Hop and drew back his arm, in slow motion, getting ready to clock the kid. "And I'm the one to do it."

"Let me," Ganeesh said, coming around the couch. "Dude, you'll fucking kill him." He reached for Richard. "Don't..."

Ganeesh altered the impact and location of the punch, grabbing Richard from behind just a millisecond before Richard's fist struck Hip-Hop in the right shoulder. I'm sure Richard was aiming for the kid's face. Ganeesh probably saved Hip-Hop's life or brain. Still, the punch hurt and the kid screamed in pain.

"Richard!" Ganeesh yelled. "Let me handle this little fucker!" He pulled Richard away from the cowering kid. "Just chill out on the couch," he said, pushing his pal towards the sectional. "Enjoy the show."

Ganeesh spun around, grabbed Hip-Hop by the shirt and dragged him across the room.

"*Listen you little fuck!*" Ganeesh screamed in Hip-Hop's face while picking him up and shaking the kid. "*Come around here again and I'll fucking kill you. One more time and you're dead!*"

The boy was crying. Sobbing. Moaning.

Ganeesh tossed the kid against the door. One of the girls screamed when Missy appeared by his side and handed him the 9 mm.

"And if you ever say a fucking thing to anyone about tonight, I will kill you." Ganeesh pointed the gun at Hip-Hop's head. Point blank. Then he spun the kid around, Hip-Hop's face pressed against the wall. "Or anything about me and pills, you will die. And I will find out because, as you know, I have sources everywhere. Understand what I'm saying *white boy?*"

Ganeesh didn't wait for a response. He aimed for the old window and pulled the trigger three times.

One of the girls screamed again and Hip-Hop pulled at the door knob and escaped outside.

"Oh my god," Missy said, scrunching up her nose, "I think he shit himself."

"You fucker!" Buffy screamed at Ganeesh. "My fucking ears are ringing!" She held her head with both hands. "And he's my fucking ride!" she wailed. "How am I gonna get home?"

"Shut the fuck up, Buffy," Ganeesh said, pointing the gun at her. "Or I'll shoot you."

"You wouldn't," she growled, wobbling. "You couldn't."

"I could," Missy said, grabbing the gun from Ganeesh and taking a couple steps closer to Buffy. "No fucking problem!"

"Get the fuck out of here," Ganeesh said. "I don't want to see your face ever again."

"Yeah okay," Buffy said. "Don't have to point guns and shit at me. You," she said to Missy. "You're lucky I don't call your dad and tell him about the losers you're hanging with."

"See if I care," Missy said with a laugh. "You fucking bitch."

"I'm leaving," Buffy said and stuck her tongue out at me. "But I don't have no way to get home."

"Like we give a fuck," Missy said. "Just leave."

Buffy opened the door and walked out.

The room went silent. I watched Missy closely. She walked to the other side of the room, ignoring me, poured herself a glass of wine, then sat at the table with Jenny and Maggie, who was crying. Savannah joined them. Both Richard and Ganeesh glared at me.

"What the fuck, Ben?" Ganeesh asked. "What did you fucking tell her?"

"Nothing," I said. "I didn't say anything."

"Well, I think it's mighty fucking peculiar that she came by with the impression you were gonna get her two pills." He shook his head. "I threw her out of here last year and she's never come back since. Until tonight. You better not be lying."

"I'm not," I lied. "Richard himself said that girl is a huge fucking liar."

"Ben," Richard said. "Wait for me outside. We're going home, but I gotta talk to Ganeesh. Alone."

"Okay," I said, very aware of how bad this looked. "Okay."

I went outside. For a moment, I considered taking off again. Just go home. To Monica. Leave this fucking scene behind. Didn't give a damn about my gear at Richard's. All of it could be replaced. But the stupidest thing in the world held me back. My almost empty gas tank. On the way back from the fields, which seemed like a million years before, the needle was on E.

I had never let my tank get this low before. Especially in rural Washington County, where there was only one gas station per hundred square miles. Was there even enough fuel to get back to Mary's gas pumps? Plus, Richard and Ganeesh still hadn't paid me. I was so fucked. Standing there outside the Grange, waiting for Richard, I had no clue what to do.

The Actual Worst Day of My Life

Woke Sunday to the giggles of a little boy and the crackle, pop and roar of a wood fire blazing in the pit. Captain and Richard were trying to get warm. Even inside my sleeping bag, in my tent, I could feel the chill and damp in the air. Gonna be slippery out on the fields. Not gonna be a good day.

A dreamless night's sleep. Thankfully. Guilt and remorse didn't taint my slumber. Awake, wide eyed and confused, my emotions spun uncontrollably. Guilt resumed, of course, mixing itself with a slurry of nervousness and fear, sorrow and self-pity. Obviously, my life was a disaster. I needed to escape this place. The Grange. The blueberry fields. These people would be my ruin. If I could just get home and tell Monica the truth, everything would be cool. Explain how the harvest had turned into a gig: chauffeur for some pill collectors. I'd have to concoct a story about why the operation imploded. I'd just have to leave out major details: Buffy, Missy and my job as a composer of soundtracks for locally-produced erotica. Then, maybe, my marriage and our dreams could be saved.

The practical reality, however, was more sobering. Floyd's tank was almost empty, again. I was flat broke. How the fuck would I make it back to Goose Island? Could Monica, over the phone, give a gas station our debit card? Or could I leave my driver's license as collateral? Probably not, since the address on the ID was Portland.

The solution came in a flash. Larry. Payday was two days away, but I'm sure he'd float me a little advance. Forty bucks. Enough to fill the tank. So I could commute back and forth to the fields, I'd tell him. He'd loan me the cash, especially since my paycheck was probably close to 300 bucks.

As soon as the cash was in hand, I'd take off. Leave the fields. (And Richard and Buffy.) Head right to Mary's and fill up. Then to the campsite to grab my gear and hightail it back to Goose Island. I'd call Larry, later, and tell him the truck broke down. Tell him I was done with the harvest and for him to mail the rest of my pay. Hopefully, he wouldn't share the address with Richard.

Fuck!

Of course they knew where I lived. Ganeesh made sure I understood that. Plus they had my phone number. What could I do? Ask Monica to move and go unlisted? Perhaps since the fellas knew I wasn't a cop, and that I wouldn't rat them out, maybe they'd forget about it. Let bygones be bygones. Only that possibility allowed me to face the day. So I unzipped the tent and climbed out into the cloudy, chilly and wet August morning.

"Gooooood morning Ben!" Captain shouted at me. "*Good morning*!"

"Morning," I said. Richard sat at the picnic table, near the fire with a cup of coffee.

"*I lighted the fire, Ben*!" Captain shouted. "Unk taught me how to use a lighter!"

"Great," I said. "Congratulations."

"Hope the sun burns off the clouds and the dew. Otherwise, gonna be greasy out there," Richard said, then sipped from his cup. "Already talked to Ganeesh this morning," he added casually. "He's not too happy about last night's party."

"Don't blame him," I said. "That turned out pretty bad."

"Yeah, well, we'll deal with it tonight." He lit a smoke and pointed toward Captain, who was gleefully poking at the fire with a long stick. "His mother ain't speaking to me." Richard gave me a wry grin. "But that's a pleasure, not a punishment. Though she don't get it."

"Yeah, well she's a lying bitch."

"Uh-uh, little pitchers have big ears," he shook his head and pointed at Captain, still playing with the fire. "Wait 'til later..."

"Unk," Captain said, turning to us. "I gotta go potty."

Richard sighed and took another puff off his smoke.

"Well, don't just stand there. A big boy like you don't need help," Richard said. "You know your way down the hill." He pointed toward the trail. "I'll race you. And I'll even give you get a head start." He paused. "Ready, set, go."

And the little boy took off.

"Better dress warm," he said. "Gonna be cold and clammy." He shivered and pointed to the sky. "Not a nice day for raking."

"Ugh." I shook my head. "Fuck."

"At least the berries will weigh more."

"Yeah, you said that the other day." I nodded. "Wondering about that. How much more can they weigh if they're wet?"

"You'd be surprised." He paused. "Couple dollars more. Maybe three bucks."

"Per bucket?"

"No." He shook his head, looking at me like I was an idiot. "All friggin' day."

A half-hour later, Buffy shot me an icy cross-eyed glare before climbing into the back of the truck with Jazz. Was I getting the silent treatment, too? Captain sat happily between Richard and I, chattering about the cartoon he'd watched just before we left. I appreciated the distraction. Anything. Anything other than the details of the night before. Anything that kept truth from seeping into my brain.

Luckily, I had three hits of speed left. So I took 'em when we got to the fields, which were wet and blue. We were definitely getting into better patches, just like Larry promised, but the raking was slow because of the slippery, slick greenery. Richard and Captain stayed about 50 feet ahead of me. Buffy was raking with Hip-Hop and a couple other teenagers. Jazz was raking with Peggy and the schoolteachers.

I'd have to wait until lunch to make my getaway. During lunch, I could get Larry alone to ask for the advance, then leave Richard and his gang behind. I visualized driving off and seeing Richard in the rear view mirror giving a half-hearted chase. Such a feeling of freedom! Empowered by my fantasy, and the speed, I kept raking. Barely stopped to drink water or lug my full buckets to the scales. Now that I was leaving the fields, I wanted to rake as much money as possible. Before lunch and my escape.

For the next couple hours, I slipped and fell four times thanks to the wet bushes and field. All the while, I obsessively tried to weave a tale to tell Monica. She knew the harvest was supposed to last three weeks. How could I explain it was over, for me, in a mere seven days? Every single conceivable scenario portrayed me as a weak, desperate man.

Around 11 o'clock, the grass was still slippery as shit. The clouds hovered low and mingled with the fog that refused to burn off. Luckily, Richard called for a joint break. I lugged my buckets, two at a time, to the scales. About 36 dollars, so far. Not bad, all things considered.

"I gotta talk to Larry," he said, "but Captain's really gotta go to the bathroom. So why don't you walk him to the sani-can? Then we'll smoke a big joint in your truck, because I'm not in the mood to share with..." He pointed to where Buffy and Hip-Hop were raking. Had been raking. "Where the frig did she go?"

She wasn't by the scales or the buckets. And we would have seen her cross the fields to the water or the port-a-potty. She and Hip-Hop had disappeared.

"That ain't good." Richard sighed and continued looking. "Friggin' girl. Where's Jazz?"

I didn't see him either. Or Peggy.

"My brother and sister are the laziest friggin' people in all Washington County." He lit a smoke. "I'll meet you at the truck."

Captain and I crossed the field, trying to avoid unraked berries. He skipped and I limped. The speed had just about worn off. My pants were soaked. So were my shirt, sneakers and socks. My feet were sore, again. Real bad. Trigger point therapy would help, I'm sure, but sitting down in the slippery fields to massage my legs wasn't gonna work.

While Captain used the facilities, I sat on an overturned bucket, rubbed my calves like Ganeesh had showed me while I scanned the fields. An even dozen humans, bent over, raking. Not a single person on a bucket break, except me.

Captain finished at the same time Richard showed up. The three of us walked toward the parked vehicles. Captain lugged Richard's rake. Richard carried two water jugs. Twenty feet away from Floyd, I spotted Hip-Hop sitting in the passenger seat of my truck. He didn't see us, even though we were in clear view. Were his eyes closed?

"What the fuck?" I pointed. "Hip-Hop?"

Richard beat me to the door, which he pulled open to reveal the boy with his pants around his ankles. Naked from the waist down, practically. Buffy, fully clothed, was stretched across the front seat, her ass in the air, the height of the steering wheel. Her mouth and right hand were on the young man's cock.

"*You frigging whore!*" Richard screamed and reached into truck, across Hip-Hop's lap, trying to grab his sister by the hair. "*Whore!*"

She screamed and sat up, turned and struggled to get the driver's side door open. She jumped out and came around the front of the truck. Fast.

"*You whore!*" Richard bellowed. "*You friggin' cunt!*" He raised his left hand and pointed at his sister. "*You no good whore!*"

"*Don't talk to me like that,*" she snapped back, "*especially in front of Captain!*"

"*You no good skanky whore!*"

Buffy sprang toward her brother and slapped him. Hard. The blurred palm print of her right hand lingered red on his left cheek. Richard, stunned, rubbed his jaw and squinted. I watched his eyes turn cold and ugly. Captain, still carrying Richard's rake, ran to his mother's side at the very moment she took another step towards Richard. Her follow-up. Her right fist was drawn back and headed for her brother's face. Richard saw it coming and shifted his stance. The punch turned into a slight glancing blow to his shoulder. The mistake threw Buffy off balance.

Then Richard back-handed her.

She fell. The slippery ground upended her. Backwards. Backwards on top of Captain, who was underfoot. As kids often are. Her feet tangled with her son's as she fell on top of him. They tripped, and together, mother and child fell. Knocked him to the ground with the force of her downward motion, multiplied by all 135 pounds of her. The boy, face down beneath Buffy, let out a quick series of surprisingly loud yelps, which turned into an incredibly loud and long scream. Buffy rolled off him. Captain, on his stomach, was convulsing. Or to be more accurate, his lower body convulsed. Captain's upper body wasn't moving.

Hip-Hop struggled to pull up his pants. Buffy, on her knees, stared in horror at her son. Richard raced to his nephew's side, kneeled and turned the boy over. That's when I saw the rake. Impaled. Without a moment's hesitation, Richard grabbed the rake's handle and pulled it from his nephew's chest. The boy let out another long yelp. A wail.

"*Oh my friggin' god!*" Richard screamed and turned to me. "Ben, he's gushing blood. We gotta get him to the hospital. He's gonna bleed to death!"

Captain's eyes were closed. His mouth, open. Huffing and gasping. Wheezing. Bleeding profusely.

"My baby," Buffy moaned and knelt, motionless, watching Richard wrap his arms around her son. "*My baby!*" she wailed.

"We gotta get him to the hospital. Now!" Richard repeated as he lifted Captain. "Open the truck door, for christsakes. We don't have much time."

"*My baby,*" Buffy screamed. "*Give me my baby!*"

I rushed to open the passenger side door, where moments before, Hip-Hop sat half-naked. Richard, with Captain in his arms, climbed in. Buffy finally rose from the ground and, still sobbing, staggered towards us. Hip-Hop was right behind her.

"*C'mon!*" Richard screamed. "*We gotta get outta here!*"

I slammed the door shut, raced over and jumped into the driver's seat and turned the key. Once more, the question of gasoline came to mind. Would we make it to the hospital? Sure as hell hoped so. Running out of gas, in all likelihood, meant Captain would die. I put Floyd into gear just as Buffy grabbed for my door handle and wrenched it open.

"*Baby!*" she yelled as Floyd lurched forward. She couldn't hold on and I pulled the door shut as we drove. Captain, laying on his uncle's lap, continued to wheeze and bleed.

She screamed "*Baby!*" one more time as we headed away.

"All this blood," Richard moaned, ignoring his sister. "He's gonna bleed to death. Step on it."

So I did. The truck bounced and dragged across the field toward the treeline. In the rearview mirror, I could see Buffy and Hip-Hop chasing us on foot.

"Gotta apply direct pressure," I said, suddenly remembering my Coast Guard first aid training. "Direct pressure stops the bleeding." Captain, desperate for air, wheezed. "That wheezing. Did the rake puncture his lungs?"

"Frig," Richard said. "I don't know."

"Gotta cover punctures." Another memory from the Coast Guard. The wheezing was probably escaping air. In first aid class, they told us to use whatever we could to seal the holes. "Your shirt," I said. "Use your shirt as a bandage."

With his nephew laying on his lap, Richard peeled off his shirt, torn, tattered and covered with mud from the fields, and folded it into a square.

"Apply pressure," I said. "That'll stop the bleeding. See if you can tell if air's coming out of his lungs."

"Oh my friggin' word," Richard said, pressing his filthy shirt against the gushing wounds. "I can't friggin' believe this!"

"Use the plastic from your cigarette pack," I said, remembering another tip from my Coastie training, "to patch any holes in his lungs."

"What are you friggin' talking about?"

"I'm telling you, I learned it in the Coast Guard. Good for bullet holes."

"Have you ever done it?"

"Fuck no," I said. "They just mentioned it, in passing, during class."

For the next 15 minutes, I drove as fast as Floyd could go. Pedal to the metal. Captain and the truck wheezed going up and down the hills of Washington County. Meanwhile, Richard worked as a paramedic. He did the best he could with our limited water supply. Unfortunately, he'd dropped his jugs back on the field. Would have come in handy to clean off the dirt and blood all over Captain's chest. Richard used our lone quart to rinse the skin covering Captain's left lung. Richard examined his nephew as carefully as he could while we sped and bounced along the back roads. Then Richard took out his cigarette pack, removed the plastic and tore it, carefully, into two pieces.

I kept my eyes on the road, occasionally stealing glances as Richard placed the patches. One on the chest and the other on Captain's neck.

"There's five holes, I think, in his lung." Richard said. "And three in his neck. But I don't think the rake hit his throat." He let out a short cry. "But I don't friggin' know. He's still bleeding."

"You're doing good," I said. "Real good. Just hold the patches in place. Keep applying direct pressure to where he's bleeding."

Captain was in shock. Or unconscious. I couldn't tell. Could have been either or both. He'd lost quite a bit of blood.

Finally, we arrived at the hospital and Richard pointed at the sign for the Emergency Room entrance.

"Get as close as you can," he ordered. "Then jump out and open my door. On the double."

I did as told.

With Captain in his arms, Richard climbed out of the truck and sprinted toward the building. The automatic door slid open and they disappeared within.

I quickly parked the truck and ran into the emergency room. Richard stood at the front desk, pointing his finger at a young woman, a girl really, sitting behind the desk. She must have been barely 18 and clearly not prepared to deal with a shirtless, hairless, bloody and filthy Richard. Understandably, she was scared. He started to sob when he saw me.

"They took Captain away. He's in real bad shape," he said, wiping tears from his mud stained cheeks. "But she wouldn't tell me nuthin'."

"Fuck," I said.

"All the blood loss," he said. "That's the worst."

"Fuck."

"His blood type is B positive. What's your's?"

"I'm A positive."

"Me too. That ain't no help."

We stood there, silent. I didn't know any words that could comfort him.

"Why couldn't Buffy get stabbed by the rake instead?" he asked. "That bitch deserved it," he sobbed. "*She should be dying*."

"Captain isn't dying," I said. "He's not gonna die."

"How do you know?" He looked at me. "How do you fucking know? He lost so much blood."

"Yeah," I said. "But they can give him a transfusion."

"Excuse me," said a man in a white coat. "Are you the boy's father?"

"His uncle," Richard said. "We brought him here."

"I was told that he fell on a blueberry rake? Is that true?"

"Crushed on top of a rake," Richard said. "Is he gonna be okay?"

"We're stabilizing him," the man said, "we need to know if he's allergic to anesthetic."

"I don't think so," Richard said. "But he's never had any. He's only five years old."

"Did you put the pieces of cellophane over the punctures?" the man asked.

"Yeah, but..."

"Good job. You probably saved his life. How deep did the rake go into him?"

"Deep," Richard said, "real deep."

"A quarter inch?" the man asked. "Or more?"

"More," Richard said, "much more. It was stuck in him and I had to pull it out of him."

The man turned and hurried down the hallway.

"Is he gonna be okay?" Richard called out. "Is Captain gonna be okay?"

The man didn't answer and disappeared through a set of double doors.

"Is Captain gonna be okay?" Richard spun around and pointed at the girl behind the counter. "*Is he?*"

"I don't know," she recoiled. Richard was a madman. "He's in good hands."

"*Damn-it,*" Richard screamed. "*God friggin' damn-it*!"

"If you just take a seat," she said. "Please."

"*I don't wanna take a seat*!" he screamed. "*I wanna know*!"

The doors slid open and Buffy and Larry came running in.

"*Where's Captain?*" Buffy screamed at the girl behind the desk. "*Where's my little boy?*"

"Buffy," Richard said. "You better shut the frig up or I will kill you!"

"*Baby*! *Captain*!" she screamed. "*Where's Captain?*"

"He's going into surgery," the girl said. "Please..."

"This asshole," Buffy pointed at Richard, "hurt him. Stabbed him."

"*You lying bitch*!" Richard screamed, lunging toward his sister. "You stabbed him."

Larry and I grabbed Richard. We struggled to hold him back. I could feel the pure energy of his anger and hate pulsate through his body as he fought to break free. If he had, he would have killed her. No question. Somehow Larry and I were able to drag him outside. Almost immediately, as soon as he couldn't see his sister anymore, he calmed down and lit a smoke. For a couple minutes, none of us spoke.

"She's a friggin' bitch," Richard finally said. "None of this would have happened if she hadn't been giving that friggin' Lil' Luke a blowjob. Whore!"

"*What?*" Larry looked incredulous. "What are you talking about?"

I filled him in on the details.

"Well, she told it way different." Larry shook his head. "Neglected to mention the blowjob. Buffy said Richard started a fight with her and pushed her on top of Captain who fell on Richard's rake. And got stabbed. That's it..."

"He was impaled, Larry," Richard interrupted. "She fell on top of Captain and crushed him." He took a long puff of his smoke. "She's the one that caused this friggin' mess. If she hadn't been sucking off that kid, I never would have called her a whore and then she wouldn't have attacked me and Captain would have never been hurt." He looked at Larry and began to cry. "And now," he sobbed, "he's gonna die."

"Captain ain't gonna die," Larry said, putting his arm around Richard's shoulder. "The staff here is excellent." He looked at me. "I should know. I know 'em all." He took a puff off his smoke. "The worst thing is the waiting. And that's all we can do. Wait. And pray, if you believe in that."

"Nope." Richard shook his head. "I don't pray."

"You?" Larry asked me.

"Nope."

"Well, me neither. Guess all we can do is wait."

"Fuck," I said. "That sucks."

"I gotta take a leak," Richard said. "And I'm gonna get a shirt. That girl offered me one."

"Okay," Larry said. "You calmed down? You ain't gonna kill your sister?"

"Not gonna kill her." He took a final drag off his smoke and flicked it toward the parking lot. "She ain't worth the prison time."

He walked inside.

"Why couldn't he use the ash tray?" Larry asked, bending to pick up the still smoldering butt and depositing it in the proper receptacle. "Someone's gonna have to clean this parking lot. This ain't the blueberry fields, for christsake."

"I was wondering about that," I said. "Out in the fields, I see everyone flicking their butts."

"Because out there, it don't matter. Part of blueberry cultivation is torching the fields after we're done raking 'em. We do it in the fall. Then the cigarette butts burn up too. Everything burns." He nodded. "You better believe it."

"Oh," I said. "That makes sense."

"Yup," he said, lighting a new smoke from his old. "I guess." Larry inhaled, sighed, then looked at me. "I'm gonna cancel the rest of the harvest, Ben. I finally decided, on the drive over here with Buffy, that I'm done running the fields. I can call a fella who'll have a crew of Mexicans on the fields by the day after tomorrow and finish 'em so fast, your head would spin. And the Mexicans get every berry too. Nothing wasted. And they don't take bucket breaks. Or constantly bum smokes. Or any of this shit." He nodded. "I'm tired of the stress. The people, not the berries. Like Richard and Buffy," he pointed toward the emergency room. "I should've known something would eventually happen. Neither one ain't ever been right in the head. The whole family, as far as I'm concerned, are freaks. Granted, I got lots of berries out of them, but they ain't worth the hassle. Or the drama." He puffed, then gestured at me with his cigarette. "You wanna buy a blueberry farm?"

"How much?" I asked. For a couple of seconds, I considered the possibilities. Monica and I could build a little cabin out in the middle of the fields. She'd still work at the high school. I'd set up a chicken shack and a pig pen. We'd plant a market-sized garden. Of course, it was a lot more land than we'd need. But next August, I could run the blueberry harvest. "How much do you want?"

"How much you got?"

"Nothing." I shook my head. Not true, of course. I had a beautiful and talented wife. My health. Three guitars and two dogs. The truck. Miscellaneous books, art and furniture. Everything that mattered. "I got nothing. That's what I wanted to ask you about. Wanted to talk to you about money."

"Huh?"

"Well, I was wondering if maybe..." I paused, hating to ask. Embarrassed. Ashamed. "If I could get an advance. Not much," I nodded, "just enough to get gas back to Goose Island."

Larry didn't say a word. Didn't even look at me.

"See, uhhh," I stammered, "I'm broke. My wife has the ATM card back home and Richard was supposed to give me gas money."

He reached into his pocket and pulled out a small wad of bills. Peeled off a 20 and handed it to me. "Enough?"

"Yes," I said. "Yes, that's enough to get home."

I was interrupted by the "blip–blip" of a police cruiser speeding into the hospital, slamming on the brakes and parking, kitty-corner, to the Emergency Room entrance.

"What the fuck?" Larry said. The door to the cruiser opened and an extremely obese cop squeezed out. "Oh great. That asshole drives me crazy..."

"You know him?"

"Know him?" Larry turned to me. "Fat Jimmy Guertin raked for me forever. Before he got hired as a sheriff's deputy." He shook his head. "Now Fat Jimmy is a major league Washington County asshole. Give a guy a badge and he thinks he rules the world. Let's get in there and see what Fat Jimmy wants."

"Standard procedure," Fat Jimmy said. "Received a call from the E-Room. Serious injury involving a child. Gotta investigate and make sure there weren't no crimes committed."

"For christsake, Fat Jimmy," Larry said. "It was a freak accident."

"Listen everyone, I'm gonna have to ask you to call me Deputy Guertin. Because I'm here on official business."

"It's all Richard's fault." Buffy pointed at her brother. "He pushed me on top of Captain."

"Jimmy, she's a cock-sucking whore," Richard said, pointing at his sister. "That bitch was giving a blowjob to Little Luke. He's just a kid, Jimmy. She should be charged with statutory rape."

"Oral sex ain't considered rape," Buffy snapped back. "Fat Jimmy, I've given you a blowjob, haven't I? Oral sex ain't rape."

"Uhhhh, Buffy…" Fat Jimmy stuttered. "Please call me Deputy Guertin. Like I said, I'm asking questions here in ahh, ahh," he stammered, "official capacity." He stared at Buffy. "What happened to your forehead?"

"A burn," she said, "all because of these assholes…"

"Listen Jimmy," Richard interrupted. "We were on the fields and I'm walking with Captain back to the truck and we catch that slut giving Little Lukey a blowjob. I call her a whore. She swings at me. Hits me twice. I had no option other than to give her the backhand. Self-defense, I'm telling yah. She tripped and fell on poor Captain, who fell on the rake and it…" Richard sobbed, "impaled him." He pointed at Buffy. "Jesus Christ, Jimmy. You know she's abusive to anyone who gets in her way. You've arrested her a half-dozen times for disorderly," he sobbed. "Plus she killed Paulie. Remember? She killed Paulie. You know what she's capable of."

"He's a fucking liar, Fat Jim…I mean Deputy Guertin," Buffy said. "And he's the criminal." She pointed at her brother. "Richard is the criminal." She turned to the cop. "Him and Ganeesh are buying up pills. Oxycontin. *Oxycontin!*" She was screaming. "Pills, Jimmy. Fucking pills. Not just weed. They're pill dealers now!"

"*Buffy,*" Richard yelped and took a couple steps toward her. "*What the fuck?*"

Jimmy dropped his notebook and grabbed Richard by the wrist. For a second, I thought Richard was gonna karate kick the cop like Zeus the dog. Instead, Richard let out a long sigh as Jimmy twisted his arm behind him.

"I'm cuffing you," the cop said. "so you don't run away."

"Jesus Christ, Jimmy." Richard shook his head. "Where the frig am I gonna run to?"

"You're out on bail, right?" Jimmy didn't wait for an answer. "Bail condition is no drugs or alcohol. What you got in the pouch, Richard?" He poked at his fanny pack. "You're gonna let me look in the pouch, ain't yah?"

Richard didn't answer.

"You know you gotta let me look. Otherwise, I just go to the judge and you end up in Machias, doing real county time."

"All right Jimmy, you got me." Richard turned around and faced me. "You gotta undo it from the back," he said. As the cop focused on the buckle, Richard looked me in the eye and mouthed, "Ganeesh."

I nodded.

Problem was, Buffy saw the exchange.

"Jimmy," she blurted out. "Ben is the driver for them. He's driving them around to get the pills."

"Who?" the cop asked, looking up. "Ben Who?"

"Ben, Ben Franklin," she said, pointing at me. My heart dropped into my stomach. "That's him."

"Okay Buffy, cut the bullshit," Larry said. "Ben just started raking last week. He lives down on Goose Island. He ain't involved in no pill dealing. He ain't no pill guy. And if Richard is messed up in pills, and I ain't saying he is, because I don't know shit, I'm pretty fucking sure he wouldn't trust this guy." Larry pointed at me. "I mean, I certainly thought he was police. Up from Portland. Working for the D.E.A. I let him rake, just to see if I was right." He shook his head. "But when he came back for the second day, then a third, I knew he wasn't a cop."

"Yeah, I ain't a cop. I mean, a pill runner, or whatever you said." I tried to sound as indignant as possible. "Buffy, you're such a liar. I don't know what the hell you're talking about."

"We'll deal with you in a minute," the cop said. He had Richard's fanny pack open and dumped it on the E-room desk. Pack of smokes. Lighter. A bag with three joints, plus another small bag of green bud.

"No pills in there," Richard said. "You know she's a liar."

"I didn't say you had 'em on you," Buffy screeched.

"Hold everything," Jimmy said, hands in the air. "Richard, you ain't supposed to have pot."

"Oh c'mon Jimmy," he said. "You can't bust me for weed. I mean, me and you, we've gotten high a million times."

"Like I said before," the cop sighed. "Like I said to your sister. I'm acting in an official capacity. Listen, I gotta place you under arrest for possession and..."

"*Possession?*" Richard yelped. "*Possession?*"

"And a bail violation."

"Dude, that weed is medicinal. I got a prescription for it."

"Lay off the bullshit," Jimmy said. "I'm just doing my job."

"I can't believe this." Richard shook his head. "You're arresting me for possession. That should just be a summons. Misdemeanor, if anything."

"Violation of bail conditions," Jimmy said. "That's why you're going to jail."

"What about Ben?" Buffy called out. "What about him?"

"Jeez, Buffy," the cop said. "I don't have anything on him. He's gonna write me a statement and that's it."

"He's part of the ring."

"Buffy," Larry said, "you'd think you'd be more concerned about your boy."

"Oh I am, Larry," she sneered. "Just trying to help clean up Washington County."

"Are you the family of the Johnson boy?" A doctor interrupted Buffy. "Are you the boy's mother?"

"Yeah," she said. "What the fuck is going on here? Where is Captain?"

"We've got him stabilized and we're running tests right now, trying to determine the extent of the damage, if any, to his heart."

The automatic door shooshed open again. Jazz and Peggy rushed in.

"Where's Captain?" Jazz cried out. "Is he okay?"

"The doc was just telling us, son," Larry said. "He's stabilized."

"What kind of damage?" Buffy asked. "Brain damage."

"We don't know if there is damage." The doctor shook his head. "The boy lost lots of blood. We've dealt with that and now we're looking for other problems."

"Doc, give it to me straight. Is Captain gonna live?" Richard asked. "Is he gonna be all right?"

"We've stabilized him and we're thinking positively about the final diagnosis. But we need to be realistic and run several more series of tests to check for organ damage. And because of the severity of the punctures, there's always the danger of infection. So," the doctor turned to Buffy, "we need your permission and you need to sign a release."

"Yeah, sure," she said, with a soft sob. For a millisecond, I felt sorry for her. "Can I see him?"

"Not right now," the doctor said. "Maybe in a little while. First, we'll run the tests and we'll keep you informed."

"Okay," she sniffled. "You can do the tests."

"Why is Richard handcuffed?" Jazz asked. "What's going on here?"

Buffy spun around.

"Jazz knows it's true," Buffy said to the deputy. "Don't you, Jazz? Ask him, Fat, I mean, Deputy Jimmy. Ask 'em."

"I know what?" Jazz asked, looking at the overweight cop. "What am I supposed to know?"

"That Richard," the deputy said, "and Ganeesh are running pills."

"What?"

"You know what I'm talking about," Buffy said. "It's okay, Jazz. Tell the truth. Tell the deputy all about it."

All eyes were on Jazz. He took a deep breath. He despised both Richard and Buffy, but his answer would show who he hated more.

"I don't know nuthin' about any pills," he said to the deputy, then turned to Peggy, who was crying softly. "Wanna go have a smoke?" he asked as she wrapped her arms around him, then kissed him on the lips. Hand in hand, they left. The chains on his boots jangled as the automatic door swooshed open.

"What the hell is Peggy doing with Jazz?" the cop asked, incredulous, eyes still on the pair.

"They've hooked up," Buffy said. "You don't know nuthin."

"Miss," the receptionist said. "We have the release for you to sign."

Buffy walked over to the desk.

I watched as Fat Jimmy started to read Richard his rights, verbatim, from a wallet-sized card. Richard caught my eye and gestured to the door with a slight tilt of his head.

I had to get to the Grange.

Luckily, there was a gas station right near the hospital. Took forever to put the whole 20 bucks in the tank, though it was a little more than six gallons. Enough to get to the Grange, then home. Knowing Ganeesh's phone number would have made everything so much easier. But I didn't even know his last name, so I was gonna have to race, on the back roads, to beat the cops to tell Ganeesh that the shit was going down.

I envisioned Ganeesh and the girls being led to a cruiser in handcuffs. Up and down the hills, I pushed Floyd, harder than I had pushed when I was bringing Captain to the hospital. Which I didn't think was possible. Which made me drive even faster. Floyd and I were flying.

I arrived at the Grange, jumped out of the truck and ran to the front door, buzzed twice and knocked hard, then looked pleadingly at the camera. The door popped open and I entered. Ganeesh stood by the pool table.

"What the fuck, Ben?" Ganeesh looked pissed. "What are you doing here? Where's Richard?"

"I've got awful news." My brain was freaking. I was elated I'd beaten the cops, but then I realized what I had to tell Ganeesh. And he wasn't gonna like it. "Captain's hurt real bad. Fell on a blueberry rake. Buffy told the cops about the pill operation. The cop was a fat guy named..." I paused again and looked into the air, searching. "His name was, uh. Uh..."

"Jimmy Guertin?" Ganeesh said, taking a couple steps closer. "You're saying Buffy told Fat Jimmy about the pill operation?"

"Yeah," I said. "Yeah."

"*Fuck*!" Ganeesh took another two steps toward me. "That racist son-of-a-bitch hates me. Would love to see me hang. *Fuck*!"

"The cop searched Richard and found his bag of weed. Arrested him for possession and bail violation," I went on, "so I raced over here."

Ganeesh reached forward and shoved me. I staggered backwards into the doorframe. I thought for sure he was gonna hit me. Instead, he just pointed and screamed.

"You're such an asshole! This is all your fault! *You totally fucked us*! You told that whore Buffy we had pills. I never should have trusted a fuckin' white man. Weak. Weak."

Ganeesh shook with rage, but still had his wits about him. He turned and moved fast. He snatched a backpack off the couch and dashed over to a cabinet on the other side of the room. He opened it and quickly brushed all the pill bottles into the bag.

This was the first time I'd been in the Grange at high noon. Little streams of sun lasered through the multiple bullet holes in the plywood covered window. Dusty beams. My initial visit to the Grange, just four nights before, seemed so long ago. Four nights. That's it. Four nights. Standing there, I was ashamed of the man I'd become in such a short time. And I realized I would probably never see Missy again. That hurt equally. Or, perhaps, even more.

"Listen here, white boy," Ganeesh said, coming across the room. "You're gonna give me one last ride, not far from here. 'Cuz I need a head start, in case the pigs are on their way. And then I better not ever see your fucking face again."

"Ganeesh," I said, putting my hands up. "You gotta believe me, I didn't tell Buffy anything."

"*Liar*!" he barked. "Fucking white man!"

"I'm sorry." I truly was. Sorry I'd ever gotten involved in this mess. Sorry I betrayed my wife. Sorry that I'd fallen in love with Missy. "I'm sorry," I repeated, tears welling up in my eyes.

He grunted and walked out the front door.

"Listen motherfucker, do not even talk to the cops. If they call, hang up," Ganeesh said, just before I dropped him off at a crossroads I hadn't noticed before. "If you even speak to them to say you don't know nuthin', I will have you killed."

He bared his teeth and growled. "You better understand me. Do not say a fucking word." He drew each syllable out slowly. "Nothing. Say anything, you will die. That simple. And I'll make sure your wife knows what a cheating scumbucket you are. I'll make sure she knows everything. So don't say a fucking word." He climbed out of the truck. "Remember, you fucking asshole, I know where you live."

Then he spit in my face.

He turned and took off, running down a trail into the woods and didn't look back.

I drove to Richard's and climbed the hill to the campsite. Quickly, I knocked down the tent and stuffed it in its sack, then rolled up my sleeping bag. I grabbed my wind-up radio off the picnic table and started to head down the path. Back to my life with Monica and the dogs. Back to the familiar tub of hot water to scrub and soak until no trace of the fields remained. Then, I would explain to Monica what happened. Almost everything. As much as I could.

But I stopped and turned for one last look over Richard's sea of green with those rich golden stripes. Marigolds, he'd said, to keep away the bugs. I'd have to remember those marigolds, when Monica and I moved to our land.

Crash Barry has worked as a columnist, reporter, sailor, bartender, demolitionist, janitor, herdsman, milker and blueberry raker. He lives in the hills of western Maine.